An Article of Lies

(Another one of those MM Arranged Marriage Stories between two princes this time)

By Lisa Oliver

An Article of Lies – Another one of those MM Arranged Marriage Stories between two princes this time.

An Article of Lies is a work of fiction. Names, characters, places, and incidents are either the product of the author's imagination or are used fictitiously and any resemblance to any actual persons, living or dead, events or locales is entirely coincidental. All trademarks are owned by the relevant companies and are used for reference purposes in this book only.

Table of Contents

Chapter One

"For goodness sake, Remy, what do you think you're doing? We've got guests arriving any minute."

"Soft voice, Mother, please. I've said it a million times before, you need to speak softly around the Orobos. They don't like loud noises." Remy, also known as Prince Remy of Bentley, smoothed a firm hand down the large reptilian creature resting her head on his knee. "Daisy is still feeling grumpy after Rudolf snapped at her this morning." The huge orange lizard yawned in agreement, showing large, sharp teeth. Rudolf had been lucky he'd gotten away with his nose intact.

His mother's sigh was familiar. Remy didn't even have to look up to know she was wearing her 'I love my son, but sometimes he makes me want to pull my hair out' expression. "Remy, you promised you'd behave while the Balenborn delegation was here. Prince Xavier's offer for your hand was admittedly unexpected..."

"That's for sure." Remy snorted quietly. "He doesn't even like me, Mother. Are you sure the papers said Prince Remy and not Princess Sophia? Maybe he was having a bad day and got confused. I hear that happens to older people sometimes."

"Remy, stop." Queen Abigail let out a quick giggle and there was a rustle of silk as she settled on a box next to where he was sitting on the ground. "Prince Xavier is only seven years older than you and by all accounts, he has amazing control of his faculties."

"That's what his PR team says, but have you seen any evidence of that?" Remy shook his head. "I don't understand why Father agreed to this," he added softly. "If things are tough, I could get a job..."

"Don't be ridiculous. You know how fortunate we are. Bentley is a prosperous country, and financial stability is never going to be a concern for our people, for us, or for you, married or not."

"Then why?" Possibly picking up his concern, Daisy gave a flick of her long tail and disappeared off his lap. No matter how fast she moved, she was still very careful with her long claws around him. She headed to the hideout Remy had made for her out of stone slabs, probably looking for the mice that frequented the stables. The Bentley royal castle never needed cats to take care of any rodent problem. Remy's lizards took care of them all.

His lap free, Remy swiveled on his butt so he could face his mother, wrapping his arms around his knees. It was said that he took after his mother more than his father in looks. They shared the same slender build, high cheekbones, and sharp chin. But where Remy's brown hair with blond highlights always looked like it needed cutting, or at least the attention of a solid hairbrush, his mother's was immaculately wound in beautiful braids around her head – reminding Remy of the crown she wore for state occasions.

"Is there any reason I have to get married right now?" He asked. "You have a perfectly studly heir in my brother, Pierre, who has already given you two grandsons and a granddaughter with his wonderful Emily. My younger sisters, Sophia and Hyacinth, are almost of marriageable age – are you sure Xavier can't wait for one of them? Sophia is barely ever seen unless she's on a horse. I understand he is much the same, so he'd appreciate that."

His mother glanced around, making sure they were alone. Barely anyone came into his outbuilding, built specifically to house his beloved Orobos, but Remy could understand the caution. Gossip about royals was rife, as in any society household. "Your father did listen to you about

Xavier, when the offer first came in," she said, her voice low.

"Your father agreed with the usual spiel about us being neighboring countries and furthering relations, but suggested that Xavier would be happier with one of your sisters instead. It's not like a royal wedding was going to be arranged in a week." Queen Abigail sighed. "By the time additional clauses had been worked through to incorporate the rights of any children of the union, Sophia would've almost been of age and your father and I didn't see why Xavier couldn't wait another year for her. So your father did listen to you."

"But," Remy prompted. There had to be a 'but'. His marriage to Prince Xavier was going to be announced at a state dinner in less than two hours, with the ceremony itself taking place in just four days. Remy's gut clenched just thinking about it.

"It was like talking to a brick wall, apparently. Xavier was adamant. It was you or nobody from our family line at all."

Remy scrunched up his nose and then asked slowly, "Would it be such a bad thing if he married into a royal family from another country? His father and mine seem to get along all right and it's not like any country goes to war with each other anymore. The World Council sees to that."

"As I said before. Xavier is all for this union." The shrug was uncharacteristic. "It wasn't said in actual words, but the implication was that if your father wouldn't agree to the marriage, then the King of Balenborn could take that as an insult to his family... and your father really didn't want to go down that route."

"It doesn't make sense. He genuinely doesn't like me." Remy's cheeks heated as he recalled their last face-to-face ten years before. Suffice to say Prince Xavier ticked most of Remy's boxes in the sexy men department. Unfortunately, Remy made an advance that had been rudely rebuffed, something Remy had never forgotten. He'd made a point of staying away from Xavier ever since, particularly during the Crown Prince's infrequent visits.

"Hey," Remy said as he had a thought that made him grin. "Maybe that's the point. He doesn't like me. He hasn't said a word to me in years. He won't want to spend any time with me, but maybe he's getting pressure from his family to get married. He is over thirty and the Crown Prince. What better way to kill two birds with the one stone than to marry a man who's not going to be falling all over him every five minutes."

Queen Abigail pursed her pale pink lips. "That's not going to be much of a marriage for you," she said slowly. "I, or should I say, your father and I, both want for you to be happy."

"I'm always happy." Remy rubbed his hands together. "Think about it. It's perfect. He doesn't want me – he'll be off protecting his country or whatever it is he does. He'll probably leave me here after the ceremony. It's not like we're going to be expected to have children. His sister took care of his heir situation for him. No one is going to have an issue with us being apart, especially when the Crown Prince is always so busy. I'd just cramp his style."

Chuckling, his mother shook her head. "If you don't think a lot of him, how do you know he's always busy?"

Remy looked over to Daisy's hideout. "It's not easy ignoring his existence. As I said, Prince Xavier has an excellent PR team. There's not a World Council newsletter that comes out that doesn't mention something wickedly heroic he's done, and our society pages are always full of gossip about him and a dozen different partners. If just half of that is true, he'll be too busy for a husband."

Remy touched his mother's arm, keen to share the latest. "For example, I heard two society ladies gossiping about him the other day, you know, after Father announced the delegation was visiting and Prince Xavier was accompanying them. They were sure he was coming to court Sophia, which was fine, I didn't mind. But one of them said," he collapsed in chuckles and slapped his knee with his free hand, "one of them actually said women swoon just seeing the Crown Prince mount a horse. What was even more hilarious was that the other woman agreed with her. They were fanning themselves with their hands, going on about how lucky the sweet Princess Sophia is going to be."

"Remy, stop it." But the queen was chuckling, too. "I'm glad to see you're going into this with a sense of humor. I think that is something Prince Xavier will appreciate about you."

"I doubt he plans on being around long enough to find out about it, but that's fine, too." Jumping to his feet, Remy brushed off his hands on his dusty pants, which didn't help get rid of any of the grime he seemed to attract, but his mother would appreciate the gesture. He held out his hand, which she took, standing beside him.

"I have far too much love and respect for you and Father to embarrass you in any way while the delegation is here. I will stand proud on my wedding day and speak my vows clearly. I will bind myself to the man and even sit by his side during the celebration dinner afterward. I may even shed a random, solitary tear as he goes riding off with his entourage, back to Balenborn without me. If I'm not too busy to watch him go, of course. You'll see, it'll be perfect, and everyone will be happy, including me."

"You have four days' worth of courting to get through first," his mother reminded him. "Your father was determined Prince Xavier was going to have to work for your affection. There's nothing sociable planned, but you will be expected to spend time with him between the announcement and the ceremony."

"You raised me to be a very well-mannered adult. So long as Daisy and her brood don't need me, I'll be as available as he needs me to be. I might even manage a smile to show his PR team I am completely swept away by his charm and wit."

"Let's get through the announcement dinner first," his mother suggested. "I'll settle for you running a comb through your hair and wearing clean clothes at this stage of the proceedings."

Remy never made promises he didn't keep. "Good hunting, Daisy," he called out to his lizard friend. "I'll be back to check on you after dinner."

"I swear, I think you love that reptile more than your sisters some days." Remy could hear the affection in his mother's tone.

"Daisy appreciates my humor, and my ability to be quiet around her when she's upset." *And I will be back as soon as I can leave the dinner without upsetting Father,* he thought as he escorted his mother back to the castle. Watching Daisy hunting was far more interesting than attending a state dinner.

Crossing the courtyard, Remy squinted as he noticed a huge bird flying overhead heading for one of the castle turrets. A common enough occurrence, although most birds didn't have a glinting collar around their necks. *Maybe Xavier has a pet. It would make sense that any pet of his was as arrogant and gorgeous as he is.*

Chapter Two

"I really don't understand why we have to stay here for a whole week, your highness. There's nothing to do... I can hardly send out notices about the antics you and that homely prince might do..."

"I beg your pardon." Sprawled against the back of a large chair, his boots resting on an ornate coffee table, Crown Prince Xavier of Balenborn's head snapped around as he glared at his secretary. He had been thinking about the conversation he'd overheard between his future fiancé and the Queen. The listening device around his hawk's neck could be very effective at times. Cecilia, his personal secretary, was always blithering on about society pages and newsletters – concepts Xavier had no interest in – so it was easy to zone her out. But insults on the other hand... "Did I hear you dare to refer to Prince Remy as homely? My fiancé, and the son of our host?"

Cecilia had the grace to blush, but she didn't drop her eyes and there was a decided set to her jaw. She had a strength of character Xavier appreciated, but he didn't like the fact she thought anyone who wasn't him was beneath her notice. "My apologies, your highness. I didn't realize you were already attached to a man you haven't met yet."

"Not that it's any of your business, seeing as you've only been in my employ for two years, but King Francis and my father have been friends my whole life. I've watched my fiancé grow up. There is nothing mundane about him and I will not have my future husband spoken about with such disrespect. Are we clear?"

"Yes, your highness." There was a two second pause, and a barely-there nod, and then Cecilia said, "With regards to what we can put out for the society sheets however, I do think your purpose here should be kept on the down low. We could suggest it's a trade mission perhaps."

Dropping his feet from the table, so that his boots hit the tiled floor with a clunk, and sitting upright, Xavier snarled, "And why would that be? Are you suggesting I should be embarrassed about some aspect of my choice of spouse? Or are you against the idea of me getting married completely? Speak freely, it will be your only chance."

"The Lady Cecilia is just annoyed that you're considering marrying a royal at all – male or female it didn't matter. When King Mintyn took the youngest Fortune son as his own, and that prince's twin sister was carried off by the Dragon Prince Sebastian, our Lady Cecilia believed the only option left for *you* was to marry a woman of good breeding from a society family."

Xavier heaved a sigh of relief as his younger brother, Luca, strode into the room. Recently he'd gotten the impression his secretary was looking at him as if he was lunch and having Luca, or his head guard Dante around always made him feel more comfortable. He understood how men thought. Women were a mystery to him, although from Luca's comments it would seem his concern about Cecilia had some foundation.

"Is what my brother says true, Cecilia? Now's your chance to have your say – it's the only one you'll get, so get on with it."

"If you must know, I don't think it's seemly." Cecilia's thin face seemed even more pinched as she pressed her lips together. "It's like an epidemic. First Prince Nikolas married Prince Syrius, then King Mintyn – a fully-fledged king – tied himself to another prince and not even a crown prince. A third son, no less."

Cecilia sniffed. "Prince Harvey from Southland had the right idea, marrying a society woman with similar interests to his own but when I took this job, I never thought I'd see the day when you tied yourself to a male as well. He's not even in the top three in line for the throne. He's fourth after his older brother and his two nephews. A decent, respectable society lady like myself would make a lot better marriage prospect for you, and marrying me would allow you the opportunity to father your own children. Why do you think I took this position if it wasn't to give you a chance to appreciate the benefits a woman like myself could bring to the table when you become king."

Resting his elbow on the arm of his chair, Xavier rubbed his forehead. "Did I just hear you correctly?" He glared up at an unrepentant Cecilia and a smirking brother. "You've been lying to me for two whole years."

Cecilia threw her shoulders back and tilted her chin up. "A gentle born lady from a reputable society family does not lie."

"Excuse me. You lied to me. You told me when you first applied for the position as my personal secretary, and I quote, 'I have no interest in marriage or having children, as I plan to study for qualifications in magical engineering' end quote. Did your plans change when you got your qualifications in magical engineering?" Tilting his head slightly, Xavier added, "You must have your qualifications by now I imagine, although I don't remember you taking time off for the exams."

If anything Cecilia's nose went higher into the air. "I found that path of study unsuitable for a lady of my breeding and discontinued it."

"I see." Xavier nodded. "When did you make that decision? And you'd better believe, I will be checking."

Two red spots appeared on Cecilia's pale cheeks, but she didn't answer.

"Did you even start your studies?" Xavier prodded.

"I think you'll find Lady Cecilia found no need to study the moment you gave her a position in your inner circle," Luca observed. He'd taken a seat on the couch, his boots off, and feet up, making himself at home. The Bentley family clearly intended their visitors to be comfortable during their stay. "I have to admit I'm surprised it's taken her two years to make her move."

"I never believed your father would encourage your plans to marry the fourth in line to an inconsequential throne," Cecilia spat out. "And I certainly thought you had more brains than to go through with this farce."

Xavier paused as he heard the court bells ring – six bells – and then he stood and made his way over to an ornate bell pull, which would summon one of the many footmen in the castle. "I appreciate your honesty regarding my plans to marry Prince Remy, Lady Cecilia. You have been very candid, which I asked you for, and I respect you are entitled to your opinion. However, the contract you signed when you took on your position clearly stated that if you were found to be lying about anything at all, your position would be terminated on the spot. I will ask the Head of the Household to arrange immediate transport for you back to your family home in Balenborn."

"You're firing me because I don't believe in same-sex marriages?"

"You clearly misheard me. You're terminated because you lied about your intentions when you took up the position as my personal secretary. Kindly wait in your rooms until your transport has been arranged. That is all."

There was a knock at the door. Xavier called out, "Enter." Upon opening, Xavier found it wasn't the footman he was expecting, but Dante, still in full uniform. "Thank goodness. Can you escort the Lady Cecilia back to the rooms assigned to her please and then ask the Head of the Household to arrange immediate transport for her back to her family estate in Balenborn. I want her gone before I finish dinner tonight."

"Ah, I see. She finally let her plans slip out about her desire to be your bride." Dante chuckled. "Yes, your highness. Lady Cecilia, if you would accompany me, please."

"We'll see how badly your reputation suffers when I'm no longer handling your press releases." Cecilia swept towards the door with a swish of silk skirts and petticoats, passing Dante with a sniff. He just chuckled as the door closed behind them both.

"That was unexpected." Unbuttoning the top two buttons of his shirt, Xavier pulled it over his head as he went through into his bedroom, dropping it in a hamper. "Was I the only one who didn't know what Cecilia was thinking about me?" He hunted through his wardrobe looking at the state tunics hanging in a neat row, before pulling out the one he wanted.

26

It was bright white with black trim on the shoulders.

"Pretty much." Luca had abandoned his seat and was leaning his shoulder on the doorframe. "You really are clueless when it comes to women, aren't you."

"I've never seen the point in learning to get on with them beyond basic politeness. I've known I was going to marry Remy for the past ten years. I didn't want to give anyone else the wrong idea."

"Me thinks you have a slight hitch in those plans." Luca chuckled. "I'm not sure the very cute Prince Remy likes you very much."

Xavier sighed. Luca had been with him when he'd played back the recording orb from his hawk's necklace. "Remy never said he didn't like me per se. He thinks I don't like him, which is a totally different situation." He pulled the robe over his bare chest and smoothed it over his skin. "I have a horrible suspicion he might have thought I was rude to him when I rebuffed his advances ten years ago."

"You *were* rude to him back then," Luca chuckled. "Think back to when you were fifteen. For goodness' sake, it would've taken all his courage to approach you in the first place – you, a grown man of twenty-two at the time, and then you slapped him down faster than a mosquito biting your neck."

"It was the shock. I was so sure he didn't know I'd been watching him. He was cute even then." Xavier glanced down at his black pants – they were close fitting, but not tights. Tights made his knees look knobbly. The pants would do for dinner. "Besides, what was I supposed to do? It's not like I could give him any encouragement when he was still a kid, or he'd think I was warped in the head."

"Oh, I know that, but there is the little matter of you having had ten years since then to make it up to him."

"I think we can all agree making small talk is not one of my skills, despite what the promotional material about me might say." Looking over at Luca, Xavier shook his head. "I can't believe Remy has been reading all that guff about me. Just what has Cecilia been posting?"

"Apart from swooning women, or how you're a man of mystery, probably to cover the fact you struggle to hold a polite conversation, and that you have 'hidden depths' relating to the complexity of your emotions and empathy." Luca had the gall to use the sign for air quotes around the hidden depths' angle. "Cecilia clearly thought your personality and good deeds needed bolstering, probably so it would look like she'd gotten the catch of the century when you married her."

"Why didn't she mention something before we came here for the wedding?" Xavier clicked the two hawk eyes embellishing a large wooden box sitting on the dresser, releasing a hidden drawer. His hand hovered between the medals he'd been given when his father named him heir, and the crowned pin which had originally belonged to his mother. She'd passed it on to him to be given to Remy. He picked up the pin and attached it just below the collar of his white tunic.

"You should wear your medals too," Luca suggested. "As for Cecilia, you heard her. She seemed to genuinely believe that when you saw Remy again, you'd turn to her as a better option as a spouse. That's probably why she also fixed you up with all those dates from hell over the past two years."

"I did wonder." Xavier clipped the medals to the other side of his top. Working quickly, he braided his dark hair, so it fell down his back, and ran a hand over his facial hair.

"Will you stop primping, we'll be late for dinner," Luca protested as there was a knock at the door. "That'll be Dante. Come on."

He disappeared, presumably to answer the door. Xavier looked critically at his reflection. "You're not going to woo him with your looks," he warned his reflected self in a low voice. "So you'd better start learning to talk to him." Somehow, Xavier didn't think his typical quiet broody persona was going to work with someone like Remy.

Chapter Three

After giving himself a private and very stern talking to, reminding himself he was no longer the blushing, stammering fifteen year old that had last faced Crown Prince Xavier directly, Remy was enjoying the state dinner more than he thought he would. His father, King Francis, greeted Xavier and his brother first, as was proper. Then Xavier bent himself in a courtly bow over Queen Abigail's hand, in a very respectful gesture which Remy could and did appreciate. Xavier's tunic was short enough to show a flex of thigh, but not show off what Remy knew was a shapely ass. Some things hadn't changed in ten years.

The moment Xavier stood in front of him, Remy held his breath, letting it out very slowly as Xavier air kissed first one side of his cheek and then the other. The hand clasp between them was enough to send tremors to Remy's knees, but he held his cool, managed a small smile, and was grateful when his mother said it was time to go into dinner.

Although the years had been very kind to Xavier, there was something different about him. Remy got the impression there was an underlying sense of nervousness in Xavier's demeanor as the man offered Remy his arm to escort him to dinner. It was almost as if… *is he trying to be nice to me?* Assuming it was all for his parents' benefit, Remy decided to go along with it, keeping his responses brief, pleasant, and polite. It helped that Xavier was expected to converse with the numerous guests his father had invited. It gave Remy a chance to observe the crown prince without being obvious about it.

"You're looking very well." The eating part of the dinner was almost over when Prince Luca broke into Remy's musings about why Xavier was being so nice. "Getting older has agreed with you."

Remy chuckled. Luca was a quieter, and in Remy's opinion, a friendlier version of Xavier. The brothers shared some physical similarities. Xavier was taller and broader than Luca and had more of an edge to his ruggedly handsome face. Remy always believed that when Xavier was crafted, someone used an actual straight edge to ensure the noble nose didn't deviate from a perfect line. His high cheekbones, dark intense eyes and brows, and even the way his facial hair was clipped close to the skin gave the impression of someone tightly controlled. Luca's features were softer, and he wore his black hair loose instead of tied back in a braid like Xavier's was.

King Francis liked for his guests to talk to each other, which was why, instead of using long dining tables that Remy had seen in some society houses he'd visited, the King arranged for family groups and friends of up to ten people to be seated at round tables. Walking around between tables was encouraged.

The only exception was the royal table, which was a large rectangle. It was significant that for the state dinner hosting the dignitaries from Balenborn, Remy was seated at the place of honor at the foot of the table – Xavier on one side of him, and Luca on the other. The spot at the head of the table was reserved for the King, of course, with Remy's mother sitting to his left, and Pierre, as the heir, to his right.

"I could say the same about you." Luca was safe to talk to – he didn't want to marry anyone from the Bentley royal family. "How have things been in Balenborn? I take it your parents are well?"

"They are both enjoying robust health," Luca said with a grin. Resting his elbow on the table, he leaned closer and added in a low voice. "Are you worried you'll be King Consort of Balenborn before you and Xavier have a chance to get to know each other?"

The assumption was enough to make Remy laugh out loud, and he made of point of not noticing how Xavier turned his head from the person he was talking to, to glance at him. Okay, so he might have noticed a little bit. Manners dictated Xavier couldn't ignore the woman who was plucking at his sleeve, however. Lady Blanche was not a fan of being overlooked and for once in his life, Remy was grateful for her.

"As far as I'm aware," he said, turning his attention back to the friendlier brother, "the plan is simply that Xavier and I will be married. I don't recall any suggestion we were going to get to know each other."

"That's kinda what married people do." Luca wiggled his eyebrows, making Remy chuckle again, even if the implication heated his cheeks. "What sorts of things are you interested in? I see you're in uniform this evening – do you spend a lot of time with your father's troops?"

"I am an officer in my father's army and I train with them for an hour most mornings," Remy admitted. "My father believes all of us should know how to look after ourselves in times of trouble. A few years ago we had a bit of trouble with outlaws, and in one instance they gained access to the royal grounds. Sophia was only eleven at the time, and had run off to the stables, as she does quite often if she wants to get out of lessons. She was captured, but before the ruffians could leave the grounds with her, Daisy raised the alarm and Pierre stopped them. The day, and the princess, was saved."

"Daisy?" Luca looked puzzled. "I thought Pierre's wife was Emily?"

"The lovely Emily is Pierre's wife. Daisy is my Orobos. For saving Sophia, my father allowed me to build a stone house and enclosure for her and her occasional brood, including a pool."

"A pet guard lizard. How intriguing. What else can you tell me about her and her brood."

As Daisy and her care was one of Remy's favorite topics, he soon had Luca roaring with laughter as he shared some of Daisy's less lovable attributes such as her need to chase the stable boys across the yard if she felt like the exercise.

/~/~/~/~/

Xavier had an unfamiliar feeling in his chest, and he suspected it was jealousy. Remy and Luca were talking as if they were old friends, and the excitement and animation as Remy talked was beautiful to see. Xavier still remembered how animated Remy had been when he offered to "get closer" to Xavier all those years before. The look Remy gave Luca was similar, without the sexual intent.

He knew, on a logical level, that Luca was finding out all he could about Remy, to help Xavier. Finding topics of conversation wasn't easy for him when he spent a lot of his time training, riding, or leading his troops on goodwill missions around Balenborn. People like Lady Blanche were a godsend in a way as they didn't require him to do anything but appear to listen as she waxed on and on about the many attributes of her four daughters.

"I believe your king is about to make an announcement," he said at last, interrupting the lady when she paused for a breath. "You should probably return to your seat."

"Of course, your highness." Lady Blanche patted his arm. "I hope we see a lot of you and your brother while you're visiting."

She disappeared before Xavier had to come up with a polite response. The only benefit he could see in visiting Lady Blanche and her four daughters, was because he'd likely never have to say a word. *Maybe I should throw Luca at them instead,* he thought as Remy and Luca looked at King Francis who had stood up, tapping lightly on his glass.

"My lords, ladies, and gentlemen, I am sure our esteemed guests from Balenborn require no introduction." The King's voice rang around the room easily, assisted by the slender crystal he held in one hand. Xavier recognized the magical tech from King Mintyn's team and was impressed to see it worked as easily in a crowded room, as it did at the smaller, official meetings at the World Court his father had made him attend more than once.

"Crown Prince Xavier, and Prince Luca have become familiar faces in our country for many years, but this particular visit holds a very special significance for me and my family. It marks the time our families will become joined." The look King Francis gave Xavier gave him the feeling the king could see deep into his soul. "Crown Prince Xavier has asked for, and I have agreed to his marriage to…"

It was as though everyone in the entire room held their breath when the king paused. Princess Sophia sat up straighter in her seat next to her younger sister Hyacinth.

"To my son, Prince Remy," King Francis continued. There were a spate of gasps and low murmurs running around the room, and the King waited a moment before continuing. "The contracts are already signed, and my lovely Queen has been busy with closed-door wedding preparations for the past three months. I am thrilled to announce you are all invited to the wedding which will take place in just four days' time." He raised his glass to Xavier, or it might have been to Remy. But no, Xavier knew the next words were for him.

"Crown Prince Xavier worked hard to ensure this union will take place and I have every confidence the Crown Prince of Balenborn will do everything he can to make my younger son very happy in their lives together. Please, all of you, raise your glasses and drink a toast. To Crown Prince Xavier and our much-loved Prince Remy."

"To Xavier and Remy."

"You're supposed to take my hand," Remy whispered as Xavier felt a light pressure on the back of his hand that was resting on the table. "As the older man, these society ladies and gentlemen will expect you to lead in the romance department of our engagement, especially when I am sure they were expecting my dad to call out my sister's name, not mine. So it's time to put your playacting skills to good use if you have any. This crowd is going to expect to see some kind of connection between us."

Anything Xavier might have said fled his brain at Remy's light touch.

Flipping his hand, he met Remy's palm to palm, raising Remy's hand to his lips. Making sure he caught Remy's eye, he said softly, "I am so happy you said yes," before brushing his lips quickly but purposefully, and with every respect due to a royal fiancé in a public setting, over the back of Remy's hand.

And in that moment Xavier was so glad his lips were busy, because while he was sure he was the only person who heard Remy's sharp intake of breath, his heart lifted. He really wanted to grin about that, but Luca said if he ever did, he looked like a demented monkey.

So Xavier kept his smirk to himself and savored the short, but powerful moment. The wagging tongues around him didn't bother him at all – the announcement was made, his betrothal was now public knowledge, and in a short time Xavier would have the spouse he'd been waiting ten years for.

Chapter Four

"What was with that kiss?" His hand still tingling, Remy had escaped from the dining hall not long after his father had made the announcement. The surprise from the assembled guests hadn't escaped his notice, nor did the crowds of people who made their way to talk to his sister, Sophia. Remy didn't need to get involved in any of that. He knew his mother's secretary, George, would be knocking on his bedroom door early the next morning, likely with a list of approved activities he and Xavier were meant to share. But Remy needed some processing time and the best place for that was in Daisy's pen. Very few people bothered him there.

Daisy didn't seem to be impressed, although she never got upset with him visiting. Three of her youngsters were currently chewing on a heap of chicken carcasses, likely thrown there by one of the stable boys. They were forever bribing her and her offspring, in the hopes they wouldn't get chased. Remy always laughed when he saw her scampering across the courtyard after them. The boys never understood she was only playing. All they saw was an open mouth full of sharp teeth, and stubby legs that ended in long claws.

"I'm so confused," Remy confessed to his lizard friend. "I thought I had it all worked out. I was so sure Xavier was just marrying me to take family pressure off himself, so he could keep living his marvelous life – the one that's so elaborately documented in society news and World Council newsletters. So why did he kiss my hand that way? Why did he say something like 'I'm so happy you said yes'. I mean, why would he say that?"

Flicking out her long tongue, Daisy snapped at a passing bug. "You're not being very helpful," Remy said plaintively. "Is it possible someone in his delegation can lip read? Is that why he said what he did? I mean, he had two advisors and the head of his security unit at the neighboring table. Maybe that's why he was looking at me all through dinner when he thought I wasn't watching. Perhaps they are reporting back to his father or something."

A large yawn was his only response. Remy slumped his back against the wall. His mother said he should at least put a seat in Daisy's enclosure – she didn't think it was seemly if anyone saw him sitting on the ground. But Remy tried that when the enclosure was first built. It was a nice chair, too – wooden framing, and bright red embossed velvet upholstery. Remy got to sit in it for exactly one hour – during his evening visit to Daisy. By the next morning there was nothing left of the chair but a few splinters of wood on the floor where it had once stood and a thread of red velvet hanging from one of Daisy's son's teeth.

"He's had so many different partners." Remy gave voice to the main thing that bothered him about Xavier's response to him at the dinner. "He is likely a true man of the world, if you understand the inference."

Daisy just looked at him as if to say, "I may be a lizard, but I'm not stupid. Look at how many kids I've had."

"What am I meant to think about that?" A flutter of panic sought to get free from Remy's chest. "I mean, it's one thing to throw myself like an idiot at the man when I was a kid, but we're *both* grown up now. Does he expect...? Is he going to think...?"

Remy couldn't even say the words, let alone do the actions behind them. It wasn't something he'd ever done. But if Xavier's publicity was to be believed, and Remy had no reason to think someone would put false stories out about a prince and heir to the throne, then Xavier had a very active... "Oh, my gods, I genuinely can't even say it, let alone think about it," Remy groaned.

"How could you do it?"

Remy's head shot up, and so did Daisy's. Her sons didn't lift their heads from the chicken, but Remy could tell they were wary, from the way their long tails stuck straight out hovering about an inch off the ground.

"Sophia, keep your voice down," Remy hissed. "I've told you before, Orobos don't like loud noises. What are you even doing here? I'm sure Mother thinks you're in bed."

"If your precious lizards don't want to hear loud noises then you'd better get your butt out of that pen." Remy heard the warning in his sister's tone and got to his feet. He didn't want to think what his father might say if Daisy took a chunk out of his sister – no matter how well deserved.

Once outside of the pen, Sophia grabbed his arm, hustling him around to the back garden. That specific area of the massive gardens and lawns that surrounded the palace was reserved for members of the royal family only. Soft magical crystal lights lit up rose bushes, well maintained bushes that formed the hedges around the gardens, and even some wild hydrangeas whose soft yellow petals gleamed when they caught the light.

"Did you know Father was going to announce you as Xavier's fiancé this evening?"

"Of course I did." Remy nodded. "Father mentioned Xavier's request about six months ago, or was it four, I can't remember, but yes I knew it was going to happen tonight. Why did you think I was seated at the foot of the table at dinner, if it wasn't for something so important?"

"Well, why didn't you tell me?"

Remy looked at his sister in shock. At seventeen, Sophia was a beautiful young woman, or she would be once she had fully grown. She was about an inch taller than Remy, and slender like he was. But she took after their father in coloring – with dark hair and brilliant blue eyes. She was still wearing the pale blue silk dress that she'd worn for dinner and Remy took his jacket off and draped it over her shoulders. The night air had a bit of a chill in it.

"Why would I discuss any potential marriage plans with you?" he asked gently, hoping to take some of the sting out of Sophia's attitude. "For one thing, until Xavier arrived, I wasn't a hundred percent sure it was going to happen, and secondly, Father had insisted on it being kept secret. Between you and me, I am not sure he thought Xavier would turn up either."

"Don't you be like that. You have to know what everyone has been talking about around the castle."

"Talking about what?" Remy was genuinely puzzled, but then he rarely paid attention to gossip unless it was something funny.

"Talking about Xavier marrying me!"

"Oh, that." Then Remy saw Sophia's face and added quickly, "I had heard some rumblings about it. I overheard a couple of women discussing it the other day. But given as how they were going on about how all women apparently swoon over the prince, I didn't pay them much attention. Surely you didn't..."

He took another look at his sister's face. "Oh no, come on. You surely didn't think father would enter you into a marriage contract while you're still so young? He definitely wouldn't have signed anything without talking to you first. Father wouldn't do that. Mother wouldn't let him."

"I thought it was going to be a surprise." Sophia wailed. Spinning around, she waved her arms up and down in the air. "Mother said Father had a surprise for my birthday. Then just two weeks ago, we heard Xavier was coming with his brother and entourage. I... I thought... I'm going to be mortified in front of all of my friends."

Great, Xavier causes mortification in yet another young Bentley royal, and this time he wasn't even present to do it. "Sophia," Remy put his arm around her shoulder, "Come on, it's not that bad. Your friends will be upset on your behalf, but they're not going to be mean to you about it. You never specifically said to them that you and Xavier were in negotiations to marry, did you?"

"No, of course not. I wouldn't lie. But I did tell them I was getting a surprise for my birthday, and then Rosa said that Xavier and Luca were coming to visit..." She trailed off, and then with a burst of energy said, "It was an easy enough mistake to make."

"Exactly, a mistake that's all," Remy soothed. "But tell me, how did you and your little band of friends jump from your surprise for your birthday which is still six months away, and Xavier's visit now, to a marriage contract?"

"I don't know how marriage negotiations go yet," Sophia said with a sniff. "I thought, if he was coming to woo me, then he'd probably bring gifts, and ask to speak to me privately. And then," she clasped her hands to her chest, "he would whisper how much he burned for me, but how he'd wait for me…"

"Sophia!" Remy couldn't believe what he was hearing. "The Crown Prince Xavier is thirty-two years old, almost twice your age. Where do you get these ideas?"

"I read," Sophia said with a pout. "My friends and I share an extensive library of love stories. In almost every case, there is something that keeps the destined couple apart, like our ages in this case, but they make their desires known to each other and then..."

"My goodness." Remy glanced around making sure no one could overhear them. "Where do these books come from? Does Mother know about this?"

"You are such a prude." Sophia laughed. "Rosa's mother gives them to her, and she knows Rosa shares them with me and the other girls. How else are we meant to learn about love and life, if we don't read about it? It's not like it's something we can bring up as conversation at the dinner table, is it?"

"Definitely not. Mother and Father both would have a fit."

Remy still felt uncomfortable, but then he remembered what it was like when he was fifteen and newly rejected because he didn't understand how relationships worked. *I still don't,* he thought glumly.

"I can't believe you wanted to marry Prince Xavier though," he said instead of sharing his thoughts. Sophia was still very young in a lot of ways. "Isn't there someone closer to your own age you could dream about instead?"

"Prince Xavier is in a class all of his own." Sophia sighed. "The way he rides a horse... he cuts a very fine figure of a man."

You shouldn't even be looking at Xavier's figure, Remy wanted to scream, but he reminded himself for the second time in five minutes that he wasn't so old he'd forgotten what being a teenager was like. "Looks aren't everything," he said instead. "I mean, it's not like we really know him as a person. Don't those books you read talk about how compatibility is more than just how a couple looks together? To be happy in a relationship, don't you need things in common – shared interests?"

"I've probably got more in common with Prince Xavier than you have."

And there was the teenage attitude Remy loved about his sister. "I spend a lot of time riding – I play sports, I know how to look after myself, and how to swing a sword to disarm men twice my age and size. I believe those are attributes Prince Xavier would appreciate in a spouse."

"Then he's likely to be disappointed in me then." Taking Sophia's arm gently, Remy said, "Come on, let's get you back to your rooms before Mother finds out you're missing. With the visiting delegation here, she is only going to assume the worst and imagine someone has tried to abduct you again. Young princesses should not be outside unchaperoned this time of night."

"You're chaperoning me and who better to do that, than my newly engaged brother. Do you even like Prince Xavier?" Sophia asked as they made their way back to the castle.

"I'm sure he has hidden depths." Remy chuckled. "At least that is what the last article I read about him said. It won't really matter anyway. What you're forgetting is that this is a royal marriage – an arranged one. Xavier doesn't have to like me to be married to me, and vice versa. We just have to be civil to each other in public. I am sure he will completely ignore me in private."

The snort coming from his younger sister wasn't a sound coming from a lady. "That man couldn't keep his eyes off you all through dinner, especially when you were flirting with Prince Luca."

"I was not flirting." Remy was sure his cheeks were bright red, and he was only glad of the dim lighting on their way into the castle, otherwise his sister would've noticed. "Luca is easy to talk to, and he was interested in Daisy. I'm sure we wouldn't have anything else in common to talk about."

"You keep telling yourself that." Sophia laughed as they entered the castle and made their way upstairs. "I doubt Luca was interested in lizards, and I'm not sure Xavier will be either. You might have to come up with another interest."

"Or you could just stop worrying about my engagement and get yourself off to your rooms." Remy spotted Lizzy, Sophia's maid half running down the corridor towards them. "Your escape has been found out."

Sophia groaned, but then plastered a fake smile on her face. "Look who I found, Lizzy. I was just out congratulating my brother on his engagement. Have you heard about it?"

"Congratulations, your highness." Lizzy bobbed her head and then took Sophia's arm. "The Queen has been looking for you, Princess. She came in to tell you goodnight. I didn't know what to tell her when she realized you weren't in your bed."

"It's perfectly natural for me to want to congratulate my brother, Lizzy. Mother can't be upset about that."

Lizzy mumbled something, but Remy couldn't hear her as she was already power walking Sophia back to her own rooms. Whistling softly to himself, he took a left towards his own wing of the castle, hands in his pockets, his mind tripping over the events of the evening. He still couldn't get that kiss out of his mind, and he wasn't sure he'd get a lot of sleep that night.

Chapter Five

Xavier seethed with impatience. "Are you sure he got the note about riding with me after breakfast?" Max, his advisor, was standing to the side watching him with little expression.

"If by he, you mean Prince Remy, then yes. His mother's advisor, George and I conferred well into the night while you were having dinner, working out the best possible schedule so you could spend time together before the big day. In public of course," Max added in case there was any suggestion of impropriety. Max was the model of decorum. He typically advised Xavier's father, the King of Balenborn, but given how a marriage agreement between two countries could involve contract changes and amendments right up until the vows were exchanged, Xavier's father felt it was a good idea for Max to go along.

"It was a late night last night, your highness," Dante offered. "I am sure

Prince Remy is looking forward to spending time with you. Perhaps he is spending extra time getting himself ready."

"The Bentley royal family don't consider breakfast at six early bells a suitable time to eat, good sir." George, the Bentley royal advisor hurried into the stables. "I gave Prince Remy Crown Prince Xavier's message as soon as he was awake, but the Bentley royal family doesn't usually break their fast until eight early bells. Prince Remy is hurriedly getting dressed as we speak..."

"Has he eaten yet?" Xavier demanded. "Does he plan to eat before he meets us for our riding date?"

"No, your highness." George looked pained at the suggestion. "When I mentioned the time you had asked to meet him... well, he got very upset because he hadn't been woken sooner. He wasn't going to make you wait any longer than he had to while he had something to eat. But... he's on his way," he added quickly. "He just needed help with his boots and then he was going to pop in for a quick visit to give Daisy her breakfast..."

"There's that mention about Daisy again." Luca had explained to Xavier Remy's passion for Orobos. "Dante, get along to the kitchen and ask them to prepare a breakfast hamper for four people for us, if you please, and leave a message for Luca to let him know I probably won't be back for lunch."

He looked at George as Dante hurried off. "Can you, or someone else direct me to where my fiancé keeps his lizards, please? I have a strong desire to see them for myself."

"Your highness, I'm not sure that's a good idea. They're Orobos," George spluttered. "I'm not sure if you have them in Balenborn, but they are exceptionally large and strong for a lizard, and can react badly to any loud noises. Daisy is known to chase the stable boys all over the courtyard on a weekly basis. You could get bitten or mauled."

"I'm sure Prince Remy will protect me." Yes, Xavier's tongue was in his cheek. The day a lizard frightened him, he'd hang up his coronet. "If you don't want to escort me yourself...?"

"I hope you will consider yourself fully warned. I would hate for anyone to say I was derelict in my duties. That Daisy is vicious. But as you insist, it's right this way, your highness." Looking as if he was heading to the gallows instead of a lizard enclosure, George led the way out of the stables.

"I'm off to visit lizards," Xavier said tightly to Max who was still hovering. "Are you going to accompany me, or do lizards qualify as suitable chaperones for sweet princes."

"I doubt even your seduction techniques will prove very effective in a vicious lizard enclosure, your highness." Max made himself comfortable, sitting on a hay bale. "I'll wait here for your return."

"Suit yourself." Xavier strode out of the stable block, seeing George waiting for him by a newer building on the opposite edge of the courtyard. There were warning signs plastered all over the outside – one of which suggested visitors absolutely must be quiet at all times, and then there were three signs about keeping doors and gates closed. From all accounts, the lizards, or rather the infamous Daisy would get out anyway, and Xavier got the impression that Remy tolerated the signs but didn't take any notice of them.

He quickened his step as he overheard what seemed to be quiet, but definite noises of distress, passing George who'd gotten slower the closer they got to the building. Pressing his ear against the solid iron door – yep, Prince Remy was upset - and taking care not to make any further rushed movements, Xavier opened the door, and slipped inside, closing the door behind him. He waited a moment, letting his eyes adjust to the gloom inside as he looked around.

Remy really knows his stuff. Xavier took in the spaciousness of the area, the vents allowing for cool air to keep the place well ventilated, and the cleanness of the hay covered floor. All along one wall was a structure – a form of hideaway that looked as if a full grown man could fit in it. Xavier marveled at the precision at which the flat stones had been stacked together, giving the impression of randomness, but Xavier doubted even an earth tremor could knock the structure down.

There was a pool, with fresh running water in another corner, well away from the sleeping area, and a few discarded bones in the hay that looked like parts of a chicken or something similar, but Xavier's attention was drawn back to the hideaway.

"Oh, Daisy," Remy's voice was soft but so full of caring, Xavier was touched by it. "Why did you have to do this now? Prince Xavier is waiting for me. He's going to think I'm insulting him... I haven't even had breakfast... Oh, I know, you poor thing. But you will keep doing this to yourself, or letting someone else do this to you."

"Er... Hello." Xavier kept his voice low out of respect for the apparently poorly Daisy. "Remy, is Daisy all right?"

"Eep." Xavier heard sounds of a scuffle and then Remy's face appeared in the hideaway's opening. "Prince Xavier." Remy's hand went through his hair which looked as though he had just got out of bed. "I'm so sorry, I fully planned on meeting you for our ride this morning, I promise. It's just I always check on Daisy first thing, and I noticed all her offspring were gone..."

"Did they escape?" Xavier immediately looked around the area with a more critical eye. "Orobos can climb, can't they? Is it possible someone left the door open." He eyed the vents. It was possible a lizard could get through the holes... maybe... "Should we look for them?"

"That's very sweet of you." Remy slapped his hand on his chest. "Honestly, that is a thoughtful thing to say, but Orobos young only stay with their mother until she lays more eggs. As they can be cannibalistic, Daisy would've chased them off after they'd been fed last night. I was in here after dinner..." he shook his head, "I did wonder why she was letting the youngsters eat when she wasn't." A huge sigh. "I should've known, but I had other things on my mind."

Xavier resisted the smirk, *again*, and instead said, "So the young have escaped off into the wild to fend for themselves, and Daisy is...?" He raised his voice with the question.

"Laying eggs." Remy looked to the side again, and then back at Xavier. "I know I am supposed to be riding with you this morning, it's just I'm really loathe to leave her. But she'll be at least another hour or two. I know, my mother always says females know what to do when it comes to giving birth and men just get in the way, but I've had Daisy since she would fit on my hand, and this is her fifth set of eggs. Logically I know nothing should go wrong, and honestly, I'm not sure what I'd do if it did, but..."

Those eyes were so expressive, and Xavier felt a shift inside of himself – as if he'd say yes to anything Remy asked.

"Would you be terribly insulted if I didn't accompany you this morning?"

Xavier considered his options. He could either go riding with Max and Dante or he could sit with his fiancé while a lizard laid eggs. It was no contest. "Do you think Daisy would be offended if I sat with you while you took care of her? I don't know a lot about lizard reproduction either, but I'll be very quiet, and I'd be honored if you'd let me keep you company. I do understand how special she is to you."

"Luca's clearly been telling tales out of school." Remy smiled, lighting up his face. "I'll warn you now, it'll be boring and there's no chair – Daisy ate the last one – but if you don't mind sitting on hay, or I have a box you can sit on, you're welcome. Come in and meet Daisy. I'll apologize for her now. Egg laying makes her grumpy."

Brilliant, that's all I need on day one of courting – a grumpy egg laying lizard. Xavier regretted wearing his dress uniform jacket and pants. He knew his knife in his boot would keep him safe if Daisy took exception to his presence, but somehow, he also knew Remy would make his married life a living hell if Xavier was responsible for something happening to a clearly precious lizard. Hunching over slightly so he could fit under the hideaway doorframe, Xavier followed after Remy who'd disappeared deeper into the hideaway.

On first impression Daisy was huge and had a face only her mother could love. She had bright orange skin, with paler patches under her neck and down her chest. Sharp black eyes perched on the top of a head that was twice as wide as Xavier's hand, watched him warily as Xavier moved closer.

"It's okay Daisy, this is Xavier. Remember, I talked about him. He wanted to come and keep you company, too." Remy dropped down onto the floor, a practiced move he'd clearly done numerous times. Butt shuffling closer to Daisy, he patted the space beside him. "You can sit here if you like. Just don't move too quickly."

Eyeing Daisy's bulk, Xavier crept closer, crouching down until he was close enough to sit. In his opinion, a crown prince did not butt shuffle and he couldn't imagine what his father or his brother might say if they could see him sitting on a pile of hay. But the smile Remy gave him was worth the indignity.

Xavier relaxed as well as he could, given how Daisy hadn't taken her eyes off him, settling down to enjoy being with his fiancé. Sort of. He would've preferred a different setting, but Xavier was out to prove he was not the arrogant asshole Remy thought he was, and if that meant sitting in a lizard pen while the damn thing started shitting out eggs, then that's what he would do.

Chapter Six

George is going to have a fit, and he's going to tell Father, I just know it. Remy wasn't sure what led him to accept Xavier's offer to sit with him while he kept an eye on Daisy. It would have made more sense for him to send Xavier off on his ride and agree to meet up with him later. His mother might understand, but his father would've expected him to go riding despite Daisy's predicament, because riding was an acceptable activity for engaged princes to participate in.

"I'm not quite sure what Luca told you last night," he said after they'd sat in silence for a few minutes. "I know some people here don't understand my attachment to Daisy, but she did stop Sophia from being abducted. That was why Father let me build this enclosure for her." He looked around at the stacked rocks fondly. If someone looked close enough, they would find drops of his blood and scrapings of his skin on some of them.

"Your stone mason has incredible skills," Xavier agreed although Remy noticed he was keeping a wary eye on Daisy... who was keeping a wary eye on him. *A standoff between the Crown Prince and the Lizard – who will come out victorious?* Remy mentally chuckled. But then what Xavier said hit the working part of his brain.

"Thank you, that's kind of you to say so. I'm no stonemason, but there was something very satisfying about laying the stones and seeing Daisy's home emerge."

"You did all this with your own hands?" Xavier reached out slowly, patting the rocks behind him as if reassuring himself they were real. They were. Remy could attest to that.

"I like keeping busy," he explained, stroking over Daisy's head as she shuffled as if uncomfortable. "There's not a lot for a second prince to do when they are so far down the line of succession. Emily loves traveling, so Pierre takes her on the goodwill missions where a royal head is expected to attend. Sophia and Hyacinth have their own little band of friends and spend a lot of time visiting them. I'm more of a homebody."

"A homebody who enjoys keeping busy." Xavier swung back around. "I'm seriously impressed. The sort of craftsmanship I'm seeing here would take someone else decades of experience to achieve. There's no magic here at all, you've done it all by hand."

"Daisy doesn't like magical tools," Remy explained, well aware his face was bright red. He wasn't sure what possessed Xavier to be so nice to him, but the prince did nice very well. "It makes her sneeze, so no magic implements are allowed in her area at all. That's why I ended up making her sanctuary myself."

"It's not easy finding a true craftsman anymore." Xavier hooked his elbows around his bent legs, looking perfectly comfortable. His deep voice, when used in a low tone, was soothing in its own way – melodic. Remy fancied Xavier had used his honeyed tones in many intimate situations, *which this is not,* he reminded himself firmly. Daisy gave another full body wiggle and grunted, which punctuated Remy's mental reminder.

"I kinda wish I'd taken the time to grab breakfast now." Looking over at the bones and vegetables from last night's dinner in Daisy's bowl Remy wrinkled his nose. "I'm sure Daisy would share, but I'm not hungry enough to eat the stuff I brought down for her."

"Dante, my head of security, is getting a breakfast hamper from the kitchen." Xavier looked at the hideaway doorway but there was no one there. "I ordered it when I learned you hadn't had anything to eat. Of course, he's expecting us to be at the stables..."

Remy chuckled. He couldn't help it. "You're in the most secure place in this kingdom. Very few people come into Daisy's enclosure. My mother does, Sophia won't come into this bit, but she will stand at the door and yell at me until I come out, which she knows I will do quickly because Daisy hates the noise. But I will bet you anything George is standing outside the door refusing to let anyone else in. He's probably terrified Daisy will take a chunk out of a ranking visitor. He does worry, but then Daisy did chase him when he yelled at her one time."

"I'll bet a kiss."

"I beg your pardon, you bet what?" Remy wasn't sure he'd heard right.

"I'll bet you a kiss that George is stopping Dante from coming in here." Xavier looked him straight in the eye. "You did say you'd bet anything."

My goodness, is he serious? Remy swallowed hard. "Yes, yes I did," he said slowly. "But how will we know where Dante is right now?" He made sure he looked as firm as he was able to. "You can't yell for him. Not in here. And I don't go giving kisses to just anyone who *thinks* they might have won a bet." *I don't go kissing anyone ever,* but Remy made sure that thought didn't show on his face. "How will we know if you've won?"

Xavier smirked, or rather half-smirked. It was like he really wanted to crack his face in half with a brilliant grin, but someone told him he shouldn't. "I'll go, quietly," he added as Daisy let out another grunt. "If I'm back in two minutes with a breakfast hamper, then will you take that as proof Dante was waiting outside?"

"I'll give you five minutes," Remy said, imagining the aforementioned Dante was probably eating the breakfast hamper in the stables with Xavier's advisor. "George is going to try and stop you coming back in here. I trust you to talk him around to your way of thinking within five minutes. How does that sound?"

"That kiss is mine." Xavier levered himself onto his feet and moving cautiously, headed for the open doorway. "Five minutes, starting now."

"He's awfully sure of himself, for someone who probably won't be allowed back in here at all," Remy said to Daisy as he heard the enclosure door close behind Xavier. "Now, how are you doing? Eww, yes, I can see," he added as he noted Daisy's outstretched tail. "Two eggs already. You're doing so well. Keep it up. There were five last time, so we probably don't need that many this time if it's all the same to you. In fact, if you could speed things along, that would be amazing. I seriously should've grabbed a breakfast roll before I came out here."

Daisy grunted. She'd eat when she was done.

/~/~/~/~/

"Where's Dante?" Xavier burst out of the lizard enclosure as if his butt was on fire. There were about a half a dozen people standing around George, but it was George he focused on. "What did you do to my head of security and the breakfast hamper I ordered for Prince Remy?"

"Your highness, I must protest at you being with Prince Remy in a private situation without a chaperone." George stood to his full height of about five foot five.

"You were welcome to accompany me. I wasn't stopping you." Xavier scanned the courtyard. "Where's Dante with that food? Damn it. I need that food and I need it now."

"Your highness!" George actually stamped his foot. "Please pay attention. Prince Remy's reputation is at stake here."

"Are you suggesting I'm compromising my fiancé's reputation? Me?"

Maybe it was the glower Xavier knew he was wearing or the fact he was definitely looming over George, but the stout man paled and backed up. "People will talk, your highness," he said with none of his earlier stridency. "It's my job to see..."

"It's your job to ensure that people don't know there's anything to gossip about when it comes to Prince Remy. Daisy is giving birth. I'm attending to my fiancé during this very special and rare event. I sent my head of security to the kitchen to get my fiancé his breakfast that he's still waiting for. The only one I see causing an issue for Prince Remy right this minute is you." *And me.* Xavier could feel his promised kiss slipping away by the second.

"We have to have behavioral standards..."

"Prince Remy has to have food. Damn it, man, if you can't tell me where Dante is, I'll go to the kitchen myself." Xavier knew doing that would cost him his kiss, but at least Remy would get to eat.

"I'm sure I don't know how things are done in Balenborn, but in Bentley, royal family members don't visit the kitchen."

Bending over, Xavier got close enough that he could smell what George had for breakfast. "If we were in Balenborn, my fiancé wouldn't be hungry, and advisors wouldn't take it on themselves to interfere in a royal courtship. If we were in Balenborn, you'd be in jail right now, do you understand me? In fact, stuff this, stuff you."

Straightening up, Xavier threw up his hand. "I'll go and speak to the king directly and lay my complaint right now. I will not have you sticking your nose in where it does not belong. It's people like you that ruin a prince's reputation with their own gutter minds."

I can kick that kiss goodbye. Xavier stomped over to the stables – no sign of Max or Dante although their horses were still there. *Where have they gone? Probably up to no good together in a hayloft somewhere.* Not that Xavier could blame them. He'd seen the gleam in Dante's eye when the king said Max would be accompanying them to Bentley. *I'm the one missing out here, and I've still got to find food for Remy.*

So intent on getting back to the castle, Xavier almost bumped into a woman coming in the opposite direction, accompanied by two others.

"Your majesty." Xavier stopped and bowed quickly to the most important person in the group. "My apologies. I'm just trying to get Remy his breakfast, and your advisor is being an obstructionist... an *obstructionist being*," he spat out. "He said I was compromising my fiancé's reputation, by sitting in Daisy's pen with him while she's laying eggs. I am so angry with that man right now. Is his behavior normal in Bentley?"

"Oh, dear, you are in a state, aren't you. My lady Anna will get Remy the breakfast you're looking for and George is a relic, but he knows where the bodies are buried, so we keep him around." Queen Abigail chuckled as she took his arm, turning him around so he was heading back to the stables again. "I came to see how things were going with my son. How are things progressing in your courtship?"

"They would've been progressing a lot better if it hadn't been for George's interference. Do you know what happened to Dante and Max? I can't find them anywhere."

"They're with the king – he had some messages from Balenborn. Your father wanted a progress report as well. As Max and Dante couldn't provide much in the way of details, I decided to come and see how things were going for myself."

"I didn't know I would have to factor in a lizard's biological cycle in my courtship plans." Although Xavier reasoned privately, he wouldn't have had any privacy with Remy if they'd gone for the ride that had been scheduled. "Is Daisy going to be difficult to move? Will she be happy in Balenborn, do you think? Only if she isn't, I can see my chances of making Remy happy getting slimmer and slimmer."

"You strike me as a man who can get things done, would you agree?"

"Definitely. Whatever it takes to make Remy happy."

"I knew I liked you for a reason." Queen Abigail patted Xavier's arm. "Now, because your mother's not here to advise you, I'm going to stick my nose into your relationship with my son. And you have to listen to me because I'm queen here."

"Yes, ma'am. You're definitely the only queen here." Xavier wasn't sure he wanted Remy's mother interfering, but it was a step up from the pompous George, and frankly he needed all the help he could get. "What would you advise?"

"You need to get Remy alone, and I don't mean in Daisy's pen." Queen Abigail looked up at him. The pen was just ahead. "You need to get Remy on a horse and get him away from prying eyes like George's."

"Then I have to contend with my father's advisor, Max, and my head of security, Dante." Xavier sighed. "It's not easy romancing someone in public."

"It can be done. Me and Francis are very happy, and I'm sure the same can be said for your mother and father. I've been friends with your mother for years, and we talk about things."

"That I don't need to know about," Xavier said hurriedly.

"Actually," Queen Abigail pulled him up short, just out of earshot of George who was still guarding the door of Daisy's pen like a bulldog. "You do need to hear this. For some reason, my son has the impression you don't like him very much."

"Hmm." Xavier wasn't going to tell Remy's mother why that might be.

"You also have to contend with all the PR that secretary of yours has been putting out the past two years," the Queen warned. "Remy, for whatever reason and I'm sure I wouldn't ask him why, has been following your publicity articles and news snippets. They present the image of a person I was concerned enough about to question your mother about whether you'd make a good son-in-law."

"Would you think even less about me, if I said I don't know what's been said about me all this time? It would seem my secretary thought she'd make a good bride for me..." letting out a long huff, Xavier said, "Between Daisy and my ex-secretary, I'm fighting an uphill battle when it comes to winning Remy's affection."

"You are a charismatic man, even if you don't say much." Queen Abigail stopped, and Xavier stopped with her, surprised when she twirled around in a rustle of skirts to face him. "You need to use that charisma on my son. I'm fully supportive of your marriage, I'll be thrilled to welcome you into the family. But Remy deserves to be happy and I'm counting on you to ensure he stays that way. So I want to see signs of you wooing him, understood."

"It would be easier to do if certain people didn't go around suggesting, or blatantly saying I'm compromising Remy's virtue. I would never do that."

Queen Abigail's laughter rang around the courtyard causing a few stable boys, and her attendant to look up. "You're going to have to compromise him in some way as soon as possible after the marriage, or Remy could get annoyed with you and invoke that 'bail out' clause, not that I think he will, but he could."

Xavier frowned. "How did that clause even get into the marriage contract? I didn't want it added. In fact, I specifically stated that there was to be a fidelity clause, because I wanted Remy to know I was serious about him, and that other clause was supposed to be struck from the initial draft and any future amendments."

The clause they were discussing, the "Exceptionally Unacceptable, Inappropriate, Negative Behavioral

Traits Clause", also known as the piss off clause, was instigated by the World Council and had been tweaked over the years. In its current form its main impact was that it allowed any royal or society person, in an arranged marriage, to invoke the clause any time before a couple became intimate.

The moment intimacy, or a form of penetration from one person to another was achieved, the clause became redundant. The thinking behind it, as Xavier could see it, was that it encouraged people in unhappy relationships an easy 'out' if needed. Anything from heavy snoring, or behavior that could be deemed 'distressing' was enough to invoke the clause. But it also meant that if a couple had reached a point where intimacy blossomed between the two people concerned, they were expected to work on their relationship from that point onwards. Xavier didn't need a darn clause in his marriage contract to know how important it was to work on his relationship.

"I don't want that clause in my marriage contract," he said firmly.

"I think you might find that the advisors have over advised themselves. I will inform the king of the necessary changes needed, and if you'd drop by our office just before dinner, then we can have you sign the final document before anyone else catches wind of the change."

Queen Abigail patted his arm. "Here comes my attendant with your food hamper. You should probably go and relieve her of that, and..." she turned as they both heard Daisy's enclosure door open, "there's my son now. I suggest you and he make a dash for the stables with the food, and make your escape. I'll take care of George. Make sure you are back before dinner, or you'll be facing a shotgun marriage tonight."

I'm not so sure that's a bad thing. But Xavier nodded, and went to grab the hamper, nodding as Queen Abigail went past on her way back to the castle with her attendants in tow and George scurrying up behind her. He sniffed, his nose in the air as he went past Xavier, but the prince really didn't care. He was more focused on Remy.

"It took me a while, but I did get your hamper," Xavier said, holding it up. It was heavy which boded well for a stomach-filled afternoon.

"And Daisy is guarding six eggs. Six of them. Phew." Remy shook his head as he got closer, his hair a mess as if he'd been running his hands through it. "It's times like this, when I see what Daisy goes through every time, that I am so glad I was born a male." He grinned at Xavier. "Did you win your bet?"

"I'd love to say yes, but apparently Dante and Max were called into your father's office. Or so George told me."

Xavier was determined every interaction with his fiancé would be an honest one. "So I'll have to find another way to win that kiss, and in the meantime, you look like you could do with something to eat. Your mother suggested we disappear on the horses and take some time for ourselves. Would you mind doing that with me? There'd be no chaperones unless you insist on one."

"You're carrying food. I'll follow you anywhere."

And that would have to be enough for now. But Xavier vowed, as they headed to the stables to arrange for horses and saddle bags, that in time, Remy would want to follow him for totally different reasons.

Chapter Seven

It was nice, being outside of the castle grounds, just the two of them, and the horses, enjoying a picnic by a peaceful glade, by a stream, with the birds tweeting in the trees overhead and a soft breeze rustling the leaves. It was the sort of romantic scene Sophia probably read about in her forbidden books, but Remy still felt there was something intrinsically wrong with the whole set up. *Why is Xavier being so nice to me?*

It was so out of line with what Remy remembered from before. Xavier had let him take the lead as to where they would go and when they did find what was a lovely spot, it was he who laid out the blanket and asked Remy for his food preferences. He waited on Remy... the way Remy believed a caring partner would, or at least a fiancé who wanted to make a good impression. And yet still Remy couldn't work out why Xavier was being… well he was being a perfect fiancé. It didn't make sense.

And of course, with him being who he was, because he wasn't fifteen anymore, he was a man of twenty-five, Remy waited until the sandwiches and pasties were consumed and both men were sitting in what could be considered amicable silence, before asking his question. Straight out.

"Why are you being so nice to me?"

The question fell like a stone into the silence between them, and Remy felt the tension he caused, especially when Xavier just looked at him with that hard, yet definitely handsome face of his.

"I mean, there's no one else around. You could've dumped me and gone cantering off the moment we'd gotten out of sight of the castle. And yet, here you are, sitting here with me as if…" Remy swallowed past the lump in his throat. "As if we're actually an engaged couple that likes each other," he added in a rush.

"What makes you think I don't like you?" Xavier asked, and there was something about that quirked brow of his that made Remy want to lick it – and he didn't do things like that. Daisy might lick everything in sight, but he was one for keeping his tongue to himself.

"I would've thought that obvious." Remy's cheeks were flaming, he could feel the heat, but he pushed on, the worries and thoughts he'd been having since that fateful night so long ago demanding he get the answers he'd wanted since he heard Xavier's offer of marriage. *This could be my only chance.* "The last time you spoke to me, before this visit, was ten years ago, and the words you left me with were harsh enough to be engraved on my soul."

"I have regretted those words and my tone in which those words were delivered so many times in the past ten years." Xavier's voice was soft, almost regretful. He looked out at the trees, or maybe it was at the blue sky, but Remy got the impression the man wasn't seeing the scenery at all. "You have to realize..."

"No. No." Remy put up his hand. "I totally get it. I was so far out of line that night I was storming borders. I appreciate that I was breaching any form of decent etiquette, believe me, I know that. But as that is the last memory you seem to have of me, and as I so sorely disgusted you at the time... why are you insisting on marrying me now?"

"Because!" Xavier jumped up, brushing off the seat of his pants as he strode about six steps away, before turning to face where Remy was sitting. There was tension in Xavier's shoulders, and he didn't seem to know what to do with his hands, fisting them one second and splaying his fingers the next.

"Do you have any idea how much I wanted to take you up on that offer that night? And do you have any idea how disgusted I was at myself for even considering it? Not because I was disgusted in you, but because you were still a teenager. Anything between us would've been so wrong it's incomprehensible. And I know you know that now and believe me, I'm not that old I don't remember what it was like to be a teenager with rampant hormones, but my gods, man. What if I had said yes?"

He took two steps closer, his voice dropping even further. "What if I had given in and said yes. I wouldn't have been allowed to even consider marrying you for a further three years, even when I would've wanted to, because believe me I did. Three long years when you could've realized how boring I am, how fastidious, and how annoying my broody silences could be. I was no decent partner for you then.

"Hell, I'm not sure I'm right for you now. But I haven't been able to get that night out of my head for ten long years. You offered yourself to me once. Just a kiss, do you remember? Ten years I have waited to take that kiss. Ten very long years, but by all that's holy we will be married because I want a right to any kisses you offer from the moment we are wedded onwards and anything else you care to offer besides. Ten years!"

Remy was stunned. "You actually wanted to kiss me back then?"

"Of course I did." Xavier shook his head. "Damn, I wanted to so much. But I was already an adult, and for you adulthood was still three years away. And I didn't know if I could stop at just kissing you back then. Why do you think it took me three years to come back after that night? Damn it! At least if you offered yourself to me a second time, you would've been over the age of consent, and I could've said yes."

"Is this a dream? It has to be a dream." Remy pinched himself. "Ouch. Nope, not a dream. You actually wanted to kiss me. Incredible. Just incredible."

He looked over at Xavier who still seemed to be wrestling with some inner turmoil. "In all the times I've dreamed of how this conversation might go, it never once crossed my mind that you might have wanted me in return. That's why I couldn't believe it when Father said you'd offered a marriage contract for me. You never talked to me. When you came back after those three years, and I was legally an adult then, you never said anything to me."

"Oh, Remy." Xavier rubbed his hand over his face, before smoothing out his ruffled facial hair. "What was I meant to say? I hurt you when I turned you down and I had no excuse for doing that. I was angry that night, but I was angry at myself not you."

"Because?" Remy thought he guessed why, but they'd spent ten years not talking because of assumptions he'd made, and he wasn't going to make that mistake again.

"Because I really truly wanted that kiss, and I had no right to think like that about someone who was only fifteen at the time. But then, when I did come to visit, just after you turned eighteen, I didn't know what to say to make up for it. Do you remember, your dad threw that state dinner for me and my father, and you were there.

"And when I saw you, damn it all to hell, I will never forget the look of hurt on your face when you saw me, and how you turned away and wouldn't look at me again. I should've been the bigger man. I should've sought you out and explained, but I was so damn sure I'd get the words wrong, and I'd make things worse..."

"So after that you decided to wait another seven years and then sent my father a marriage contract for me." Remy looked down, covering his mouth with his hand as he chuckled. But then he couldn't resist looking up again – and it was worth it when he did.

"It worked." Xavier showed off his lop-sided grin, his head tilting slightly as if he were a curious puppy, which was not an association Remy usually had with the crown prince. "You're talking to me again, and that's all I've wanted in these past ten years."

"It would be a very unusual marriage if we didn't clear the air about some things between us," Remy agreed. He patted the blanket. "Come and sit back down. With the arrangements George is probably making on our behalf already, we're not likely to have many moments just to ourselves until after the wedding.

"Perhaps you can explain to me why, in all the articles I've read about you over the past few years, you're always seen in the company of women, but never the same woman more than once. Never another man, but that sort of press definitely gave you the reputation of being a love them and leave them type.

"Do I want to know what you actually did with those women before we get married? They all looked old enough to kiss." No, Remy wasn't jealous, he just wanted to get an idea of how much of a man of the world his fiancé truly was.

"I'm so sorry you had to read all that. Those articles stemmed from employing a secretary who decided very early on in the piece she would make the perfect bride for a Crown Prince." Xavier sighed, but he did as Remy suggested and came and sat on the blanket beside him. "This is nice," he said, making himself comfortable. "Really nice. I don't get many moments like this."

"Peaceful?" Remy asked.

"Peaceful. Private. Away from all the hustle and bustle and expectations everyone seems to have of me." Another sigh. "I met up with your mother just before you came out of Daisy's enclosure. She told me I should get you alone and use my charisma so that you'll be happier going into our marriage. There's only one problem with that."

That sounds like mother. Remy knew Queen Abigail had always wanted him to be happy no matter what he did in life. "What's the problem?"

"I'm really not charismatic at all."

Chapter Eight

Xavier did agree with Queen Abigail about one point. He had to do something to help encourage the type of relationship he'd dreamed about having with Remy for so long. But he knew charisma wasn't going to cut it. All he could do was be himself.

"All that stuff you've read about me, all the pictures you've seen, all the quotes and crap like that is exactly that. Crap." Xavier glanced in Remy's direction, hoping his strong language didn't upset his prince. "I've just been doing what I do – mostly what my father likes me to do. I work with the Balenborn army. I command a ship in our navy. I represent Balenborn in World Council meetings at times. My father relies on me to carry out his wishes both within Balenborn and in other countries, and I do my tasks willingly. But honestly, I have the personality of a newt."

"My best friend is a lizard," Remy pointed out. "I'm sure I'd have room in my heart for a newt as well, given a chance to get to know that newt. But why are you being so hard on yourself? Honestly, I overheard two women the other day who both agreed all females swoon when they watch you get on your horse. Their knees tremble when you walk past them. I mean, when you've got those kinds of skills, how much more charisma do you need?"

Xavier shot Remy an exasperated look. "People who admire the way I get on a horse are only interested in my body, my status as an heir, or the fact they think I have a lot of money. They don't care about me as a person. I'm seen as a prize to be attained. That's what my secretary thought, I'm sure. She was literally writing posts and articles making me out to be this complex person, so she'd look as though she'd made a good catch when I gave in and went after her. Sheesh. One of these days people will stop objectifying me and understand I'm a real person, and not a very interesting one at that."

"Did you honestly just say sheesh?" Remy chuckled again. "I have to admit, I'd never expect a crown prince of a realm, and someone who makes getting on a horse so sexy to say something like that. But how about, in an effort to get to know you as a real person, I won't watch you when you get back on your horse. How does that sound?"

"I'm not sure," Xavier admitted – he sounded so serious, but there was a twinkle in his eye. "It does sound as though you're making fun of me. I think I like that, because most people are too in awe of me and just wouldn't do that. But if watching me get on my horse would make you swoon, and keener to marry me, then I'll let you know every time it's going to happen."

"I've known you were well put together physically since I was a lot younger than fifteen." Remy's grin widened. "But its not appropriate to say things like that while we're still engaged. But tell me, if your secretary, whom I assume is the disgruntled lady who gave me a filthy look as I saw her leaving the castle last night under guard, was that her?"

Xavier nodded. He couldn't think of anyone else who'd give his cute looking prince evil looks.

"Well, if she wanted to marry you, then why did you go on all those dates with all the other women that were giving interviews about how wonderful you are and were written about at great length. Was that you failing to see what she was doing, or what was it? I feel like I'm missing something."

"It was my secretary who set me up with those dates." Sitting up, Xavier tugged at his hair making sure it was off his face, and then smoothed over his facial hair as he struggled to think how to explain.

"Every date, and I mean every one of them was an absolute disaster. I couldn't talk to any of them the way I'm talking to you. One woman wouldn't stop talking about all the skills she had that would ensure she'd be a good wife. Another time, a woman I'd only just met started asking me about the succession rules for Balenborn and how many children I wanted. This was on the *first date*. This is another sheesh moment, I tell you."

Xavier wasn't sure what more he could say, but unlike his previous dates, Remy was listening to him and truly appeared interested. "I honestly believed there must've been something wrong with me. That I was giving off these signals that suggested I wanted to get married to the first woman who would give me the time of day, when that couldn't have been further from the truth." He glanced in Remy's direction. "I'd already planned to marry you. I was just biding my time waiting for you to grow up."

Squinting at him, Remy shook his head. "Then why did you date at all? I'm not suggesting for a second you should've remained pure for my benefit. But why go out on dates with people you didn't get along with?"

Gods this is so difficult. Letting out a long breath, Xavier laid back so he could look at the sky. The clouds were nice. "I only ever told Luca about my fascination with you, until recently that is. I didn't dare mention it to my parents as I didn't want them to think I was being inappropriate about someone who was effectively still a minor.

"I know marriage contracts are conducted between children and adults all the time in society families and some royals, too. But my father doesn't approve of that idea, and I didn't want to disappoint my parents. However, apparently not dating was bad for my image too – or at least that's what my secretary told me. A man in their thirties had to start thinking about settling down or people will think there is something wrong with them."

"And you didn't want to forge a marriage contract with me when I was eighteen because...?"

"Because I saw at the dinner we were at together when you were eighteen..." Xavier tried again. "I saw so clearly how badly I had hurt you and how it still stung, just to see me." Xavier gave a half shrug. "I figured I had to wait until I had the courage to speak to you properly, and to be honest, I thought by now you could be attracted to someone else."

"I didn't have the same pressures to marry that you did." Remy leaned over his bent legs, wrapping his arms around his shins. "Honestly, as a second son, I have very little value for any other royal family. When Pierre and Emily had my adorable nephews, my value slipped even further. There was a casual idea my father put to me, about looking to make an arrangement with Crown Prince Harvey from Southland, but he was away a lot studying, and didn't seem keen. My parents did want me to be happy with whoever I ended up with."

"But *you* never met anyone, you know, that you thought you could be happy with for life?"

"I did actually." Remy looked his way and actually winked at him. "I saw this guy, and thought he was someone who could really make me happy. Unfortunately, I was just a kid at the time and had to wait until I grew up before he could express his interest."

Xavier must've looked shocked, because Remy laughed, his happy sounds ringing around the glade.

"Oh, come on." Remy was still chuckling. "I'm not a fickle person. I knew my own mind at fifteen, even if it was overridden with hormones at the time. I just wasn't blessed with patience and for the longest time I thought I'd ruined any chance I had of being with you. Until a messenger came from Balenborn with a marriage contract."

"You were happy about it?"

Remy was still shaking with mirth. "I thought you were bidding for Sophia."

"Sophia? Your sister?"

"Well, you had been dating women. There had never been any talk of you enjoying the company of men except your brother and your guard Dante. It was an easy mistake to make. I didn't know you'd been waiting for me."

"And now you do know." Xavier sat up, mimicking Remy's pose. He could barely believe the man was actually talking to him, or how relaxing that could be. "Do you think you could be happy with me?"

"I think if you waited ten years in the hopes that I could want to be with you eventually, and I spent ten years holding you as the ideal all other men fell short of, then we've got a jolly good chance of making things work between us, don't you? Now we've talked things out, I'm happy to try."

The weight Xavier had been carrying for ten long years fell off his shoulder, making him feel almost giddy. But he couldn't forget how that pompous advisor, George, had suggested for a second that he'd compromised Remy's virtue. He wouldn't do that. With a rueful glance at the way the sun was lowering in the sky, he said, "You have no idea how happy our talk has made me, but I guess we'd better get back. Your mother said if we returned after nightfall, we'd be having a shotgun wedding."

"And that wouldn't please her after all the effort she's put in to planning the wedding we will be having in three days' time." Jumping to his feet,

Remy held out his hand. "Do you need help getting up?"

"No. I'm not that old," But Xavier grabbed Remy's hand before his fiancé could withdraw it and pulled himself to his feet, keeping hold of the hand. "I really, really want that kiss, but I am prepared to wait three more days."

Remy's cheeks reddened – it was a good look on him. "As I've never kissed anyone before, perhaps we should wait. If I'm lousy at it, then you could call off the wedding leaving me mortified and my parents horrified. I'll amuse myself by watching you get on your horse, shall I?"

He's never even been kissed. Xavier gave Remy's hand a quick brush of his lips and then nodded as he let Remy's hand go. "Try not to swoon, or I'll have to get off my horse again to catch you."

"Darn, you see through my dastardly plan. But it's okay. I'm sure I can contain myself." Remy was still grinning, and Xavier made a point of slowly getting onto his horse. Remy clasped his hands to his chest, a fake dreamy look on his face, and Xavier let out a full grin. Yes, the one that Luca said made him look like a demented monkey. From the way Remy's eyes widened when he saw it, it was possible the Bentley prince liked monkeys as well as his lizards.

Chapter Nine

Remy checked out his reflection in the long silver mirror his mother had bought him for his eighteenth birthday. He'd decided on one of the state robes the Bentley family had commissioned in the family colors of emerald green with gold trim to wear for dinner. Combined with black pants, even Remy could agree he didn't look half bad. He ran his hand over his hair and grimaced. No matter what he did, how he had it cut, or how many products he used, he could not get his hair to sit straight.

"It's not like Xavier expects me to look any different," he reminded his reflection. On the outside, he looked like a prince who had dressed up for dinner. On the inside, however... His insides were a mass of emotions – like someone had just handed him his wildest dream and it was so amazing, he wasn't sure how to process what had happened.

Remy hadn't lied to Xavier. He'd noticed the man when he was just a boy – well before he'd tried to cadge a kiss from him. *And thank everything that's holy that little issue has been discussed and put away.* Remy couldn't have imagined in his wildest dreams that Xavier had actually wanted him, too. *But he did, and he does.* Remy did a little soft shoe shuffle, in his bare feet, across the tiled floor.

A knock on the door to his suite of rooms had him frowning. He was expected down for dinner in the main dining hall at six bells, and Remy had been dithering about what to wear for at least thirty minutes. He was due to go downstairs very soon.

"Enter," he called out as he went from his bathroom, into his main room. He tilted his head and smiled as his father came into the room. "Father. Is something wrong? Did I miss a message from you? I was just about to come down for dinner."

"No, no message." His father smiled, closing the door behind him and making his way to the two-seater couch Remy had placed by the window. "I thought, with your wedding just a few days away... well, in fact your mother thought I should have a wee talk to you. Come and sit down a moment."

Feeling a bit anxious, because Remy couldn't remember the last time his father had come into his room since he'd become a teenager. Queen Abigail and King Francis were good people – devoted to each other, and they spent a lot of their energies managing their small kingdom. They had spent a lot of time with their children when Pierre and Remy were both small, and again with Sophia and Hyacinth when they came along one year apart, seven years later. But one of their key lessons to their children was how to be independent.

"You're worrying me," Remy admitted as he sat next to his father who was already dressed for dinner in a robe of the same color as Remy's. "Have I done something wrong? Has Daisy been in trouble again?"

"No, nothing like that, although you're probably going to have to talk to your fiancé about arrangements for moving Daisy to Balenborn."

"Shoots. I hadn't even thought about that." Daisy's eggs would hatch within the next fourteen days, but Remy wasn't sure if it would be easier to move her with the eggs or wait until she'd had her young. "I don't want to leave her behind if I can help it. I hope Xavier understands that."

"Apparently, he's already mentioned thinking about transport arrangements with your mother."

"Phew. That's a relief." Remy smiled at his father. "So, I haven't scandalized anyone, Daisy hasn't bitten anyone today, I understand Xavier had words with George earlier today, but apparently Mother smoothed those ruffled feathers."

"George overestimates your fiancé's powers if he thinks you'd be interested in mucking about in Daisy's pen." His father smirked reminding Remy that underneath the crown was a man who cared deeply for him.

"Well, maybe if Daisy hadn't been laying eggs at the time, and if I thought I could get away with it without Daisy biting Xavier." Remy returned the smirk.

"Yes, well, that's sort of what I wanted to talk to you about." King Francis looked like he'd been sucking a lemon. Remy had tried that once. It wasn't pleasant. "As you may or may not know, I called Max and Dante from the Balenborn contingent into my office this morning after receiving messages from King Dare, Xavier's Father."

"Everything's all right with Xavier's family, isn't it?" Remy was suddenly anxious on Xavier's behalf.

"Yes, yes. They sent their regards. Dare wanted to come to the wedding, as did his wife, Selena, but their daughter Imogene is due to give birth in a matter of days, and Selena wanted to be with her which was totally understandable. They are very keen to welcome you into their family after you and Xavier marry. *If* you and Xavier marry."

Remy didn't have butterflies in his stomach, he had bats – agitated bats. "What do you mean if? The contracts are already signed. All we need now is to say our vows and record our marriage with the World Council." Those bats were making Remy feel sick, all the good feelings he had since he'd left Xavier at the stables after their afternoon together fleeing faster than a straw in a cyclone. "Did Xavier say something? Does he want to pull out for some reason?" *Was everything he told me a lie?*

If that was the case, then all Remy wanted to do was curl up under his blankets and not come out until the Balenborn delegation went home. And then he was hit with another thought. *My gods, my father has already announced our engagement. I'm never going to be able to face anyone again. I'll have to run off and join a pirate ship. I hear the new king of Gunkermal has a brother who's a captain of a pirate ship. Perhaps he can arrange a passage for me.*

"Remy, the only change Xavier insisted on to your marriage contract, that he passed on through your mother, was that he wanted the piss-off clause removed. Apparently, he never intended for it to be part of your agreement. He seriously wants the two of you to work on your marriage and make it work over the long term."

"He does?" That made Remy feel marginally better. "Then what's the problem, Father? No disrespect, because you are my King and all that as well, but maybe you should've sent Mother to speak to me instead. I admit, I'm a bit confused."

Sighing, the king reached into his robe and pulled out a piece of paper. "You need to see this. It would appear Xavier's secretary wasn't keen on being fired. Your mother explained to me the situation concerning the woman, and Dante, Xavier's guard confirmed it. The secretary was terminated because she lied about her reasons for employment in the first place. But apparently, she was also particularly scathing of Xavier marrying another man. She retaliated publicly."

Remy scanned the piece of paper. It was the copy of a newsletter article put out by one of the gossip sheets – the sort of thing Sophia would read and titter over. But there was nothing amusing about the headline which screamed, "Prince of Deviance seeks to hide his vile actions through marriage to low-ranked royal son."

"This woman is sick – she has a form of mental illness, she must have," Remy murmured as he glossed over the pertinent bits. From the way the article was written, the reader was expected to believe that Xavier, the hero heir of the Balenborn throne was actually a monster from the pits of hell who pressed his deviant sexual needs on any hapless female he came across.

Apparently, if the article was to be believed, to hide his affliction, his father, King Dare, had insisted Xavier marry a male, so as to help curb the malicious rumors that were bound to follow since his actions had been found out. The writer promised more facts would emerge about Xavier's scandalous behavior in the coming weeks.

"If it helps, King Dare saw this and immediately contacted me personally. Lady Cecilia, the author of this article, has been taken into custody by the World Council and questioned under a magical spell. Thanks to her responses she will be charged with spreading malicious rumors among other things. She definitely won't be in a position to write any more gutter trash like this. But I'm afraid the damage has been done. Xavier, on hearing about this, came to me and your mother and said he would retract the marriage contract, taking full liability, if that was your wish."

Remy didn't even have to think about it. In his head, if anyone could be considered being deviant in behavior, it would've been him when he was fifteen years old. The fact that Xavier didn't press on him to follow through with his bravado was a testament to just how honorable the man was. Not that he would share such news with his father. But he knew what he had to do for Xavier. What he *wanted* to do for Xavier.

"I'm going to marry him, Father." Remy looked up from the piece of paper and met his father's eyes. "You might not realize this, but I found out this afternoon both Xavier and I had hoped for ten years that this union would take place. I'm not backing out now because of a few hastily written words by a woman scorned."

He inhaled slowly, and then added, "I understand this could have repercussions for everyone in this family, too. If this scandal is too much for you, and Mother – I don't want it to impact Sophia or Hyacinth's chances of making good matches, then you can publicly disown me, and Xavier and I will be married quietly somewhere discreet, and I'll just leave with him as Xavier originally planned." *I hope that's what he was planning.*

"Don't be silly, son. We'd never disown you and we'll welcome Xavier into our family, the same way Dare and Selena will welcome you into theirs." The king patted his knee. "My only question is whether or not you'd prefer a quieter ceremony, or if you would still want the wedding your mother has been arranging for the past three months." He quirked an eyebrow, and Remy knew what he was expected to say. His mother had worked really hard on creating the perfect wedding.

"We will have our wedding with all the trimmings and if no one comes, well they aren't going to be missed."

Somewhere across the courtyard the bells sounded for dinner. The king stood up, smoothing down his robes. "I will understand if you and Xavier want to excuse yourself from dinner this evening."

"We're not hiding away, Father." Remy stood up too. "That just gives the gossips more to talk about. If you wouldn't mind sending a footman with a message to Xavier, asking him if he can meet me here directly – he can escort me to dinner, and we'll see what the wagging tongues have to say about that."

Chuckling his father nodded. "I'm proud of you boy, and for what it's worth, I do realize none of this tripe in the article is true. I've known Xavier since he was a small boy and I consider myself a good judge of character. Honestly, the people who truly care about you will see this ruse for what it is and sooner or later it'll be forgotten."

"I'm not so sure." Remy chuckled to show he was joking. "I'm more worried about Lady Cecilia's article causing more men and women to swoon and throw themselves at my husband-to-be now they think he has insatiable lusts. Xavier just isn't equipped with the verbal skills necessary to fend them off with any success."

"Then it's probably just as well you agreed to marry him after all."

Striding across the room, his father paused by the door. "For what it's worth, I do intend that the World Council prosecute Lady Cecilia for her damming description of my younger son. We might be a small country, but she's still grossly insulted royalty and we can't let things like that slide."

"Thank you, Father." Remy inhaled and then patted his hair which somehow was sticking up all over the place again. "I'll see you at dinner once Xavier comes to escort me. It'll be fun."

"That's not the word I'd use, but then it probably helps you see it that way."

Actually Father, that's not how I see it at all. But Remy could well imagine how poor Xavier was feeling, having someone tell such terrible lies about him. *I'm going to stand by my damn man whether he wants me to or not.*

Chapter Ten

"We should be packing. The king will want us gone now Cecilia's ruined me for life. We need to be packing. Where's the footman? Will they send a maid? Probably not, given my apparent reputation as a deviant, but by gods. Stuff it. Don't just sit around doing nothing, find out what happened to our bags."

Xavier couldn't imagine how Remy was feeling. His fiancé, or should that be ex-fiancé, was probably cursing his existence and calling him every name under the sun for being a bounder and a cur *and a liar*. As Xavier felt he couldn't do what he wanted to do, which was find Remy, fall to his knees, and beg to be believed, he just wanted to get out of Bentley and back to Balenborn where he could find out how the gossip rag that printed Cecilia's story could be prosecuted and shut down. There had to be some perks to being a crown prince.

It didn't help that Luca was just sitting on the couch, feet up, showing no signs of moving.

"Have you gone deaf in your old age or something. Has all this luxury got you thinking the couch won't survive without your butt carving a space on it?"

"Unlike you, dear brother, who's running around like a headless chicken," Luca said calmly, "I'm waiting patiently for a message from King Francis. You remember, the king who happens to be the father of your fiancé? The one who said, and I believe him, that he would go and talk to Remy, discuss Remy's options with his son, and then send word as to Remy's decision on whether or not he wants to go through with the wedding his mother has spent three months planning."

"There won't be a wedding." Flushed with excitement at having spent such an amazing afternoon with his intended, Xavier's mood had plummeted the moment Max met him at the stable and informed him of what his ex-secretary had done. Her methods of ensuring that no one would consider Xavier a serious choice for a marriage partner, or a reputable king in due course, had been harsh and effective.

Just walking through the castle Xavier could feel the weight of condemnation on the faces of the staff he passed on his way to the suite he'd been given. "Everything I've dreamed of over the past ten years gone in a puff of smoke." Leaving the pile of clothes he'd collected in a heap on the bed, Xavier slumped down, burying his face in his hands. "What in magic crystal's name am I going to do now? You should've seen Remy this afternoon. He actually talked to me."

"And surprise of surprises, you talked to him as well," Luca said. "I know. Huge surprise. Who knew the broody enigmatic crown prince could actually talk to anyone, but you proved you could with Remy. So, if the afternoon was as magical as you claim it was, then why are you doubting your fiancé now?"

"It's not just Remy who's got to be considered here." Xavier groaned as he jumped to his feet and started pacing. Feelings of rage and frustration were racing through him, and there was nothing he could do. The damage was already done, and with Cecilia already in the World Council's custody, thanks to his father, Xavier didn't even have the pleasure of wringing her damn neck.

"Remy has his family's reputation to consider. Having any association with me is going to impact the Bentley royal family. Think of Sophia and Hyacinth. They'll be eligible for marriage contracts of their own in the next few years. No, you'll see. We'll get the message. It will be very polite and filled with regrets that they wish things could be different, but then I'm going to have to suffer the fact that eventually Remy will marry someone else. And there's not one damn thing I can do about it!"

Needing an outlet for his frustration, Xavier reached the bed and picked up his clothes in both arms, flinging them against the wall. They were cloth. The most noise they made was when a button hit the wall, and Xavier got no satisfaction from the mess they made on the floor, or the knocking sound... the knocking sound.

"Someone's at the door," he said urgently.

"I guessed that from the knocking I heard." Taking his own sweet time about it, Luca got up and sauntered to the door, opening it slightly and having a murmured conversation with whoever was on the other side. Moments later he closed the door again and turned, holding a piece of paper. "The king sent a message, as he said he would." He waved the paper.

"Oh, my gods." Xavier warred with wanting to know what was in the note and hanging onto his dream of marrying Remy for one second longer. But he'd never gotten anywhere in life by ignoring what the world threw at him. "You read it. How long do they give us to get out of the country?"

With deliberate slowness, Luca opened the seal on the note and then seemed to take far more time than necessary to read it. Looking up, he said, "Five minutes."

"Five minutes?" Xavier looked at the mess he'd caused with his clothes as his heart plummeted through his boots and then through the floor. "It'll take me more than that long to pick that lot up."

"You misunderstand, brother dear. You have less than five minutes now to get your ass to Remy's room as he's asked that you escort him down to dinner. It seems he fully expects his fiancé to be at his side as he's going to be by yours."

"He can't do that," Xavier yelled even as he checked his reflection in the mirror. "You saw what that woman wrote about him. This could ruin his reputation for life."

"It would seem the wonderful Remy doesn't care, provided he can spend his life with you." Luca lowered his voice and smiled. "It certainly looks like you did the right thing in waiting for Remy all these years. Don't throw away his selfless gift in a fit of misguided morals. Remember, success is the best form of revenge and while I know you are probably seething with the need to do physical violence to Lady Cecilia, her family, and any children she will probably never have now, your revenge is far better served in the form of a long and happy marriage with Remy. A very public long and happy married life with Remy."

"I know you're right, although I'm not sure I want to go through the process of interviewing another secretary. But yes, I was blessed the day Remy said he wanted me, and I've been blessed again today." Running his hand over his facial hair, Xavier let out a long breath. "Will I do?" He indicated his outfit. He was still wearing the pants he'd gone riding in, but had changed out his robe for his uniform jacket.

"With this sort of gossip, no one is going to be looking at your clothes, brother." With a smirk firmly in place, Luca waved his hand at the door. "Time to go and meet your prince. I'll see you downstairs in the dining hall, and I will make sure Max and Dante can pull their faces out of each other's behinds long enough to attend dinner as well."

"Luca! There are some things we do not need to be thinking about, and what Max and Dante are up to is one of them." But Xavier was feeling a teeny bit more lighthearted as he headed out of the room. Remy believed in him, and for now, that was a gift Xavier was going to cherish.

/~/~/~/~/

Dinner was as much of a nightmare as Xavier thought it would be. He barely touched his roasted quail or small green things that looked as though they should've been cabbages but hadn't made the grade. The sauce was a blend of sweet and sour that would normally have him looking for a second helping, not that royals did that sort of thing, but if the chef on his ship had put something like that meal in front of him, he'd have gone for third helpings.

But the weight of social disapproval sat heavily on Xavier's shoulders and everything he put in his mouth tasted of ash and dung. Remy chatted away about inconsequential things to Luca and to him, acting as if it was just another regular dinner. And for the most part it was.

The king and queen were holding court at the same rectangle table they'd sat at the night before, as were Crown Prince Pierre and his consort, Princess Emily. Xavier noticed the two younger siblings weren't at the royal table, but King Francis made their excuses. Apparently, they were visiting friends that evening – a longstanding engagement.

Food was served on long platters that weighed down every table. It was fresh, beautifully cooked and smelled amazing. Quiet, respectful, and well-dressed attendants kept glasses topped up and plates full. No one dropped anything on Xavier's lap, so he counted that as a win.

In fact, it was a simply perfect evening, if a person discounted the fact that at least forty pairs of eyes kept looking in Xavier's direction as if seeking proof of a man who was governed by deviant lusts. He found it difficult to sit up straight under the scrutiny.

It didn't matter that the owners of those eyes would already know about Lady Cecilia's trial by the World Council or that she was found to have lied about every word she'd written. The men and women who sat around enjoying the king's hospitality would be muttering behind their napkins about how 'she had worked with him for two whole years so she must know something', and that 'there's never smoke without fire', which Xavier knew for a fact wasn't true, because he'd seen a smoke machine made by a mage once, and there wasn't a flame or fire in sight.

"You've barely eaten anything." Remy had a wide smile on his face as he leaned in Xavier's direction as the plates were being whisked away. "Can I get the chef to bring you something else?"

Xavier shook his head. "I was actually thinking, we should probably go and visit Daisy. Make sure she has enough food and water and ensure that nothing is bothering her eggs."

"That is a very sweet thought, and we will do that. However, I thought we could enjoy a dance together first." If anything, Remy's smile got brighter. "We wouldn't want the dancing lessons I'm sure your mother made you take go to waste, would we?"

Groaning under his breath, Xavier gave in to the inevitable. "I can dance, as I'm sure you've read about me but..."

"Nope." Remy's fingers landed lightly on Xavier's lips tapping them before moving away. A totally flirtatious gesture that was sure to have been watched by everyone. "I want to learn the bits about Crown Prince Xavier of Balenborn that are not written about over the past two years in particular. I have a suspicion that the person who was written about was a figment of someone's overactive imagination, so let's focus on the real relationship between you and I."

Xavier knew what Remy was doing and his heart warmed at the selfless gesture. Just dancing with him was going to open Remy up to gossip. Standing, he gave a courtly half bow and offered his hand. "Can I have the pleasure of this dance, please, Prince Remy."

"How very kind of you to ask, Crown Prince Xavier." Remy couldn't hide his smirk as he took Xavier's hand and got to his feet. It might not have shown on his lips, but his eyes were shining, and it was as if he beamed with the fun he was having. And it was genuine. Remy had told him when he'd gone to his suite to escort him to dinner that they were going to have a good time, and Remy was showing the joy he felt in Xavier's company.

Now, if only I could do the same. Xavier was determined to make more of an effort.

Chapter Eleven

The moment Remy had answered the door to Xavier just prior to dinner, he'd felt a huge sense of relief. There was a good chance Remy would have had to chase Xavier back to Balenborn before the man would have anything to do with him again. A person's reputation was the backbone that determined an individual's position in society. Among the royals and high-born social families, people had been known to have become lifelong hermits after a night of unacceptable behavior, especially if their behavior impacted someone else in a negative way.

Lady Cecilia had known that and tried to twist that to her advantage. It didn't matter that she'd been found guilty by the council and would likely face jail time for what she'd done. She probably didn't care her own family would spirit her off to a rural estate somewhere if she was ever given her freedom again. All she wanted was to inflict the worst possible damage on Xavier's reputation and she'd already done that.

Lies or not, people were going to wonder if anything she'd written was true. It was likely she anticipated Xavier would withdraw from public life completely, and become a recluse, rarely seen in public again. Perhaps she even hoped they could become recluses together, although Remy didn't know the woman and couldn't say what she had been thinking. He doubted Lady Cecilia had cared for Xavier in any way at all, to write the things she did.

So the fact that he was being held by the crown prince in question, who could dance divinely, was a huge step in the right direction. In public no less. Admittedly, the crowds moved out of their way on the dance floor, but in Remy's head that was them providing respect for the royal couple. He refused to see it any other way.

"Did I mention you look very handsome tonight?" Remy looked up at his prince who still managed to look foreboding even when dancing.

"I don't believe it was mentioned but thank you for saying something now." Was that a twinkle in Xavier's eyes at last. "I should say the same about your fine self. You're looking very well put together this evening."

Remy chuckled. He couldn't help it. Xavier was trying hard, but his lack of dating skills was showing, which made Remy feel more confident about them working as a couple. If Xavier had practiced moves he'd seen in quite a few society men and women, it would be difficult for Remy to take him seriously. *Maybe I should encourage Sophia to loan him a few of her books.*

"Thank you. You know, one thing I did notice this afternoon is that you rarely smile with your whole mouth. On the odd occasion where I have been sure you're going to crack a beautiful grin, you like only do it halfway and stop. Is there a reason for that?"

Xavier glanced away, swept them around, and then focused back on him, which made Remy feel good – being the focus of such an intense man. Leaning closer, he murmured, "Luca told me I look like a manic monkey if I grin, so I stopped doing it. A future king shouldn't look like a jungle creature."

"He said that about you?" Remy shook his head, enjoying how Xavier was leading their dance. "You do know that was just a younger brother poking fun at you, don't you? Siblings do it all the time."

He glanced around making sure no one could overhear them, and then added, "When I was a lot younger, Pierre told me once my hair resembled that of a porcupine and I was going to wake up one morning and it would have all fallen out. Admittedly, I was five at the time, but I went to bed every night for about six months convinced I was going to wake up bald."

Xavier chuckled, but then he did it again – that slightly endearing lop-sided grin. Remy was just about to let him know it was fine to smile when he felt a tap on his shoulder. Looking over his shoulder, he saw Palin, the eldest son of the Plantagenet household.

"Excuse me, your highness. May I cut in?" Palin had an oily smile.

"No." Remy shook his head. "If you don't mind, my fiancé and I are having a private conversation." Xavier had stopped moving, although he was still holding Remy as he had been while they were dancing.

"You misunderstand me, your highness." Palin leaned closer. "Your refusal is not a viable option here. If you are to have a chance of saving this farce of a marriage everyone is talking about, then your fiancé will need friends in low places, if you get my drift. I can be helpful to him in that regard. So, if you'll just run along then nothing I say will hurt your delicate ears."

The way Xavier stiffened meant that he'd heard every word. But Xavier was tied by societal rules that deemed he couldn't say or do anything to stand up for himself. He was in a foreign country and anything he did or said against Palin could get him into a lot of trouble.

Remy, on the other hand, wasn't bound by such restraints. "Can you wait here, just one moment please," he asked Xavier, removing a hand from the man's waist and the other from his shoulder. "This won't take a moment."

Turning, he faced Palin who clearly thought he'd gotten what he wanted – his greasy hands on the crown prince. "When a prince of the realm, the son of your ruling king, tells you no then it pays to listen to him."

Swinging his arm back, Remy formed a fist and punched the man right under the jaw.

Palin was a lot taller and bigger than Remy, which is why Remy had missed the nose he was aiming for, but the man still went down like a stone. Resisting the urge to cradle his hand, because *damn that hurts,* Remy faced the crowd who'd stopped dancing to watch the scene, his features firm. "I need someone to pick this mess up off the floor. He's impeding everyone's enjoyment of the evening. And musicians, if you could continue playing, please, I'd like to continue my dance with my fiancé."

There was a lull, that moment when everyone froze as if they were still processing what they'd seen. Then Xavier's guard Dante came over, shadowed by Max and one of Remy's father's guards, Boris. It was Boris that spoke to Remy. "Sir, are you all right? Did this man insult you?"

"Yes, he did, and he insulted my fiancé, Crown Prince Xavier from Balenborn, as well." Remy nodded. "I'd prefer to carry on enjoying my evening, and I'm sure everyone else present feels the same. But if my father wants to discuss this matter further in the morning, I'll make sure I'm available." Turning to Xavier, he forced a smile, "Shall we continue our dance?"

Xavier's aloof expression didn't change, but he did take Remy back into his arms, and swung them away from where Boris and Dante were dragging Palin away. Remy just hoped Xavier didn't notice that he couldn't flatten his hand against Xavier's waist as he'd originally done. *I have a horrible feeling I've broken a knuckle.* At the very least, it was definitely swelling. *Worth it though.*

Chapter Twelve

It felt like days but was probably only another hour or so before Xavier and Remy could make their excuses and leave the dinner. Xavier was now escorting Remy to Daisy's enclosure holding a dubious smelling bag of food for the lizard in one hand, the other tucked under Remy's elbow. Remy had been quiet since the altercation with whoever it'd been who had decided being rude was the way to get what he wanted, but Xavier wasn't sensing any upset as such.

Although, there was something going on, beyond Remy up and punching someone. Xavier just wasn't sure what it was. He was just glad they got a chance to be alone for a moment or two, even if it was from visiting a lizard. He'd had all the condemning glares he could handle for the evening.

"Are you all right? You've been a bit quiet this last hour or so." Xavier gave a self-conscious chuckle. "Are you regretting deciding to follow through with our wedding plans? I can assure you, no one would blame you if you had a change of heart."

"What? No, nothing like that. I... I'm sorry. This is so embarrassing."

"More embarrassing than being considered a sexual deviant? I'd love to hear about it."

"Yeah, it's nothing like that, but still..." Remy trailed off and for a moment Xavier thought he wasn't going to add anything more, but then he asked, "Have you ever punched anyone... you know, like on the jaw, if you were angry with them?"

Xavier had to think about it. "Can't say that I have. I have been in fights before, when I was younger, and I learned how to wrestle when I was still a boy. I still train when I get the chance. But boxing was never something I enjoyed and once I became an adult, punching someone was generally frowned on, too. That's what I have Dante for."

"That's a shame, not that I like the idea of you fighting or anything." Remy sighed. "It just would've helped if you'd had some embarrassing story about swinging a punch at someone to protect their honor, and then... oh, I don't know... possibly broke your knuckle doing it, or something silly like that."

"Broke a knuckle? Why would you say such a thing? Remy!" Dropping the bag of food on the cobbles, Xavier whirled Remy around and took hold of his hands. The wince on Remy's face told enough of the story, even in the dim light offered by the crystal lights along the pathway.

"I wasn't aiming for a bone," Remy flinched again as Xavier brought his hands closer to his face so he could see a bit better. "I thought the impact would've been more impressive if I'd hit Palin on the nose to make it bleed.

But I caught his jawbone instead. Ouch."

"Punching anyone is going to hurt if you're not used to it. You need ice on this, now." Xavier wanted to kiss the puffiness he could see, and he'd never felt like that before. "Come on, we'll head back and see the healer. That's more important right now than visiting Daisy."

"Nah, uh, we're going to see Daisy." Remy pulled on his hands and Xavier reluctantly let them go. "I spent an hour having the time of my life dancing with you, I spent ten minutes I'll never get back listening to my father explain why a prince should not hit a man in the middle of the dancefloor."

"You hit him on the jaw not the dancefloor." Swooping down, Xavier picked up Daisy's discarded food bag and held onto Remy's elbow with his other hand.

Remy chuckled, which Xavier had hoped for. "According to my father, doing things like punching Palin in public is not good for promoting the diplomatic image royals are meant to aspire to."

"I don't think that guy would've listened if you'd tried talking to him." Xavier had been mortified and freaking furious when he heard what Palin said to Remy. It wasn't even so much the words, but the tone. Palin talked to Remy as if he was twelve instead of twenty-five and that angered Xavier more than any slur on his own character.

"No, and father agreed with that." Remy stopped by Daisy's pen's door. "He just said next time I felt the need to avenge both mine and my fiancé's honor, I should invite Palin into the royal's private garden and punch him there. He reminded me you and I both had images to maintain."

"If there's any punching to be done in Balenborn, let me do it," Xavier suggested. He pointed at the door. "Are we going in? I really want to get your hand seen to."

"Hold on a moment." Remy knocked on the pen door. Waited a minute and then knocked twice.

Xavier scratched the side of his neck. The mosquitoes in Bentley weren't bad, but there were a few of them around in the warm night air. "Are you expecting someone to be in there with Daisy?" Maybe Remy had someone sitting with his lizard while she was looking after her eggs.

But Remy shook his head. "Not a someone as such, a *something*. Mr. Daisy."

There's more than one? "I thought you only had the one lizard who occasionally gave birth to others."

"Yes and see that's what most people think. But not long after she came into my life, Daisy started acting all weird. At the time, I used to lock her in securely at night because I was

159

always worried about someone stealing her. Then this one morning I noticed there were scratch marks on the door when I went to let her out – scratch marks on the outside of the door."

Xavier frowned. "Someone was trying to get in?"

"*Something*. Mr. Daisy, to be exact." Remy chuckled. "It was Reggie who runs the stables that told me the facts of life according to lizards. That's why, when I built this enclosure, I put vents in it. That way she can get out…"

"And Mr. Daisy can get in. Makes sense." Hefting the bag with the food in, Xavier suggested, "should we just toss this in and leave this for her and her friend?"

"No, no. We'll go in. I heard the scrabbling on the walls, so I know he was there, but is now gone. For some reason, he doesn't like humans at all, but then most Orobos are like that."

Remy opened the door and slipped inside. "Come on."

Bending his head, Xavier ducked under the doorframe, and reached back so he could close the door behind him. Thinking it would be pitch black in the enclosure, Xavier was surprised to see the whole place was dimly lit with what seemed to be magic crystals.

"I thought Daisy doesn't like magic? Don't the crystals bother her?" Remembering to keep his voice low, Xavier raised the hand holding the bag, pointing at the wall.

"It's an easy mistake to make." Husky voiced Remy struck a chord in Xavier, just below the belt. "The light doesn't come from magical means, it's a luminescent powder. One of the army engineers came up with the idea – a way of providing light without triggering any magical wards, or alarms. Everyone in the army carries a jar of the stuff, and when I needed help with designing this place, he recommended the idea. As you can see, it works really effectively in providing enough light to see by, without being annoying to Daisy or any of the other lizards around."

"It is a great idea." Remy's face seemed to glow in the amber light. Xavier thought of things like smelly foods and swollen knuckles in an effort to prevent himself from acting inappropriately in a lizard pen. Fortunately, Remy couldn't read his thoughts, and was already heading through into the hideaway.

"Hello, Lady Daisy, are you keeping well this evening?" Xavier heard a grunt and hurried through in case she didn't realize he was there. "Look at this, you pampered young mother. You have a Crown Prince serving your food this evening. You're definitely spoiled."

Daisy was perched on a mound of hay, that probably held her eggs. It was quite incredible how much she'd moved presumably by herself. The floor had barely any scraps of hay left on it, leaving just dusty boards below.

"We won't put anymore hay in this particular part of the pen now until after the eggs have hatched," Remy said, keeping to his low tone, while Xavier emptied the contents of his bag into Daisy's bowl. "There's a special enzyme in the Orobos saliva that causes the hay, or other grass products to break down really quickly. As the grasses decompose it offers warmth to the eggs which are buried in the mound she's made."

"I never knew that about lizards, or that they could do that." Xavier made sure he stood well away from Daisy's food bowl. She did look hungry. "What's going to happen to Mr. Daisy when we go to Balenborn? Will we have to catch him and bring him, too? That could be difficult if he doesn't like humans."

"I wouldn't even try and do that. Mr. Daisy is a confirmed wild being."

Remy was scratching the top of Daisy's head with his uninjured hand. "To be honest, I am not sure if Daisy will come with us either. I'm thrilled that you're even considering that she should, and to be honest I had been thinking about it, once I realized you were serious about marrying me and wanting me with you."

You haven't been thinking about it long then. Xavier was well aware since Remy had been honest with him, that his fiancé had originally believed their marriage was going to be one of convenience only. He was just glad he'd been able to convince Remy that he wanted a real marriage and he was genuine in his feelings.

"Put simply, despite her love of scritches from me, Daisy is still a wild animal at heart. Sure, she loves this pen, and she considers this enclosure and the whole stable courtyard her territory, but that's part of the reason I think she's going to have to stay behind."

Xavier wasn't surprised at the sadness in Remy's eyes. His fiancé had a warm heart and his affection for Daisy was unprecedented.

"I'd love that she could come with me." Remy looked down at the lizard who could take his face off with one bite, and then back at Xavier, "But she'd have to be completely contained to move her, and her eggs, and then there's the fact she'd probably miss Mr. Daisy. A pining lizard is no joke."

"What do you think about hawks?" Xavier offered. "I'm sure mine wouldn't mind a new friend."

"The one with the fancy collar." Remy smirked. "How much of that conversation with my mother did you hear thanks to that?"

Wow, look at how that hay is arranged. Such a clever lizard.

"Xavier?"

"My hawk wasn't intentionally overhearing anything," Xavier said quickly. "The stables are just a good place for her to find mice and other small furry creatures."

"And the fact that she flew back to you the same time me and my mother left Daisy's pen was totally coincidental."

"Did she?" Xavier knew that's what had happened. "Creatures such as birds or lizards are so much more intelligent than we give them credit for, don't you think?"

Seeing Remy's knowing smirk, he quickly changed the subject. "Can we go and get your knuckles looked at now, please? If you did break a bone, it will need resetting so it can heal the right way."

"Seeing as you asked so nicely." Giving one final scritch across Daisy's broad skull, Remy headed back outside the hideaway, brushing against Xavier's body as he did so.

Please, give me patience until our wedding day. Xavier wasn't sure who he was praying to, but he hoped someone could hear him.

Chapter Thirteen

"You're an absolute hero." Remy was just tugging his boots on when Hyacinth came bursting into his room with barely a knock, followed closely by Sophia. "Everyone is talking about how you punched creepy Palin for being horrid – right on the dance floor for everyone to see. We didn't think you could even do something like that."

"And he went falling to the ground like a dead tree," Sophia added, her bright eyes sparkling as she was clearly imagining it. "No one knows what he must've said to upset you so much...?" She trailed off, looking at him expectantly.

Finally getting his feet seated in his boots, which wasn't easy onehanded, Remy stood up and brushed off his jacket. He was going riding with Xavier. Dante, Boris, and Max would be accompanying them. His father thought it best, after the incident with Palin the night before. Personally, with two days to go before the wedding was due to take place, Remy couldn't wait. Maybe then people might understand Remy was committed to Xavier, and then they could start a long and happy marriage together.

"You know very well, I'm not about to upset Mother by repeating anything to you two, especially something that might have been said by a rude and uncouth individual who was likely jealous Xavier wants to marry me, not him or scum like him," Remy said firmly. "Suffice to say, I simply did what Xavier wanted to do, if he hadn't been so polite, and respectful of his position as an honored visitor to this country."

"I think the whole thing is swoon-worthy," Hyacinth said, flopping over Remy's couch in a mass of petticoats and skirts. "Pure swoon. The sort of thing a person might read about if they were allowed to read the same books their older sister has always got their nose buried in."

"You're not old enough for those books yet," Sophia replied with her nose in the air, but she dropped her airs soon enough. "But truly, Remy, what on earth possessed you to punch someone. You've never acted like that in public before."

"There are times when a gentleman has to do the honorable thing," Remy said firmly. "It's not romantic, or heroic. Punching someone to make a point could be considered boorish and the behaviors of an uncouth lout. But in that instance, I was so very angry – not for me or how Palin's words affected me – but for poor Crown Prince Xavier who, simply because of his position and the fact he was a visitor to our country, had to take the insults on the chin without being able to say or do anything about it. I don't believe that is fair."

"I don't care what you say," Hyacinth said staunchly. "I think it was totally romantic. You must have a lot of feelings for the handsome Crown Prince."

Remy felt his cheeks heat up. "My feelings about Xavier are my personal business as well, young missy. They are something else I will not be discussing with you. Mother would have a fit at me."

Sophia sighed. "I hope, when I meet the man I'm contracted to marry, that he will do something equally dashing to protect my honor." She flopped down beside her sister. "I have a horrible feeling father might contract me to some accountant, or someone equally staid and boring. My life will stretch ahead of me as nothing more than being someone to grace my husband's arm, looking pretty but not allowed an opinion. I'll be lucky if I'm ever allowed on a horse again."

"For goodness' sake." Remy chuckled. "Is this another one of those ideas from the books you keep reading?

You know all to well that father would involve you in any discussion regarding your future happiness, and the onus will be on you to ensure your future husband is aware of your wonderfully creative and bright personality, not to mention your strong opinions, before you are married. You have a voice, sister dear. Don't be afraid to use it."

"See?" Sophia said to Hyacinth. "Just like that. That's how I want my future husband to be as well." Looking at Remy, she continued. "How come we didn't know you could be so gallant and supportive. Honestly, I thought the only thing you were interested in was lizards, and yet listen to you, supporting me as your sister – supporting my right to have a voice."

"We don't live in the dark ages." Remy made shooing motions with his one good hand. "Now move along. Xavier will be at the stables waiting for me, and it's not good form to be late for a date. Another piece of advice you can have for free. If you are interested in a person, then don't make them wait while you're fluffing your hair or choosing your dress colors. Being tardy shows a lack of interest in a person. Being on time on the other hand…"

"We're going. We're going." Sophia jumped up, holding out her hand to her younger sister. "Come on," she said to Hyacinth excitedly, "lets go and see if Rosa can come and visit us today."

"You just want to see if Rosa has any more of those books," Hyacinth grumbled, but she followed Sophia out of the door, leaving Remy to take a moment to compose himself. He meant what he said. He hated the idea of anyone being late for an appointment as to him it showed a lack of respect.

But more importantly in Xavier's case, Remy didn't want anyone like Palin to have the chance to insult his fiancé again. Once was quite enough.

He wasn't sure what he was going to do with the new feelings of protectiveness he felt about Xavier, but he was going to roll with those feelings and see where they developed into something more.

/~/~/~/~/

"Your father was surprised to hear you were still going ahead with the wedding," Max said as Xavier pulled on his boots. "While he is more than happy to welcome Remy into the family, there has been a few suggestions made..."

"By father's other advisors that run amuck when you're not there to keep them in line. I know. Go on." One more tug and his second boot was on. "Where do father's advisors suggest I go to wait out the scandal caused by Lady Cecilia?"

"They are well aware that everything written about you was untrue." Max's face took on a deep red color. "I made it plain myself that your behavior since being on this trip was more than exemplary despite any provocations you might have had to act otherwise."

"Much appreciated." Xavier pulled on his jacket and checked for loose buttons. "So you are supportive of my marriage – my parents are supportive of my marriage. In theory there should be nothing stopping my marriage, but that's not what the look on your face suggests."

"Your father has to be seen to listening to his advisors, even if he doesn't give a damn about their idiotic opinions."

Max's strong language was enough to attract Xavier's attention. "The news you have for me seriously bothers you. What is it?"

"Your father has been given the advice that it might be best if you spent some time aboard your ship," Max said shortly. "No mention was made of Prince Remy, but then those silly fools probably never considered the amount of honor that young man has, or that he's clearly devoted to you. However, the feeling among the advisors is that if you arrive at Balenborn with the young prince as your consort, then you are helping to give Lady Cecilia's made up gutter trash stories some credence."

"So they are trying to stop my marriage." Xavier started to pace. "They have no idea the years I've waited for this, or how much it means to me that Remy has committed himself to me now. For all that's holy, man, if I back out now, leave him as those fools clearly believe I should, then I'll dishonor everything we've shared and what he did for me last night."

Fisting his hands, Xavier strode over the window. The courtyard below was full of people going about their business. Remy would be on his way to the stables, eagerly anticipating their riding date together. *He's probably already there, wondering where I am.*

Turning to face his father's stricken main advisor, Xavier took a deep breath. "I am going to inform Prince Remy of what you have said. I will not make a blithe assumption that my fiancé will commit his life to living on a ship for the foreseeable future, but nor am I going to leave him like a thief in the night. My fiancé has shown incredible courage since Cecilia tried to do her worst. I will not demean that. I will not demean him."

"I did point out to your father this morning that if you did leave Prince Remy at the altar as such, that in itself could be skewed into people considering that Lady Cecilia was right, and that as soon as you'd been found out, for the want of a better term, that you'd ditched him because the rubbish she wrote was true."

"If I wasn't a crown prince this wouldn't have happened," Xavier fumed. "If I didn't have my title

Cecilia and those of her ilk wouldn't give me the time of day. Where is it written that individuals have a right to impose their will on others? What if I give up my legacy? Would Remy and I be left alone then? Could I ever go home to visit at least?"

"Your highness!" Well, that was just brilliant. Xavier had succeeded in doing something no one else had ever done. He'd shocked Max to the core. Hearing a knock at the door, Xavier went to open it, expecting a footman with a message from Remy probably wondering where he was.

"Remy," he said in surprise as he saw his fiancé standing in the hallway. "Come in. Come in. Your reputation is perfectly safe. Max is here."

"Has there been more bad news?" Remy swept in, his hair a mess, his outfit crisp and well fitting. "Lord Max, good morning. Are there further impediments to our marriage I should know about? Has some woman produced a love child claiming it to be the illegitimate offspring of my fiancé, or perhaps it's been revealed my fiancé owns a pleasure dungeon or some other such ridiculousness?"

"How could you suggest such things, your highness?" Remy took the dubious honor of being the second person to shock Max speechless in as many minutes. Max recovered quickly. "You two are of similar minds, I admit, which makes you well-suited it would seem. But Prince Remy, if you'll forgive me being forward, a marriage to the Crown Prince is likely to be fraught with social disapproval at least in the short term."

"I'm aware of that." Remy held his head proudly. "I am a second son, and my brother already has his heirs. My parents are prepared to accept and support my marriage despite recent events."

"Even if we can't go back to Balenborn in the foreseeable future?" Xavier's heart sung at his fiancé's staunch support, but his soul was still hurting at the idea he couldn't go home, and Remy deserved to know his fate if their marriage took place.

At the look of confusion on Remy's face, Xavier hurried to explain. "My father's advisors suggest I spend time at sea. They likely feel I should be chasing pirates that have no wish to be found. Perhaps since Prince Nikolas of Westland has become King Consort of Gunkermal, the pirates are getting restless and encroaching on people's land and livelihoods. Who knows, but the advisors have informed my father that I shouldn't be allowed home, either with you on my arm, or alone until the gossip has died down."

"Oh, Xavier, I'm so sorry." Remy crossed the distance between them, and suddenly arms were around Xavier's waist. "You must feel awful especially when none of this is your fault."

He's hugging me. Xavier couldn't even think to formulate a suitable response. He was so taken by the feel of Remy in his arms. The hug was short lived and when Remy stepped back, his face was bright red.

"So," he said, tugging at his fetching black jacket with his uninjured hand. "What does a person wear on a ship? Will I need much in the way of a wardrobe?"

Chapter Fourteen

Remy insisted they go riding, as they'd originally planned. After the shocking morning he'd had, Remy believed Xavier would benefit from doing something normal, something already arranged, that was considered suitable for a couple getting to know each other. Dante came with them, along with Boris. But after speaking with Xavier in huddled whispers before Xavier left his room, Max stayed behind. His comment, "I think you're wrong, but I'll inform your father, and await his instructions," had Remy's curiosity morphing into high alert, but he bided his time. Xavier would tell him if it affected him soon enough.

His hand was still in some kind of cast that the healers had insisted on, but Remy wasn't feeling any pain. Remy suspected, the way the healer fussed over him, that the only reason he was wearing a shield over his knuckles was that if he had to punch someone again, it would hurt his opponent a lot more, and do less damage to his poor swollen knuckles.

In the meantime, he spent time pointing out areas of interest, and talking about Daisy and her protectiveness over her eggs. "There's always an incident," he said with a chuckle, looking in Xavier's direction. "One of the stable boys nearly always has a friend with him, and they'll encourage each other to go into her pen to see the egg mound."

"What Daisy has done with that hay is pretty impressive," Xavier agreed, gently encouraging his horse around a fallen log on the trail. His hawk, that had been kept with Dante was flying overhead, the gleam of her collar catching the sun as she glided along the wind streams.

"I know but they should know better. I mean, Daisy will chase them half the time for sport. I think she likes to see their little legs flying as they dash across the courtyard. But she's not playing when she's in her protective mode." Remy shook his head. "You'd think they would learn, but if you tell young boys they shouldn't do something it seems to make them want to do it more."

"You don't remember being a bit like that yourself when you were their age?" Xavier did that half grin thing that he did, and Remy smiled with his full mouth.

"Maybe."

Looking ahead to where Boris and Dante seemed to be in a heated conversation on their respective horses, Xavier pulled his mount to a stop. "Hold up a moment," he said, keeping his voice low. "I need to talk to you about something really quick and we might not get another chance before the wedding."

As he slowed his own horse, Remy checked the area around them. Dante and Boris clearly didn't think they were in any danger as they kept going, Boris's flying arm, and Dante's mirroring move suggesting their conversation was reaching argument stage. On one side of them was the gentle downhill slope covered in grass, while to their left was a sparse group of trees.

"Let's head over here," Remy suggested, nodding in the direction of the trees. "I think it will take a while before those two notice we haven't kept up with them."

"Hmm. Not necessarily a good thing, but it works in our favor for now." Xavier looked after the two men too, and he didn't seem impressed, but he moved his horse off the trail. They could still be seen by anyone else that came up or down the trail, but Remy felt happier that he could also see if anyone else was using the trail in either direction.

"All right. We're alone. What reason are you going to give me for breaking off our engagement this time?" Remy smiled, but he was only half teasing. The set of his shoulders, and the grim look on his face had Xavier looking really intense. Hot in an untouchable way. Handsome definitely. And intense.

/~/~/~/~/

"Are you marrying me as a person or because I'm a crown prince and might rule Balenborn one day?" Xavier didn't know any other way than blunt, but he wished he'd rethought his opening lines when a flash of hurt crossed Remy's face.

"I thought I'd made it perfectly plain that I wanted to get to know you as a person – a man I've been attracted to for far longer than you were aware of. Is there a reason you've decided not to believe me? Was your morning before I arrived really that horrible?"

Yes. I seriously should've rethought how I asked. But it was a good thing Remy felt that he could speak honestly, and even take Xavier to task.

Xavier half-bowed. "I apologize. I've offended you. That was not my intention. I've been wrestling with this issue of the rumors Cecilia has sent flying around the land, and how to deal with them. It's been difficult to think of anything else. I fear my insecurities are showing."

Looking out across the sloping hills of Bentley, Xavier thought of his home with its rugged cliffs and the scent of the sea in the air. "I never thought for a second that my father's advisors would suggest to him I'd be better off staying away from home. Sending me out to sea like a renegade pirate. All I'd need is a huge skull belt buckle, a crystal sword, and my gorgeous husband of course, and I'd be spawning a whole new set of rumors about us."

Remy chuckled and the sound was so surprising, Xavier had to take a double look. "I can see you as a pirate," Remy explained when Xavier was caught looking. "You have the build, the facial hair, and that forbidding expression you do so well. It would be an interesting career change."

Xavier sighed even as he appreciated Remy's humor and compliments. "Thank you, but you should know this is a serious matter. It's not just my reputation I have to consider now, but yours as well. I honestly feel if I wasn't a crown prince, Cecilia's lies wouldn't have gotten any traction at all."

"I believe a lot of the problem is the amount of publicity your ex-secretary generated about you prior to the lies she spread." Remy wasn't disputing what Xavier was saying, which made it easier to say what he had to say next.

"I realize I should've talked to you about this first, but I wanted you to know before our vows were exchanged." He inhaled sharply. "I told Max that if the advisors were so adamant that whether I married you or not, I would still be fueling Cecilia's rumors, then it might be better if I give up my title and allow the line of succession to go through to my brother or my eldest nephew." Xavier said it all in a rush, and then waited, his heart in his throat as he waited for Remy's reaction.

Holding his horse steady with the one hand, Remy raised his hand with the cast on, indicating the 'wait' symbol. "Do you mean we would live our lives as non-royals?"

Xavier nodded.

Frowning, Remy was clearly thinking things through. "We'd have to elope. Our marriage contract is only valid if I marry the Crown Prince of Balenborn. I would discuss our renewed plans with my parents first, with your agreement of course, as I'd like for both of us to be able to visit here sometimes."

"So you'd consider marrying me, even though I'd be untitled?"

"I'm not going off with you to parts unknown without being married." Remy gave a snotty look as if he were shocked at the suggestion. Then, to Xavier's relief he cracked a smile. "My mother is going to be so frosty with you. She's planned our wedding for *months*. And we're going to have to consider what we're going to be doing if we no longer have to be royal figureheads. I mean, I can handle living on a ship for a while... I think. But are you going to think I'm being particularly precious if I insist on having a home at some point?"

He's taking this all so well. Xavier had known his news would be a shock. A gentleman was raised from when he took his first steps to appreciate and understand the importance of a man's station in life and their reputation – royals more so than most. But it seemed Remy's major concern was being able to have a home, that

Xavier could and would provide, and how much his mother might be upset because of the planning she'd done for their official wedding.

He couldn't help himself. Reaching over, one hand still holding his horse's reins, the other hand needed to make contact with his fiancé. The cast was problematic, and Xavier could hardly expect Remy to stop controlling his horse, but he allowed himself to let his hand linger as it stroked down the top of Remy's arm.

"I know it's not going to be the life you expected," he said slowly, pleased beyond words that Remy edged his horse and himself closer, not further away. "To be honest, I enjoyed my life as a crown prince, barring the rumors that seemed to follow me everywhere. But traveling, meeting people, representing my father whom I respect above all... I haven't given any thought as to what we might do instead."

Remy leaned slightly in his direction. "A problem shared is a problem halved, and as this does impact me, too..." He paused for a moment, and then Xavier felt the hint of his hair against his jacket. "We need to speak to my parents. It might pay to see if there are any messages from your father as well. I can imagine this is going to be a huge shock for him."

Taking care not to spook Remy's horse, or Remy, Xavier wheeled his horse around so he could see Remy's face. "In all the years I dreamed of us being married, I never imagined something like this would happen. I swear on my parents' lives, I have conducted myself honorably in every interaction I've ever had since you and I met. I wanted to be someone you could be proud of being with when it could finally happen."

Remy fixed him with a glare that could only be described as steely. He liked that look on his fiancé. "I am only going to say this once and I'm only saying it now because I believe you've probably said more words this morning to me, than you ever said to Cecilia, your parents, or anyone else in a personal capacity. I respect and appreciate that."

Remy was right. Xavier rarely spoke personally to anyone except maybe his brother. Remy also hadn't finished.

"We, that is you and I, are going to have an amazing life together. Crown Prince, pirate, or bookshop owner, I don't care. We're going to have a wonderful life as a married couple and nothing and no one can take that away from us. I have…" Remy looked around, but Boris and Dante had disappeared from view and there was no one else around. "I have followed every word ever written about you," he continued in a lower voice. "I have an embarrassing collection of likenesses of you that will never see the light of day."

Xavier's eyes widened as he realized what Remy was saying.

"Since our misunderstanding, and until very recently, I truly believed you didn't like me, and it broke my heart. But the reason it broke my heart was because I developed a crush on you when I was ten years old, and that crush has evolved into deep, grown-up feelings that are much stronger now. I am fully confident those feelings will grow even more once we've joined our lives together."

"That's why you've never considered marrying anyone else?"

"I resigned myself to a very lonely life, watching you from afar with your beautiful princess." Remy's cheeks glowed pink. "Not in the manner of a stalker, you understand. Just as a hobby."

Xavier let out about an hour's worth of breath. "Quick. We must be quick. We have to get back to the castle."

"Why so quick?" Remy gathered up his reins as best he could and encouraged his horse to face the way they'd come. "Is there someone coming?"

"I made you a promise that we'd be married when I kissed you for the first time, but you're not making it easy for me to keep that vow. We need to be married as quickly as possible."

Remy didn't seem upset about Xavier's rash declaration. Although he did look back up the trail. "What about Boris and your man, Dante? And didn't you bring your hawk with you?"

"Your man and mine are probably comparing appendage sizes at the top of the hill, waiting for us to get there. You'd better believe I'll be saying something to my head guard about his lack of attention to his duties, after you and I are married. As for my feathered companion, she'll be hunting, but she'll return to Dante when she's done."

Dante could look after himself. Boris looked like he could, too. The only person Xavier was interested in looking after was Remy who was already heading back down the trail.

This is the right thing to do. Xavier could feel it in his bones... and a few other places. He would swear, if ever asked, that his lips were quivering in anticipation of their first kiss. He just hoped it didn't show.

Chapter Fifteen

"It's not as simple as Xavier just giving up his title and the two of you running off into the sunset like a pair of love-blind fools." Queen Abigail wasn't being unkind, but Remy still flinched. "Xavier has a position to upkeep, and so do you, my son."

"Xavier is willing to give up his title," Remy insisted. There was no point in querying his mother about his role in life considering he was not only a spare heir, but in accordance with the Bentley laws, his two nephews came before him in the line of succession for the Bentley crown. "This marriage already meant I would be leaving home. Nothing has changed in that regard."

"That's not strictly true," King Francis said. They were all in his office – Remy's mother and father, and Max, who kept trying to catch Xavier's eye. In fact, he'd tried to talk to Xavier before they'd even got into the office. Xavier wasn't interested, but apparently Remy's father thought what he had to say was important. "Max, seeing as both Xavier and my son are being stubborn, perhaps you could explain the situation with the King of Balenborn and his other family members."

"Thank you, your majesty." Max rearranged the pages of a sheaf of paper he was holding. "My apologies your highness, but I did attempt to discuss this with you before your announcement. If I can be frank," he looked up, "Your father thinks your idea of giving up your title is the biggest load of crock he's ever heard. Obviously, those are his words, not my own. His advisory team suggested that Prince Luca might be happy to take on the role of Crown Prince given your nephew is still so young, but Prince Luca had conditions on taking up the appointment which could not be met. Your sister, the Princess Imogene absolutely refuses to have your nephew take your place until he's at least twenty-one years old…"

"That's fifteen years away…" Xavier looked ready to hit someone, and Remy glanced down at his cast. *Perhaps I can…* Glancing up, Remy saw his mother do a minute shake of her head as if she could read his mind.

"Why can't Luca take the title?" Given how agitated Xavier was, Remy hoped his mother and father wouldn't mind him showing a bit of support. He rested his good hand in the middle of Xavier's back.

Max didn't answer. He looked at King Francis instead.

"It would appear there was only one condition Prince Luca would insist on if he were to take the title of Crown Prince," the king said slowly. "And I have already refused his request."

Remy tried to work out what his father was talking about, slotting in one situation after another before coming up with the only one that made sense. "Did Luca want to marry Sophia?" he asked. "Would that be so awful for her? She'd get to be queen one day. I'm sure Luca would treat her with kindness once she was of age."

"He would if it was Princess Sophia he was interested in." Xavier glowered. "He wants to marry my fiancé, doesn't he?"

"Prince Luca was perfectly reasonable in his request," Max said quickly. "Prince Remy is contracted to marry the Crown Prince of Balenborn."

"I won't," Remy said quickly, and then his face flushed as he realized how rude he was being. "I do beg your pardon for my outburst Father, Mother, Lord Max. While the contract may be between Prince and Crown Prince, in the meantime I have given my personal promise to Xavier, not his title. I will stand by that promise with everything I am."

"Something Prince Luca fully understands. He is not insulted by what he knew would be an immediate refusal," King Francis said. "But King Dare and I have been communicating while you were out this morning, since Max came to us with your idea, Xavier. While I understand your motives for making such a selfless act, and your father asked me to convey the same understanding from his side of things as well, his message to you, which I hope you will appreciate coming from me, is 'suck it up, marry the boy', and I am assuming he means you, Remy, 'and bring him home.'"

"And before you mention it, the World Council won't allow for you to just blithely give up your title, either your highness," Max added.

Remy was more worried about Xavier who seemed stunned, standing like a handsome statue, with very little expression on his features. Max didn't seem to think it was an unusual stance because he just kept talking.

"Apparently, the World Council believes that you rejecting your title, when there is no imperative reason for doing so..."

"No imperative reason!" Xavier exploded. "Cecilia has ruined my reputation through her slanderous lies..."

"Which the council has punished her for," Max said calmly.

"Her punishment will never make up for the embarrassment caused to my family, and more importantly to my fiancé and his family. The damage is done, and she knew that the moment she put pen to paper."

"Nevertheless, the World Council believes that your actions would constitute an unhealthy precedent that could undermine the stability of the various ruling families around the world. The only way they would consider allowing you to step away from your duties and responsibilities as the heir of the throne of Balenborn, is if you were deemed mentally unfit."

"Mentally unfit!?"

Remy could see Xavier's anger. It emanated like a cloud around his body. His teeth were clenched, and lines of strain showed in his neck and fisted hands.

"Xavier, please calm down." Remy kept his voice low, pressing harder on Xavier's back. "Your father's advisor is simply relaying the messages he's been told. He has no authority in this."

"They want to deem me mentally unfit."

"No, Xavier, that's not what was said." The more Xavier seethed the more important Remy knew it would be to stay calm. It was the only way his fiancé would listen to him. "Neither the council, nor your family, nor anyone else would ever consider there was anything wrong with your mental faculties. Lord Max was simply explaining the only conditions the World Council might consider letting someone in a position similar to yours relinquish their titles and responsibilities. Not you personally. Those are just the guidelines they operate under."

"Luca has become an unmentionable word I won't repeat in mixed company." Xavier nodded at the Queen. "He didn't have to impose any conditions on becoming Crown Prince. I thought he and I were as close as two brothers could be."

Sheesh. This is difficult with an audience. Both his mother and father were watching him closely. Turning so his back was to his audience, Remy rested his cast on Xavier's chest. "Look at me," he said in a low voice. Yes. There was definite hurt in Xavier's eyes.

"The reason Luca, and your sister Imogene, and likely your mother and father too have passed on these messages to you, is because they do care about you. Can't you see that?"

"Then why aren't they helping us?" Xavier seemed genuinely confused by what he considered a betrayal by those closest to him. "Mentally unfit?"

"That was a World Council term, and it doesn't apply to you. Xavier…" Remy paused as he worked out how to put his thoughts into words. "Luca could've taken your place as Crown Prince, but he knows you're the best man for the job, which is why he included his ridiculous condition. Likewise, your sister Imogene has already agreed that her eldest son will be your successor in years to come. I'm sure she could've accepted the Crown Prince regent title and raised her son accordingly. But she didn't want you to lose the position you were born to fill. They did this because they believe in you, and they care."

"Xavier," Remy heard his father speaking from the desk behind him, but he kept his focus on his fiancé who was watching the king over Remy's shoulder. "Your father and I are friends. Remy's mother and yours spent many hours when our families were small, sharing the trials and joys that come from raising young children. I hope you'll believe me when I say on behalf of your family and my own, we all sincerely believe you are the best Crown Prince for Balenborn. You can't let the words of a definitely deranged person wreck your life."

"You know my father's right, don't you." Remy allowed his fingers to pat Xavier's chest very briefly.

To his surprise, Xavier held his arms, looking directly into his eyes. "We could've been married today," he said, his voice low. "Tiny ceremony, just your parents as witnesses. Married today, on my ship in another five days, our whole lives ahead of us. No titles. Nobody caring what we did."

Remy allowed the words to sink in for a moment, weighing up what had been said since they'd been invited into his father's office, against what he and Xavier had shared under the trees. He knew he and Xavier had to do the right thing, but just for one moment he thought about the future they could've had.

"Yes," he said, with a nod, still holding watching Xavier's face. His heart sank, but he said the words that had to be said. "Instead, we'll be married in two days, and you're going to take me to Balenborn in style. We're going to ignore your father's advisors, because that sounds like what your father is doing, too.

"We're not going to hide away. We're going to live as a crown prince and his consort would live if their reputations were not besmirched by someone with an evil mind. We will show, by our behaviors towards each other and others, that we are good people, who in time, will rule the country of Balenborn as you've been raised to do."

"I'd rather be a married pirate who ran bookshops as a sideline." Xavier's grip tightened for a moment, before he dropped his hands.

So would I, Remy thought, but he turned and faced their audience again. "Is there anything Xavier and I need to do before our wedding ceremony?"

Chapter Sixteen

It seemed like there was a huge list of things that needed doing before Xavier could marry his fiancé. During one of the few private moments he'd been allowed – even a crown prince needed to use the bathroom – he came to the conclusion that his parents had gotten together with Remy's, and they were determined that Xavier and Remy would be so busy, any further talks of them eloping just couldn't happen.

He and Remy were never alone. At all. It seemed during their collab, King Francis and Xavier's father determined they should solidify their merging of families with a treaty between the two countries. A treaty that took two full days of meetings as every single word from both parties had to be debated.

At one point, Xavier was ready to storm out of the office when Max and King Francis were debating at length whether to use "although" or "and" to join two sentences that could've equally stood alone as two phrases. The conversation just went on and on, and it was only his father's teachings that kept Xavier from leaving.

Remy was equally busy. Originally Xavier had suggested that he should sit in on the treaty negotiations. He was going to be King Consort one day. But he was told that Remy was needed to help his mother with the last-minute preparations for their big day - which seemed to take all day.

Dinners, which were the one time the entire royal family got together were almost painful. Xavier was always seated next to Remy, which he appreciated. But he either had Sophia on his other side who seemed to talk about nothing but horses, or Remy's attention was being monopolized by Luca.

The same Luca who had refused to take his position when it'd been handed to him damn near on a silver platter. Xavier had discussed that issue with him. He'd made a point of going directly to Luca's room after dinner the night of their family intervention. Yes, he was calling it an intervention. When two families got together and made decisions unilaterally for him and Remy, when he and his fiancé were both adults, that constituted an intervention.

Luca wasn't at all put out that he'd upset Xavier's plans of having a free and happy life with Remy. He'd even laughed, slapping Xavier on the back, and saying, "I knew if I threatened to take away your darling, you'd shut me down real quick. And it worked."

It worked. That was all Luca had to say. Xavier wasn't sure what had worked exactly. His reputation was still in ruins. Fortunately, Queen Abigail was so busy with a thousand different last-minute details that went into his and Remy's wedding ceremony, they hadn't any social events planned. The next time Xavier and Remy would be seen together publicly was when they were standing in front of the Minister of Marriages.

The night before the wedding, the urge to talk to Remy became overwhelming. He understood, and had picked it up from his fiancé's tone when Remy had made the decision to stand with him, that he was as upset to be marrying a crown prince, as Xavier now was in *being* the crown prince.

Figuring Remy would go and visit Daisy, Xavier snuck out, on the pretense of going to the bathroom yet again, and hurried over to the stable block to check out the lizard pen. Which was empty except for a judgmental looking lizard sitting on her hay mound. Ignoring Daisy's expression, Xavier found a box and got comfortable. The lizard was surprisingly easy to talk to, but she didn't have a lot to offer in terms of advice. Spotting a stable boy on the way back to the castle about an hour later, Xavier learned Prince Remy had visited his lizard before dinner, not afterward.

But now it was time. He was dressing for his wedding. By the time the giant clock in the courtyard struck the next set of bells, Xavier and Remy would be married. The fluttering he had in his gut could've been eased if Xavier had been given just one chance to check in with Remy and be reassured the marriage was still something his fiancé wanted.

Without being able to talk to him, Xavier was struggling with the idea of whether he'd done the right thing in pushing for the marriage in the first place. Sure, in most cases men of his position married someone they barely knew. Caring for someone wasn't a prerequisite – that would either come over time or it wouldn't.

Xavier had always wanted more than that – with Remy. He'd dreamed of the life they could share together. And now he'd spoken to the Bentley prince and felt they had a chance at a true connection, he really wanted that connection to be real. But in his lonely bed at night, tired and restless, Xavier had relived every mean word he'd said ten years earlier, and the hurt look on Remy's face the first time he'd seen him after that. His memory wasn't doing him any favors, and that was without a few tidbits of gossip Dante had shared with him, and so he worried. On the inside.

Fortunately, he'd spent more than a decade perfecting the art of looking confident, when inside he felt as agitated as a wood fairy on mushrooms. But of course, Luca would pick up that something was wrong, even if he didn't know what it was specifically.

And his brother was going to say something. Luca wasn't very good at not prying about things, which was why he was the only person prior to coming to Bentley who knew about how much Xavier had thought about

Remy over the years. It didn't take him long. "You're awfully quiet," Luca said, strapping Xavier into his ornamental harness showcasing medals and other badges of office. "I thought you really wanted this marriage."

"I've dreamed of this day for ten years. That hasn't changed." Xavier turned, holding his arms up so Luca could do up the six buckles that held the leather together down each side.

"You couldn't show a bit more excitement?" Luca finished on one side and moved around Xavier's back to the other. "Anyone seeing your face would think you were attending your own funeral."

"I can't help thinking I've pressured Remy into a situation he can't get out of." Spinning on his heel, his remaining undone buckles clanging against each other, Xavier glared at his brother. "What if he doesn't want to be married to me after all? I need to speak to him. Now. Before the wedding. He has to be given the chance to back out before it's too late."

"You are not seeing your fiancé until he arrives for the wedding, so don't even think about it." Strong hands were on Xavier's back and he found himself turned around again. "I know you've been kept busy…"

"I knew that was a ruse from the start," Xavier muttered.

"Maybe so, but it also means you haven't been able to keep tabs on what's going on in the rest of the castle while you've been stuck in that office. For example, Remy spent four hours at the healers last night trying to get his hand working to the point where he could get his cast off, just so he can hold your hand during the ceremony."

Xavier frowned. "Is that why he didn't visit Daisy after dinner?"

"That's right." Luca tugged Xavier's last buckle, so it sat snugly at his waist, and then patted it as he moved out of Xavier's personal space. "He's also arranged for a World Council magic user, you know, one of those boffins that know when you're lying. Well, Remy got one of them to turn up for the ceremony, so it can be put on permanent record that you and he are marrying because you care about each other, instead of for whatever other reason people might suspect."

"How in crystal mountain's name did he arrange that?" Xavier looked around for his boots. Spotting them by the armchair that was placed by the window, he crossed the room, using the chair so he could tug his boots on for himself. "The World Council pride themselves on not interfering in society affairs unless a dispute has been declared."

"It was a true stroke of genius on young Remy's part, at least in accordance with what Princess Sophia told me. Apparently, Remy is friends with one of the council clerks, who happens to share his interest in Orobos. Remy contacted him, apologizing for presuming on their friendship, asking if there was anything he might do about the terrible injustice his fiancé was facing, given that the injustice was due to actions outside of your control, and yet could cast a negative cloud on what was supposed to be a happy day."

"I still can't see why anyone on the World Council would want to help me, or Remy, even if he and this clerk are friends."

"In normal circumstances, I would agree." Luca tilted his head to one side and then the other. "You need your black boots, otherwise your footwear is going to clash with your harness."

"Damn it.'" Xavier tossed the brown boot in his hand to one side and started looking for his black ones. "You still haven't explained why a

World Council member is coming to the wedding."

"Ah, yes, well Remy's two younger sisters are a true font of information. If you want to know anything that is going on, you only have to ask them. It would appear that despite the Lady Cecilia's rather tragic fall from grace after writing a completely untrue story about you, she did do you some good prior to her brain melting. The numerous stories printed in the World Council newsletter about the dashing Crown Prince Xavier increased their readership by more than forty-two percent in just two years. The council appreciate that and hope to continue to foster positive relationships with you and your new husband."

"That is an incredible act of diplomatic strategy on my fiancé's part." Xavier stood and inhaled, straightening his shoulders. "I think I need to go and marry that man before someone else gets their hooks into him."

"Er… just one more thing." Luca put his hand up.

"What? I can't afford to be late for just one second or Remy will think I don't want to do this."

"You haven't put your boots on." Luca pointed to the black pair resting on a shoe rack by the door. "Bare feet does not work with all the fancy trappings you have on, and you don't want to set tongues wagging about your state of undress. You've also forgotten your coronet. Father would have a fit about that."

"Damn it. Bring them here if you don't mind." Xavier sat back down again, his nerves only slightly calmer than before. *This is it. This is finally it.*

Chapter Seventeen

For Remy, the vow exchange ceremony went by in a blur. From the moment his father escorted him to the great ballroom, and he saw Xavier waiting for him in full dress uniform, Remy's brain switched off and he floated along on autopilot. He'd seen Xavier dressed in accordance with his position before. In fact, Remy didn't recall ever seeing Xavier out of uniform.

But the harness was a new addition, looking very official, regimented, not to mention difficult to get in and out of. It had the added bonus of molding Xavier's jacket to his chest and shoulders, to the point Remy was ready to swoon like the ladies he'd joked about with his mother. Was that only a few days before? And that was without the impact of Xavier's tightly tailored pants and knee-high black boots. A plain gold coronet sat nestled firmly in Xavier's dark hair and his look was as forbidding as it had been ten years before.

Remy only felt the slightest twinge in his injured hand as it was taken from his father's and passed over to Xavier's waiting palm. The healers had worked miracles in Remy's opinion. Once Margorie, the head healer, realized Remy was excited about marrying Xavier, despite 'that dreadful business', she worked her magic crystals so hard one of them shattered. He was warned there would be an ache for about a week, and that he really shouldn't use his hand for anything strenuous – words that sent Margorie's young helper into a fit of giggles – but he was cast free and that was all he'd worried about.

The whole event was all very prim and proper. Remy was determined his wedding day wouldn't be marred by the dreams he'd had of him and Xavier eloping. The pomp and pageantry of the ceremony, the vows that were made in accordance with the marriage agreement already signed, even the presence of the World Council representative who stood like a hulking crow in the shadows – they were all for the audience.

An audience who had turned up in their finery to see if Remy and Xavier were going to go through what many of them believed was a farce. Remy stood proud throughout, even as he felt the weight of their judging stares on his back. He said the words when prompted, he listened to Xavier's deep tones as the Crown Prince made his vows, and when Xavier's lips brushed his cheek, Remy knew that was his fiancé's... his husband's promise of more to come. He could wait, because after what seemed like an interminable time, the Minister of Marriage finally declared the two of them married.

"You look very handsome this evening," Xavier said in a low voice as the two walked hand in hand back down the aisle, following his parents to the large family dining table.

"So do you, devilishly so, in fact." Remy kept his eyes straight ahead, as he added, "If you need help getting out of that harness later, I do hope I'm the one who'll be doing the helping."

Xavier made a slight miss-step, although he recovered quickly. It was enough for Remy, knowing he could affect someone in *that* way. He'd worried that maybe Xavier would go running off into the night, before the ceremony, and not being able to talk to him in any personal fashion had caused a few anxieties.

But they were well and truly over now. Remy and Xavier were bonded in front of his family, judgmental visitors, and a member of the World Council. Remy's concerns about Xavier leaving him at the altar were now replaced by new and more pleasurable flutters of anticipation for the wedding night to come.

All we have to do is get through dinner. He'd promised his mother they would stay until after the first dance. After that... Remy had been busy with a lot of things for his mother, but he'd also had a chance to put a few private plans into action while Xavier had been occupied on official matters.

And now it was time - the first dance. It was customary in Bentley, whether a high society couple knew each other well before the wedding or not, to at least share one dance. Like the wedding, the dance was for show, at least that's what Remy thought. It was a way for a couple to show their audience that for at least five minutes they could be amicable. As Xavier took him into his arms, Remy remembered his cousin Clara's wedding that he'd attended the year before and grinned.

"You look happy. Are you enjoying yourself?" Xavier started to move, and Remy followed. The music could easily be heard, but it was low enough conversation was still possible.

"I was thinking of my cousin Clara's wedding," Remy admitted, glad of an excuse to look up at Xavier's face. The man's expression had barely changed at all. "She had never met her husband before the wedding. They had barely gotten through the first dance, and she fell into a delicate heap on the floor, declaring her new husband – they'd only been married an hour – but she declared he was an absolute brute because he held her too close during the dance. She spent the rest of the evening in hysterics while her parents tried to explain that dancing in public with her new husband was not a justifiable cause for invoking the piss off clause."

"That sounds very dramatic. You do realize we don't have a piss off clause in our arrangement, don't you?" Xavier's chin was in the air again and while Remy could admire the fine cut chin bones, even when they were covered with closely cropped facial hair, he preferred it when he was seeing Xavier's eyes.

"I wouldn't use it even if we had one." Remy used his newly healed hand to press more firmly on Xavier's shoulder. "I am hopeful that by tomorrow morning, neither one of us would be able to use the clause even if it was in our marriage contract."

There it was again, that slight hitch of breath that a person would have to have eyes of a hawk to notice. "Remy, my husband." Yes there was a definite undercurrent of something going on in Xavier's tone. "I'm not sure… is it even seemly…" Xavier unbent enough to lean closer, "Are we sharing a room tonight? Here? In the castle?"

"Yes. No. No." Remy whispered back, wiggling his eyebrows quickly.

There was a pause. Remy could almost see Xavier joining the dots.

Then he was back, leaning in as he said, "We're not spending our wedding night here?"

Remy's head shake was slight. The weight of the eyes around him hadn't lessened as the evening had progressed. "We're going to finish this dance. We may even finish two, so people have more time to dance around us, and it will be recorded we were having a perfectly pleasant time. And as the end of the second tune approaches, you are going to ensure we're at the far corner of the dance floor, over by where the musicians are playing. Can you do that?"

"If it gets us out of here, you can count on it." Xavier's expression didn't change, but Remy fancied his husband felt lighter and definitely on a mission as they slowly danced their way across the floor, dodging other couples, as they moved ever closer towards the corner of the room Remy had indicated.

/~/~/~/~/

"We did it. Quick. Quick. Follow me." Remy was chuckling with excitement as they escaped the ballroom. He was thrilled the first part of his plan had gone off without a hitch. Not too many people paid attention to what he was doing. He was a prince, just not an important one. But getting Xavier out from under the judging glares and curious stares of the people of Bentley, not to mention Xavier's guard and advisor, and his mother and father... that took precision timing.

Keeping hold of Xavier's hand, Remy shuttled him along the servant corridors, heading for the kitchen. "Don't make eye contact with anyone. We're not doing anything wrong. Just walk as if you know where you're going."

"I don't know where we're going," Xavier muttered, but he didn't sound unhappy, and he kept pace with Remy easily enough.

"Just a simple stroll, husband of mine, through the servant corridors, into the kitchen." Remy leaned his shoulder into the huge swinging doors that guarded the chef's domain to push it open. "Ignore everything and everyone, we're just passing through..."

"Did you need to get food for Daisy?"

"It's sweet that you thought of her. Luca offered to feed Daisy for me tonight." Remy risked a quick look at his new husband. "He thought I might be busy."

Xavier's lips tightened, but his eyes were bright, and he firmed his hold on Remy's hand.

"Dinner was amazing, Chef Jerry. You outdid yourself, thank you," Remy called out as he pushed on another door, leading outside. As soon as Xavier was through, he closed it. "Now, a brisk walk through my mother's rose gardens, and keep your ears peeled for giggling."

"If we're making a getaway, shouldn't we be heading for the stables?"

Remy wasn't surprised Xavier asked. He doubted his husband had ever trusted anyone enough to blindly follow them anywhere.

"Your men will head straight for the stables as soon as anyone realizes we're missing." Remy veered left, and Xavier followed. "Did you ever find out what Dante and Boris were fighting about that day on the trail?"

"A brief idea, not that I want to talk about it now. Let's just say that he and Boris had a difference of opinion. Dante was annoyed we'd come back to the castle without him, but I reminded him I wasn't in the habit of chasing the person who was supposed to be guarding my person."

"Ooh, using fancy phrasing and snobby tones, I'm sure." Remy chuckled again. He'd never felt so lighthearted. He was under no illusions. He knew until the scandal of

Lady Cecilia's writings had died down, he and Xavier were going to be judged, and every minute of their relationship scrutinized. After his parents kindly, but very deliberately kept him and Xavier apart before the wedding, Remy was determined to take charge of their wedding night. His grin widened as he heard his sister's giggle. "Hear that? That's our cue. Behind the hedge there."

Ducking around the side of the hedge that was taller than Xavier, Remy dropped Xavier's hand and hugged Sophia and Hyacinth. "You two are the absolute best, you truly are. Lady Rosa," he turned to Sophia's best friend who was holding the reins of two horses. Although she'd clearly forgotten about them and him, her eyes wide and her mouth dropped open as she saw Xavier in all his finery. "Have you met my husband, Crown Prince Xavier of Balenborn? Xavier, may I present Lady Rosa Blanche, Princess Sophia's dearest friend."

Xavier, bless his caring soul, nodded, and stepped forward, taking Rosa's free hand and raising it to his lips. "A true pleasure to meet you, my lady." He released her hand gently and took the horse's reins from her. "I won't forget your help this evening."

"Oh, my gods, it's true." Released from holding the horses, Rosa fell into Sophia's arms, hugging her madly while still managing to hold up the kissed hand. "He genuinely made my knees weak. I've never wanted to swoon so badly in my life. Handsome and a true gentleman. The stories are true, I tell you. True."

"You lovely ladies are amazing." Remy had seen Rosa's dramatics before, although he wasn't sure what Xavier made of them. It wasn't easy spotting red cheeks in a dim light. "Xavier is right. Your help won't be forgotten, but you'd better get back to the castle before you're missed. Is the key for Lady Blanche's cottage still in the same place, Rosa?"

"She double checked it this morning and the staff have been instructed not to go near the place for at least two days. It's well stocked with provisions, so you won't starve."

Giving her a quick kiss on the cheek, Remy got on his horse, watching as Xavier did the same. The cottage wasn't far, but it was enough off the beaten track no one would think to look for it. And for all her faults, Lady Blanche would not disturb them. Waiting until the girls were safely on their way back to the wedding party, Remy gently coaxed his horse into a canter, following the trail leading out from the castle grounds. A second later, he could hear Xavier's horse following him. *Finally we can get some privacy.*

Chapter Eighteen

The horses had been tended to and left with plenty of food and water in a small stable block that only had four stalls. Xavier noticed Remy seemed to know his way around but didn't say anything about it until Remy had located a key, and opened the door to a small, but very sweet cottage.

"It's not much, but it offers a lot in the way of privacy." Remy seemed almost shy as he ushered Xavier in and closed and locked the door behind him.

"What is this place?" Xavier looked around. The front door had opened directly into a living space that had a large couch along one wall, and two armchairs arranged around a warmly glowing fire. The rug on the floor looked thick and comfortable, and there were a couple of pictures on the walls which Xavier recognized from prominent artists. "Did I hear you mention Lady Blanche earlier? Isn't that the same woman who spent a lot of time talking with me during our engagement announcement dinner?"

"Monopolizing you, you mean." Remy chuckled as he nodded. "Lady Blanche is a very dear soul who believes risqué reading is perfectly suitable for an impressionable princess among other things. She is also a woman who talks a great deal, but never gossips. No one will find out we're here from her lips."

"Does she use this place for...?" Xavier's mind went to words like affairs, assignations... terms not usually discussed in polite company. Hopefully Remy would understand what he was saying without him actually saying it.

Grinning, Remy went over to inspect the contents of a covered tray sitting between two armchairs, placed to catch the benefit of the warm fire. "She's left us some of her famous mulled wine. Have a seat while I explain the wonders of the life of

Lady Blanche. It will give us a chance to relax after a busy day."

Xavier wasn't one for sitting and relaxing as a rule, but as he sank into an armchair that seemed built for a man of his size, allowing his back muscles to relax into the soft cushions, he could feel the tensions of the day disappear. The feeling of comfort was enhanced with Remy sitting next to him. The man's joy was infectious.

"If you've talked with Lady Blanche for any length of time, you will know she has four daughters. It was her younger daughter you met this evening – the one who swooned in your presence."

"Lady Rosa." Xavier nodded. "A very bright young lady, if a bit..." again words failed him.

"Enthusiastic," Remy filled in for him. "I'm sure Lady Rosa was raised to believe the stories in romance novels are all totally true and I don't doubt at least one of the daughters will run off with a pirate one day, simply for the romantic value." Remy had poured two large goblets of a delicious smelling liquid. "Here. Try this. Lady Blanche is famous for her mix of spices in her mulled wine."

Taking a cautious sip, Xavier's eyes widened as a delicate balance of flavors infused every part of his mouth. It gave the initial impression of being a relaxing brew, and yet Xavier got a zing of energy from it, too.

"No one knows Lady Blanche's secret recipe." Remy had clearly noted Xavier's reaction. "But mages and chefs alike have spent years trying to recreate it."

Xavier sank further into the chair and stretched his legs out towards the fire, cradling the goblet in his hands. "She could make a fortune if she ever divulged her secret," he said, taking another sip. "I haven't felt this relaxed in days. How does she come to have this place?"

"Ah, well, as I mentioned, Lady Blanche has given her husband four daughters, of whom he is inordinately proud. General Blanche is a lot older than his wife, a lot, lot older, and there came a time when the nature of his position meant he was required to spend large chunks of time at his apartment at the World Council. General Blanche bought this cottage for her, it is said, so that his lovely and very devoted wife could have somewhere to explore hobbies in her own time."

Glancing around the walls and furnishings, Xavier's eyes landed on a picture that at first glance seemed very innocent, displaying a group of people in scanty clothing playing games in a woodland setting. They reminded Xavier of depictions of wood nymphs. But then as he lingered on one specific group of *nymphs*, he started to see more details.

"That painting was given as a gift to Lady Blanche by one of her hobbies." How Remy managed to keep a straight face, Xavier didn't know, but his eyes sparkled with merriment.

"And she is still a loving and devoted wife to the General?" Bed hopping wasn't unheard of. Infidelity clauses were rarely added to arranged marriage contracts, although Xavier had insisted on one for his and Remy's.

"She genuinely is." Remy nodded. "When you see them together, you can tell they have very solid feelings about each other. Lady Blanche has never done anything that would cause a scandal, and she's extremely particular about her occasional hobbies. She adores her husband, and he is clearly proud of her. I like to think this cottage was the General's way of showing his trust that his wife would never do anything to rock the foundation of their marriage so to speak, while appreciating her need to have time with special friends once in a while."

"Then it was very kind of her to loan it to us." Letting his head fall back with a sigh, Xavier added, "It is very peaceful here. It's been a hectic few days."

"I think this is the most relaxed I've ever seen you." Remy was settled back in his chair too, his legs curled under him, his hair flopping over his brow. He reached up, unbuttoning the top two buttons of his dress jacket. "It's nice to just stop and breathe isn't it."

"After the past two days, definitely." Twisting in his chair so he could see more of his new husband, Xavier reminded himself again of just how lucky he was. No matter what was happening, or what would happen outside of the walls of the sturdily built little cottage, they were now married, and Xavier vowed to himself they would find time to just be with each other. "Did you know about your parents and mine coming up with ridiculous excuses to keep us busy after we said we wanted to elope?"

"I guessed it when Mother asked me to go into town and see the candlemaker about the center pieces for the tables," Remy said with a ready smile. "I pointed out to her that there was already a box of them, clearly marked, in the supply cupboard she'd sent me to earlier in the day. I think my parents were worried I was going to convince you to run off with me, and ruin your future chances of being king someday."

"I got the impression Max had the same idea," Xavier said glumly. "I appreciate treaties are very important documents and it's imperative that all words can be clearly understood. They have to fit the purpose and the intent behind the treaty. But honestly, at one point I thought your father and Max were going to put me to sleep with their incessant debates over wording that made no difference to the intent behind the treaty at all."

"They were definitely keeping you busy then." Remy laughed. "Father absolutely hates treaty negotiations and it's not like he didn't already have an informal agreement with your father that has worked for both countries benefit for years. But tell me something."

"Anything." It was not in Xavier's nature to lie to people he cared about.

Remy's smile was sweet, and one could say, innocent. "Why are we talking about Lady Blanche, wedding arrangements, and treaty negotiations? I want to know how you're feeling now the vows have been said. Any regrets marrying me?"

Setting his goblet on the table, Xavier reached over for Remy's hand, smoothing his thumb over Remy's slender fingers. "I have no regrets about marrying you, none at all. Hearing you say your vows and agree to be with me for the rest of our lives is the culmination of a ten-year dream."

He looked down at the large ring on Remy's finger. "I'm only sorry the scandal of the past week turned what could've been an event where people would've been happy for you, into one where they were watching our every movement looking for signs of my deviancy and your complicity in my degenerate ways."

"They really were like that, weren't they. It was worth it, though, to know no-one can tear us apart ever again." Remy was looking down at their joined hands too, his cheeks a faint red under the glow of the fire. "Of course, if you wanted to be absolutely sure of that..."

He trailed off, but Xavier immediately understood his meaning. It was virtually impossible for a couple who'd been intimate with each other to separate once their marriage had been confirmed by the World Council, which Xavier made sure of the moment the vows were finished. Even if Remy left him for whatever reason, they would always be married, and both of them would still be bound by the contract they signed. The penalties for breaking a marriage contract were severe. No matter what happened Xavier would be responsible for his husband for life – not that he had any intention of giving Remy a reason to leave him.

"Remy, husband. I want nothing more. I have waited for so very long…"

"I was rather hoping you'd know what we'd be doing, when it comes to cementing our marriage in the final way." Remy's quirky shy smile was fast becoming Xavier's favorite thing. "I'm afraid I have no experience at all in any intimate situations. I kinda got shot down the first time I attempted a move on anyone, because I was far too young to know what I was doing at the time. I've never tried it since."

"Oh, Remy." Xavier knew he should be feeling guilty that Remy had led such a sheltered life from an intimate situation perspective, but there was another part of him that was a raging beast at the idea he would still be Remy's first despite waiting ten years for the opportunity.

"I had done some stuff..." Xavier wasn't sure how to phrase it, so he didn't upset his new husband, "before... prior to you being fifteen," he added in a rush. "But since that night, no. Nothing. I told you before, I wanted to be a man you could be proud of being with when it finally happened."

"Good." Remy nodded. "At least one of us knows what to do in circumstances like this. Now where's that kiss you've promised me? You told me once we were married, all I had to do was ask."

In Xavier's head, when he pictured his first kiss with Remy, he was standing and given the table was between his chair and Remy's, it seemed like a good idea to do that. Getting up, still holding Remy's hand, he encouraged his husband to his feet. Remy came easily, that same quiet smile still dancing on lips Xavier longed to taste. Remy released his hand, sliding his arms around Xavier's waist, and Xavier felt it when their bodies just clicked together as he always dreamed they would. Remy had always belonged in his arms.

As he leaned down, Remy met him halfway, standing on tiptoes, their height differences not something Xavier had factored in when dreaming of their first kiss. But he was committed now, and he wasn't going to pull back. Not when there was still a hint of uncertainty in his husband's eyes.

The brush of lips meeting lips was just as Xavier dreamed but it wasn't enough. He had to have another, and then another. Xavier decided then and there, he could live on Remy's kisses alone. There was so much more than lip action going on though. Xavier hadn't even considered how Remy's body would feel pressed against his, the feel of taut muscles down Remy's back, the way Remy's arms clung around his waist – the hold getting tighter as Remy's breath quickened.

Xavier was on the fast track to losing his mind. He was a normal healthy man – a gentleman in word and deed, but a man nonetheless - and it had been a very long ten years. Ten years fueled with dreams of Remy as he'd gotten older, privately lusting after those slender legs and tight behind. As Remy flicked his hair back and dove back in for another kiss, Xavier even found that erotic, capturing Remy's unruly strands in one hand and burying his fingers in among the wavy hair while the other hand was cupping Remy's butt, hoisting him closer until Remy's weight was almost fully supported by him.

Finally, when Xavier had to get some air in his lungs, he pulled back, panting out a question he had to have answered. "How far do you want this to go? I will not push you for more than you are ready for."

"I want to feel your skin against mine." Remy's chest was heaving, his eyes glittering in the firelight, his face flushed, his lips puffy. Xavier had never seen anyone so beautiful. "I don't know what else we can do, because I have no knowledge of these things, but that has to be a good start, right?"

"Definitely, a good start. We need a bed."

Chapter Nineteen

Remy itched. It was as if his skin didn't fit, and his clothes were too tight. His need overcoming his nerves, he led Xavier through to the small guest room Lady Blanche had set up. Taking a quick look around, he felt his cheeks heat further as he spied the small bottle of oil set on the bedstand.

Discreet lamps, a chair by the covered window with a small table beside it, big enough for a book and a cup but not much more. The bed took up most of the room. High, it was covered with a discrete patterned coverlet that promised comfort and practicality. Remy caught the faint hint of magic wafting from the threads. *Probably to keep it clean,* he thought.

He turned to see Xavier struggling to get his harness buckles undone. He'd gotten the lower two on one side open, but the one tucked under his armpit was proving difficult. *We're married now,* Remy reminded himself. "Can I help with that?"

"If you'd be so kind." Xavier huffed holding out his arms as Remy moved closer. "Honestly, I'm sure my mother included this in my wedding outfit because it's so difficult to get out of."

Chuckling, Remy ducked under Xavier's arm so he could see how the buckles fitted together. The leather of the harness was stiff and new, lending proof to Xavier's complaint. "She was protecting my modesty from afar. I take it your mother didn't know we both wanted this wedding," he said as he tugged on the stubborn strap.

"If I recall, when this wedding was planned, only one of us wanted it. A little bird of mine suggested you might have been quite the reluctant groom." Xavier's chuckle was deep and full of promise. "But no. My father guessed how keen I was, I think. When I'd mentioned marrying into this family originally, he'd made a case for me waiting for Princess Sophia to be a bit older as he was in favor of a marriage alliance with Bentley... I would have never done that to you," he added quickly, as Remy finally got that one stubborn strap free and moved to the other side.

"I have to admit. I'd never considered that as an option, although I probably should have." Remy got the two bottom buckles undone in quick succession. The material under his fingers hinted at the hard body that lay beneath as he ran his hand up Xavier's torso to the final buckle. "There aren't that many royal families with daughters of a marriageable age. Would you think me insensitive if I mentioned I'd previously thought Lady Cecilia was right and that you'd marry a local society lady – someone from Balenborn, definitely."

He tugged at the final buckle, trying to get the leather free from the brass.

There was always one that was stubborn. "I used to think, to wonder how I'd feel when I'd read of your inevitable joining with someone else." He peeked up to see Xavier was watching him. The heat in his eyes couldn't be ignored. "I've never been so glad to be wrong in all my life."

There it was. That quirky half smile. Remy tugged even harder on the errant bit of leather that just did not want to come free. He wanted to feel Xavier's bare skin so bad he could almost taste it.

"Here, let me." Xavier had gotten a knife from somewhere, its thin stiletto blade gleaming in the soft lights. "If mother requires for me to wear another one of these, she can have a new one made for me." Before Remy could blink, Xavier slid his blade under the annoying strap, flicking his wrist and slicing it through.

"Oh, that feels a lot better," he said as he pulled the harness over his head and dropped it on the floor. "Is there anything else you want me to slice my way through?" The wink was highly suggestive.

"I'd rather use my fingers," Remy admitted as his hands moved towards the row of gleaming buttons down Xavier's front. They were beautifully carved with the Balenborn's royal family crest, but all Remy was interested in was how quickly he could get them undone.

Very quickly, it would seem, but perhaps not fast enough for his new husband. Xavier was shrugging his jacket off almost before the last button was free. Remy swallowed hard as Xavier stood proud, his chest covered in nothing more than a thin white shirt of soft material that left very little to the imagination.

"You're definitely well built," Remy managed to say without a stutter, his hands flitting over the shirt. He longed to trail his fingers over the tanned skin showing above the V-neck of the shirt. "I don't have anywhere near the same build as you."

"I'm not attracted to men like me." Xavier reached for Remy's jacket buttons. "But I've wanted to see you without clothes for a very long time. Would you deny me now?"

Wordlessly, Remy shook his head.

/~/~/~/~/

Xavier had always been a study of patience. He had to have been to have waited for Remy for so long. Although it was true, part of the delay in reaching the moment he was now in was his own doing, Xavier had always been determined their wedding would take place.

Intimacies were another matter completely. Given the ten years they didn't speak, and the reluctance Remy had to even believe Xavier had wanted him for all that time, Xavier expected a chaste kiss and to be sent away after the wedding to sleep alone. At least until Remy got to know him better.

The trust Remy was showing, as Xavier carefully peeled away his husband's jacket buttons one by one – Xavier couldn't imagine how Remy was feeling. He knew how he was feeling though – like every special day in his life had come at once.

"Look at you." The buttons undone, Xavier eased Remy's jacket off his shoulders and carefully draped it over his on the floor. Like him, Remy wore a thin white undershirt with the same V-neck, and it was fitted – very fitted. The bulge in Xavier's pants was becoming impossible to ignore as Xavier trailed his fingers down Remy's neck and watched his husband's eyes half close as he shivered.

Dropping to his knees, which wasn't one of Xavier's better ideas as he was tempted by the bulge Remy was hosting in his pants, he managed to say, "Put your hands on my shoulders, so I can take off your boots."

Still not a word, but Remy's hands were hot, and they gripped rather than rested on Xavier's shoulders. Sliding his hand down one of Remy's legs, his husband lifted his foot and let Xavier tug off his boot. A moment later the second one was gone, and Xavier put them carefully next to the draped jacket. Standing again, Xavier hooked the toe of one boot against the back of the other to toe them off. It wasn't easy – they were tall boots. A smirk started to form as Remy watched him.

Boots finally gone, and still going with his instincts, Xavier quickly stripped his own shirt over his head, dropping it wherever. "We should be more comfortable on the bed now, don't you think?"

Remy gave an audible swallow, that Xavier ignored, taking Remy's hand, and leading him over to the most obvious piece of furniture in the room. It was high enough Xavier would have to climb on it, and Remy was shorter, so he picked Remy up and plonked him on the middle of the mattress.

Finally, he thought, praying not too many of his lecherous thoughts were showing on his face. Climbing up, Xavier kept moving until he was looming over Remy who'd lain back, his eyes wide. Using his hands flat on the mattress to keep his weight from smothering his husband, he leaned over, keen to resume kissing again. Something Remy seemed to want as well.

Xavier lost track of time and space. All he could think of was the man writhing beneath him, on top of him, side by side against his body – the man in his arms, the one he would never let go of. Kissing was so much more important than breathing, and Remy's hands running patterns up and down his bare skin was setting Xavier's skin on fire.

Remy's shirt was long gone. Xavier needed to touch his new husband's skin everywhere. With his big hands, it wasn't easy getting them down the back waistband of Remy's pants, but Remy's moans got even louder when the tips of his fingers grazed across the bare skin on the swell of Remy's butt.

"Roll back, roll onto your back." Pulling his hands out of Remy's pants he coaxed his husband onto his back and attacked the buttons hiding under a discreet flap. One flew off under his fingers, pinging against the wall, and Remy chuckled, and then gasped as Xavier achieved his goal. The front of Remy's pants were spread wide, and only undergarments in royal green sat between his hand and Remy's cock that was clearly outlined against the satin.

Looking up, Xavier could only stare. His face flushed, his breath ragged, Remy was looking at him as though he'd hung the moon. "I don't know what you're planning, but keep doing it," Remy panted.

Oh, yes!

Bending to a task he'd only done a handful of times in his life, Xavier carefully peeled away the green silk, exposing the flesh below. Remy wasn't big – it would be difficult to imagine he would be - but in Xavier's eyes he was perfectly formed. The slim cock was pale against Remy's curls, with a tip that looked red and angry enough to burst.

And it will in a minute. Xavier knew it wouldn't take long – they'd both been on a weeklong tease with each other - and that was enough to make him proud, and damn aroused all at once. Cupping the length, it fit perfectly against his palm, he tilted up the head and licked across it.

"What the...?" Remy's eyes were blown. "I didn't know people could do that to each other. Again. Again.

Gods of steam and magic, that feels so good."

It gets better, babe. Xavier obligingly gave the cockhead another lick and before Remy's groan had finished, he opened wide and slid his mouth, so it sealed around the redness. One suck, then a second one and a tiny tickle of Remy's tight balls, and his mouth was flooded with salty essence, as Remy's body trembled and shook. *Damn, it's been so long,* Xavier thought. He swallowed quickly, coaxing Remy through his climax, and not letting his husband's cock go until Remy's whole body slumped into the mattress.

His instincts still ruling his brain, and feeling horny enough to rut the blankets, Xavier reared up, tearing his pants open. Shoving his underpants below his balls, he gave his cock one tug, then two before he was spurting all over Remy's creamy belly. "Oh, damn that was so worth the wait," he groaned as the climax shot through his body, causing tingles everywhere from his hair to his toes. Slumping to the side, making sure not to trap Remy underneath him, Xavier checked his husband's face to make sure he was comfortable. He didn't think Remy could've ever imagined being climaxed over, but Xavier honestly hadn't been able to wait a second longer.

Remy was watching him, his smile lazy this time, and there was no sign of any wariness in his eyes. "Crown prince you may be," he said softly, "but you made the mess. You can get me a cloth to clean it up."

"I knew you were perfect for me," Xavier chuckled, because in that moment everything was right in his world. "Just give me a minute, and I will, I promise."

Chapter Twenty

"What do you want us to do now?" Remy asked. It was the next morning and after another delicious mess was made earlier, simply by kissing and rubbing their semi-naked bodies together, which Remy had thought was a lot of fun, he'd gotten up, and went to find them food. It wasn't difficult. The wonderful Lady Blanche had left them a stock of bread, cheeses, and plenty of fresh meats and sauces kept in a hamper that had magical crystals to keep the food chilled. Squeezed fruit juice completed the simple but ample breakfast menu.

Sitting with Xavier, both of them still bare foot and wearing undershirts and pants, no jackets – Remy knew he was being strange, but to him, just sharing a meal and dressed so casually with his new husband was as intimate as the antics they got up to in the bedroom. And he loved every minute of it.

"Apparently our dream of running off on a pirate ship and operating a book shop on the side has to be scrapped." Xavier took a large bite of his chunky sandwich. A few quick chews and he swallowed. "I have a feeling Crown Princes and their Crown Prince Consort aren't supposed to do that sort of thing."

Remy was momentarily distracted by the idea that Xavier's mouth that was wrapped around his sandwich, had also been wrapped around his cock the night before. *Not princely thoughts,* he reprimanded himself. *Pay attention to your husband,* and yes, Remy was using the word husband a lot in his thoughts, because... it made him feel good.

"Crown Prince Consort. That's a bit of a mouthful. But you are likely right. So, did your father send you any messages at all? Are we meant to head off to your ship, or..." *Are you allowed to go home now?* But Remy couldn't bring himself to say something so brutal. If he got banished from home, especially for something he didn't do, Remy would be devastated.

"I've had a few messages, yes. I haven't seen you to speak to for two whole days." Xavier smirked to show he was teasing. "Mother has overruled father's advisers and said if it's good enough for Queen Abigail to host a royal wedding for their sons, then she was going to host a celebration of our nuptials herself." Xavier speared a piece of meat with his knife and popped it into his mouth.

"To be honest," he added after he'd swallowed, "I got the impression that my parents are furious that any suggestion from any quarter was made that I might not be suitable to rule Balenborn someday. Just as your mother welcomed me, and stood by me and our relationship, my mother fully intends to do the same. According to Max, she came close to actually swearing at father's advisors, especially when one of them suggested that maybe she should go and lie down, when she was arguing our case."

"Goodness." Remy tried to imagine his mother doing such a thing and realized he could. Queen Abigail didn't put up with any nonsense from father's advisors either. "All right then. So, we travel back to Balenborn in style, and prepare for another state function. Is there anything else I need to know before we go?"

There was a pause, and a look Remy couldn't decipher crossed Xavier's face. "There is one more thing," Xavier said slowly, "and I hope you'll forgive me for not telling you any of this before the wedding." Putting down his knife, Xavier reached for his hand. "It concerns the fight between Dante and Boris, or rather the reason why they were fighting."

"Dante and Boris?" It took Remy a moment to remember that there had even been a fight, but then he remembered their time on the riding trail, when he and Xavier dreamed of running away together. "I did wonder about that, but you said you hadn't wanted to talk about it when it was mentioned before. I couldn't work out why your guard and my father's head of guards would have enough in common to fight at all." He smiled at his husband. "We had a lot of other things to discuss at the time."

"There's no easy way to say this." Xavier reached for his hand across the table. "Dante seems to believe there's a threat against you relating to the man you punched before we got married and his having a connection to Cecilia. The man you punched was spouting a whole lot of stuff when he was dragged away from the reception, and from the limited amount Dante has been able to pick up, it would seem we need to take his threats seriously."

/~/~/~/~/

Xavier hated how Remy's face shut down, and hated even more that he was the one who had to tell his new husband that his life could be in danger, purely and simply because of the gossip generated due to Cecilia's written rant.

"I think you need to explain," Remy said slowly, looking at their joined hands. "I can't see any reason why your guard would fight my father's guard over a threat against me. That would suggest they had a difference of opinion about whether or not I would be safe."

"Boris felt, and you have to realize how difficult this has been for both Dante and myself, but Boris refused to accept there was any threat to you at all when Dante tried to discuss it with him. All Dante asked, when they were riding together, was if Boris had made a report about Palin's comments to your father. Boris said he hadn't and then he made some comments..." Xavier really didn't want to repeat what Dante had told him.

Remy held up his free hand. "Let me guess. Boris made comments along the line of I wasn't important, I was nothing but a lizard lover, and why anyone who would imagine me important enough to target clearly needed their head examined. Am I close?"

"Not word for word, but very close, yes." Xavier was stunned. "Do you mean you've known about this threat and..."

"No, no." Xavier was glad of the interruption because he'd been sitting on the knowledge for two whole days, worried sick about how Remy would take the news and if he already knew about it... "I just have a, let's call it gossip-knowledge, of how Boris feels about me. You have to understand, he is very good at his work, fiercely loyal to my mother and father, and he would lay down his life for Pierre and even Emily to a point."

Well, that's something, I suppose. But Remy hadn't finished.

"By the same token, to Boris, my sisters are a noisy nuisance who bother his soldiers and I'm just a waste of space he was responsible for training three times a week and who he had to stomach as one of his occasional officers. I'm not even the spare anymore." Remy shrugged. "When Pierre and Emily had their first son, my importance dropped to zilch in Boris's eyes. I imagine Dante, who is clearly loyal to you, was trying to find a way to warn my father's guards about threats he'd learned about concerning me, and Boris had fobbed him off." He looked up and Xavier could see the worry in Remy's eyes. "Please tell me my father doesn't know about this."

"Not yet, no. But I really feel he should." Exasperated beyond words, Xavier got up from the table, striding over to the window, looking outside. "To me the whole situation is appalling. Boris was sent with Dante, to guard you and me. He's the head of the king's guard and he's supposed to follow orders. He and Dante actually came to blows when Dante said he'd inform *me* Boris wasn't being protective the way he's paid to be. Boris's behavior was belittling to you in so many ways."

He turned, and saw Remy looking around the little kitchen area, a rueful look on his face. "I didn't realize there was any threat to my person when I set this up," Remy said, indicating the room. "My only thoughts were that we'd been deliberately kept busy so we couldn't run out on the ceremony, and I truly wanted us to spend some time alone. But if Dante's worried about your safety in all this..."

"Not just mine!" Xavier wanted to scream his frustration. Two days, actually three, and he'd kept quiet, waiting for a chance to talk to King Francis alone, and that opportunity hadn't presented itself once. "Dante's worried about you, too. Apparently, the uncouth personage who insulted me, by suggesting I needed friends in low places, has actually got friends in low places, including it would seem, a connection to Cecilia's second cousin."

"I didn't understand why he'd even approached you the way he did."

"I can only imagine it's because he knows Cecilia's cousin. They're distant family members, related through marriage. Apparently, and Fates know this whole thing is second and third hand according to Dante, Cecilia's plan was to ruin my reputation so soundly that I had no choice to do anything but become a hermit, thereby isolating me from my family to the point where I'd be that driven by despair, I would welcome new friends from low places."

"Hang on a minute." Remy got out of seat, coming to stand by his side. "Are you telling me Cecilia actually believes the rubbish she wrote about your so-called deviant behavior?"

"I don't know what to believe anymore." Xavier reached out, touching Remy's shoulder, amazed when the younger man came to him, wrapping him up in a hug Xavier didn't realize he needed. "I just know that Dante's so angry he wants us out of the country immediately. He's concerned we don't have the backup needed to ensure your safety. Boris knows there's a threat to you and doesn't care. The man you punched..."

"Palin. Lord Palin to be exact. He's the eldest son of the Plantagenet line. His father..." Remy trailed off. "I really don't like gossip, and I make a point of never repeating anything I hear if I can possibly avoid it."

"Remy, husband. If you can shed any light on this situation at all, it would be helpful to me and Dante in assessing how troublesome this threat might be. Honestly, we're flying in the dark at the moment, and that doesn't lead us to making sensible decisions. Please."

Nodding, Remy said, "That makes sense, but please understand I will not repeat gossip for gossip's sake. I find that practice untenable."

He's grown into such a decent and passionate man with values equal to my own.

With a sigh, Remy continued. "The older Plantagenet has had issues with drinking and illegal substance abuse for most of his life. He has a mage, specifically on his staff to find new and interesting ways he can attain a form of higher mental state which, as you can imagine, has had disastrous results. His family work very hard to keep his behavior confined to their estate. That was why the younger Lord Palin was at our engagement function. The older Lord Plantagenet hasn't been seen at a society event since he almost set fire to his wife's skirts, and that was at least four years ago.

"It is said, and this is just hearsay – I don't know how true this is at all – but it has been rumored that Palin encourages his father's behavior and emulates him in a similar way, especially in the lack of respect he shows women. If I'd been asked to come up with an example of anyone among our society members who might have ties to places where deviant behavior is encouraged, then it would be him."

"That is interesting," Xavier said, slotting that information into the brief facts he'd been given from Dante. "That would suggest that when he approached me on the dance floor, he was genuine in his offer to introduce me to low-born friends with similar interests to those he presumed I enjoyed. He wasn't being intentionally insulting to me, just crass in his approach, although definitely rude about you."

"Oh, no, no." Remy shook his head. "He was being deliberately insulting both to you and to me. To you, in assuming the trash his distant cousin wrote was true, and to me – the Plantagenet's have an issue with royalty. The general consensus among their family is that the royal families worldwide are too inbred, they don't serve a purpose and should be fazed out entirely, or at least they should marry into a wider range of families, to help strengthen their ties with the communities they serve."

"That's public knowledge? And they were still invited to our engagement announcement?"

Looking up at him, Remy smirked. "Are you going to tell me that when we're in Balenborn attending the celebration Queen Serena is arranging for us, every person there is a fervent admirer of the royal family and all they stand for?"

Xavier screwed up his mouth. "I would advise you to stay away from the Cathaways – the eldest daughter of that family was one of the disastrous dates Cecilia set me up with. And everyone in Balenborn knows that the Valorian's have no time for me or for anyone in a position of authority. But they do appreciate free food."

"See." Remy tightened his squeeze around Xavier's waist. "You have similar issues in Balenborn as we do here. I always used to think the most difficult thing my mother had to do in her position as queen was to be polite to everyone. I was lucky, people used to mostly ignore me."

"They won't be ignoring you anymore." Xavier thought for a moment, and then said, "I think I need to kiss you now, and then we should probably go and find Dante. He's probably pulled all his hair out by now. I know you had hoped we could be here the full day together..."

"No, no. It's all right. I don't like causing anyone any worry." Remy tilted his neck and pushed out his lips. "Kiss me," he said, and Xavier wanted to laugh at the put-on accent. But he didn't, because kissing his new husband was far more important. Remy might believe he was usually ignored, but Xavier had been Crown Prince for long enough to know that was going to change.

Remy's lips were still new to him, and yet there was a familiarity already blossoming between them and that warmed Xavier, alongside his husband's closeness. They had explored some the night before, although they still hadn't been fully naked with each other, but Xavier knew it would happen, and soon. But for now, with no way of knowing how long their private moment might last, Xavier wanted to enjoy it with everything he was.

So caught up in Remy's lips, his moans, and the way their bodies seemed to be seeking each other out, Xavier wasn't aware of anything else, so when the door burst open, he went straight into a fighting stance. He had Remy behind him, and a knife in his hand before his lips stopped tingling.

"Damn it all to Hades' world and back. I thought you two had been taken." Panting, Dante leaned over, resting his hands on his knees. His face was pale, his dark hair was sticking in all directions and there was a tear in his uniform jacket. "While you've been here sucking face with each other, I've been frantic. Why didn't you tell me where you were going?"

Remy's face was beautiful in the morning light. His lips were swollen as their kisses had become heated, and in his undershirt and pants with his bare feet, he looked like every one of Xavier's dreams had come to life. "Sorry, my sweet," he said softly. "It looks like duty calls."

Chapter Twenty-One

After Dante had burst in on them and brought their intimacies to an abrupt end, the move to get them to Balenborn went quickly. Hyacinth's red face, and the way she wouldn't meet his eyes let Remy know how Dante had found them, because he knew Lady Blanche wouldn't have said anything.

But after his entrance, Dante was being so pushy about getting his prince and consort back to Balenborn... well, Remy didn't like to make a fuss. He would've liked the time to say goodbye to Sophia, but she was staying with Rosa and wouldn't be back until the next day.

His parents had been informed they were leaving within the hour, Max had hustled Xavier away the moment they'd returned to the castle, presumably to reprimand him in private for causing concern. The wink Xavier gave him as he walked away was as good as a promise in Remy's opinion. He just wondered when he could cash in on that promise.

Maids were packing Remy's belongings that would be transported by carts Xavier had thoughtfully provided, and Remy's horse was being saddled and prepared for the five-day journey. There were people everywhere and they all had something to do.

Remy had only one thing he knew he had to do. Nobody else had even thought of it, but then they didn't understand, not fully. Wandering through to the kitchen, he nodded at Jerry who handed him a bag as he went past. "I'll see to it she gets fed, your highness," the big man said somberly. "I haven't had a mouse in this kitchen since she came and to be frank, sir, I'm glad she's staying."

Taking that for the endorsement it was, Remy nodded, blinking hard as he left the warmth of the kitchen. It didn't take him long to get to Daisy's pen. He'd trodden the path hundreds of times both during the building of her pen, and then at least twice daily since. As he trod the pavers one last time, Remy imagined anyone considering his friendship with Daisy would think him a rather pathetic figure – the fact that he counted an Orobos lizard as his dearest friend.

But there was something so special about her. There had been since she'd intruded on his solitary picnic lunch one day and climbed on his leg looking pointedly at the chicken he was eating. He'd given her a piece of his sandwich and their friendship was born. She'd never judged him. Never hurt him.

Admittedly, she wasn't very good at offering advice, but Daisy was an excellent listener. She didn't flick her tail up and run off, like so many society people seemed to do when he entered a room. Unlike many people who considered him unimportant, Daisy seemed to like him in her own cold-blooded way. Given how long

Orobos could live, Remy had fully expected Daisy would be his constant companion for life.

She has Mr. Daisy, he reminded himself as he opened her pen door. Daisy had heard a lot about Xavier over the years. If it was possible for lizards to be understanding, she would be. She embodied every quality Remy wished a friend could have. *Well, apart from the fact she can't talk, she really has no love of people, and she chases people she doesn't like.*

Daisy blinked lazily at him as he ducked his head under the door frame marking her personal space. Remy spoke softly as he put her food in her bowl and made sure her water container was full.

"Someone else is going to be feeding you from now on." Remy could barely say the words before his eyes were leaking. "I'm off on that great adventure we always used to talk about. Of course, I didn't think you'd be sitting on eggs when I was due to leave. I thought perhaps, in my innocence when we'd dream of my being swept away by a dashing husband, that you'd be coming with me. I guess I never expected it was better for you to be left behind."

He looked around. There were a lot of his time, sweat, and blood on the stone walls. Building the pen had given him purpose – looking after Daisy had done the same thing. She had proven countless times she was more than capable of caring for herself, but Remy liked to fancy she understood it was important to him to spoil her, and it was easier having food carried in for her, as opposed to having to hunt for it, although she did that, too.

Setting down the bag the food had come in, Remy sank down on the floor next to the nest where Daisy was guarding her eggs. "Everything's happened so fast. You're the only one who knows how long I've been carrying a torch for Xavier. I never dreamed he might have feelings for me. Last night was..." Remy let out a long breath. "It was as amazing as I imagine your time with Mr. Daisy can be. You certainly get pregnant often enough."

He smiled at his friend, although it was difficult to see her through his tears. "I'm not that good with change. You know that. There's a part of me that's so excited, but people have been so cruel since that article came out, and now that guard Dante seems to think someone's out to harm me in some way because I made the choice to stand by my man. Face it," he chuckled in Daisy's direction, "I waited for Xavier long enough. It's still like a dream that he was waiting for me, too."

Daisy let out a burp and then flicked her tongue in his direction. "Fair enough, am I being too mushy for you?" Remy tilted his head, listening. He could just make out the sounds of people moving around outside. "I guess it's time for me to go. You know, if you or any of your offspring find yourself in the Balenborn region, look me up, would you? I'll be the one pretending to be a crown prince consort and hoping no one notices how hopeless I'll be at it."

Getting up, Remy brushed the dust off his pants, moving closer to the nest, but not too close. "I will miss you every single day, my friend. Try not to bite too many stable boys while I'm away. I'll be back to visit before you know it, and I don't want to hear of you misbehaving. The chef promises me you'll be fed regularly, and I believe him."

Remy desperately wanted to pat Daisy's head one last time – to feel that leathery skin under his fingers. But while she was sitting on eggs it wasn't safe. Even though he trusted Daisy explicitly, he wasn't going to push her out of her comfort zone. Turning, he heard a faint hiss of hay moving, and turned back to see Daisy was off her nest and standing behind him, her head raised as if waiting for a pat.

"You do know I'm going, don't you." Remy could barely see for the tears as he laid his hand on the head of his Orobos. "I will always count you as my dearest friend. Don't let those little ones of yours give you any grief." *And please*, he thought, *please be safely here when I return.*

Brushing the evidence of his tears from his face, Remy ran his fingers through his hair, and hoped he looked semi-decent, before moving through the enclosure and pushing the door open.

Outside there were people milling around as Remy had suspected. His mother and father were there, Boris a hulking presence behind them. Dante was bossing four guards in Balenborn uniform to finish packing the carts, looking particularly dashing with the hawk tethered on his arm. Max was already on his horse, watching Dante with an indulgent grin and Luca was also on his horse, watching Max with a mischievous look on his face. But the only person Remy wanted to see was Xavier, and finally, over by the stables, he spotted him. In full uniform – Remy missed the casual look already - Xavier was on his horse holding the reins of Remy's mount.

Hurrying over to his parents, Remy gave his mother a brief hug. "Don't forget who you are," she whispered as he held her close. Sometimes Remy thought that was part of his problem – he did know who he was – but it wasn't the time to debate that with the woman who'd been nothing but kind to him growing up. He kissed her cheek briefly and let her go, stepping forward to shake his father's hand, only to be pulled into a hug from him too.

"Don't be a stranger," the king said fondly. "I expect to see you as often as I've been seeing Xavier all these years."

Nodding, because by now he was beyond speech, Remy did manage a smile as he sniffed. "Promise."

"And make sure that Xavier keeps you safe," his father warned. "If there's any trouble at all..."

"I'll let you know for sure." Sniffing again, Remy stepped out of his father's embrace. As he got on his horse and swung the reins so he could fall in beside Xavier, Remy took away the feeling that he would always know he was loved and that no matter what happened, he and Xavier would be welcome at the Bentley castle. But for now, he had a five-day trip to contend with. *I've never camped out before. I wonder if Xavier and I will be sharing a tent.*

Chapter Twenty-Two

Xavier had traveled the route between Bentley and Balenborn at least thirty times since he was twenty-one and Remy had been fifteen. Sometimes Luca had come with him, other times it had just been Dante and a couple of guards. The roads were wide, they had plenty of scheduled stops along the way, and Xavier had never really given the trip much thought before. He just focused on the end result – either hoping to catch glimpses of the elusive Remy to feed his memory until he'd gotten the courage to open his mouth, or thinking about the fact he'd had to leave Remy behind as he made his way home again.

This time it was different, obviously. He hadn't left Remy behind – the man had married him. Remy was now Crown Prince Consort of Balenborn, and the trip home should've been a celebration. Lady Cecilia had wrecked that, and Dante hadn't helped. His nervous energy and almost angry responses to the simplest of questions had Xavier making a mental note to pull the man aside and have a serious talk to him when they got home. It wasn't like Xavier was a porcelain doll or something equally fragile. He was capable of looking after himself and Remy if necessary, but Dante's mood had been infectious.

While Xavier was trying to get his gear together, his mind still on the kiss he'd been sharing before he'd been interrupted, Max was filling him in on information that had come to light while he'd been enjoying his honeymoon night which didn't make him feel any better at all. Xavier needed some private time with Remy so he could discuss all he'd learned and see if his husband could provide any context. Remy seemed clever like that and could apparently think of things in a totally refreshing light that Xavier found fascinating... and helpful.

On the trail, having that private talk was proving impossible. Remy was riding on his left side, while Luca was flanking his right for the most part. That in itself meant even expressing a quiet, "are you all right" was impossible without Luca butting in.

Xavier knew Remy had gone to say goodbye to Daisy. He didn't have the same affection for his hawk that Remy had for his lizard – he certainly hadn't built his hawk's living quarters and most of the time his hawk master or Dante was the one responsible for feeding her.

Remy had tried to hide it, but he was visibly upset when he'd emerged from her pen and while it wasn't in Xavier's nature, he found himself wanting to hug his husband close and let him know how much Xavier appreciated Remy giving up everything, including Daisy, to be with him. It was humbling what Remy was doing for him.

But he couldn't do that. Not with everyone listening in and watching them as closely as his hawk, as if just waiting for any signs of issues between himself and his new husband.

/~/~/~/~/

"We'll pull off here," Dante yelled, slowing his horse to a stop as they approached a small town Xavier remembered passing through many times although he'd never rested there. They were only an hour from the Bentley castle. Dante and Max had been riding in front, while the other four guards were behind with the two carts. "The carts will continue on with Prince Luca, Lord Max and the rest of you – your highnesses, if you can follow me," he pointed to a small trail on that disappeared into some trees. "We'll go around the townships as much as we can."

Xavier saw Remy's frown and felt much the same way. Pulling his own horse to a stop, he fixed his guard with a glare. He counted Dante was one of his closest friends, but the man still worked for him. "Is there a reason why you want me and my husband to go skulking around townships instead of just riding through where it would be safer and quicker?"

Now it was Dante's turn to look at Max. "I thought you explained to the prince the dangers we face on this trip home."

"They weren't discussed with me," Remy muttered.

"It's not like I can get you alone for even a minute, although I sorely wish I could." The faint pink on Remy's cheeks let Xavier know he'd been heard.

"Your highness," Max said in that calm tone that meant he was going to say something Xavier wouldn't like. "Dante believed, and I had to concur, that public opinion of you in Bentley, especially now Prince Remy is your husband, might cause our group to be attacked, or molested if we move through populated areas."

The look of shock on Remy's face would remain etched in Xavier's memory for some years to come, he was sure of it. But his husband's words when they came snapped with the anger of a prince who'd had his last nerve tweaked. "Are you insulting the good people of Bentley? Suggesting they might act in a manner unbecoming of them because of a few slanderous lies written in a gossip rag? Have you proof of these allegations?"

"No, sire," Max replied quickly, probably taken aback at the way Remy was talking. "Nothing but rumor and hearsay admittedly, but we are moving through uncharted times. There are many people, worldwide, who would prefer to believe gossip about a good man's reputation than believe a short press release about how it was all lies afterwards. That's just how people operate."

"It will be some time before I can visit these parts again," Remy said tersely. "I accept that gladly as one of the many prices I pay for wanting to be with my husband. However, I will not skulk among the trees, in my own country, when there is a perfectly good road in front of me, and I don't expect my husband would want to do that either. Now, if you don't mind, perhaps we can move on."

Xavier nodded. "You heard the Prince Consort, Dante. Move on."

There was a tense moment. Dante seemed to freeze as though shocked Xavier would countermand him. Xavier instinctively put his hand on his thigh – he always carried a knife in his boot. But then, Dante whirled his horse around again and they headed into town. Xavier let out the breath he was holding as Luca said, "Well, that was a bit unnecessary, don't you think?"

Xavier couldn't agree more, but he was more concerned with the rigid set of Remy's shoulders and the way he fixed his gaze on the road ahead.

/~/~/~/~/

Remy was silently fuming. He didn't dare look at Xavier or he was likely to have more than few choice words about the man's head of guard. Boris, his own father's head of guard was rude about him, but never *to* him, but Dante's behavior had a distinctly edgy vibe that got Remy's curiosity senses sparking.

He couldn't do anything about the man's attitude on the road, and he wouldn't say anything without talking to Xavier first. But he was determined that the advisor Max's attitude at least would be adjusted as soon as they reached Coolarly.

Like most of the smaller towns in Bentley, Coolarly enjoyed a proximity to the main city and the castle, and yet an independence to rule on most local matters. It was only an hour's ride from the city, and the distance could be covered faster if a person pushed their horse.

The people who stayed in Coolarly were retired social family members looking for a quiet life, along with trades and crafts people who enjoyed the community feel of the small town with their families. Magically infused crystals took care of things like lights and hot running water in most houses, but it was the hand crafts that stole the show in Coolarly.

Remy remembered from his previous visits that there were a lot of quaint shops and stalls that held a vast array of practical and decorative pieces. The town's business area was set in and around a large courtyard, making it a meeting place for family and friends as they went about their days. He'd originally gone to Coolarly looking for a stonemason to build Daisy's pen but had returned many times since for some of the truly amazing carvings the place sold. He wasn't the only society member, or indeed even the only royal who would take a day trip to Coolarly. Emily in particular was another avid shopper among the various wares on offer.

It was clear Dante wanted to ride as quickly through the courtyard area as possible, which in Remy's mind was rude. A number of locals recognized his face and he smiled and waved at people he'd dealt with before. Determined to start his mission of showing people how happy he was in his marriage, and how perfectly normal Xavier was, Remy let Dante and Max move on ahead, while he pulled his horse to the side of the courtyard that held a railing used to tie the horses, too.

"You really can't go through Coolarly without meeting some of the artisans we have here," he said in a deliberately loud and cheerful voice. Dismounting, he was quietly thrilled Xavier and Luca did the same thing.

Taking Xavier's hand, which was the only acceptable touch permitted in public between royals, Remy scanned the stalls. The market was busy, but he had a specific vendor he wanted to visit.

"I come here as often as duty allows." Spying the stall he wanted, Remy led Xavier and a curious Luca over to meet the man who was watching with a hesitant smile. "Mr. Godfrey, has business been well?"

"It has, your highness, thank you." The bow was respectful, the smile morphing into the genuine one Remy remembered. "And you've brought new friends with you this time. I'm honored."

"I have indeed. I'm not sure if you've met my new husband, Crown Prince Xavier of Balenborn, and also with us is his brother Prince Luca. Gentlemen, Mr. Godfrey has the most incredible wood sculptures that he and his two sons create. They are simply remarkable as you can see."

Remy was prodding. A crowd was gathering which Remy had hoped for. He knew Xavier didn't enjoy small talk, *but he's going to have to make an effort*, he thought fiercely. "I recently commissioned Mr. Godfrey to create a sculpture of my Orobos, Daisy, but alas, Mr. Godfrey, I will have to presume on you to transport it to Balenborn if that's at all possible."

"Of course, your highness, it would be my pleasure." Mr. Godfrey, who had to be seventy if he was a day, turned with surprising grace and indicated a table behind him. "I have started your commission if you'd care to see what I've done so far."

"Oh, Xavier, you have to see." Remy made sure his smile stayed firmly fixed, although he was tempted to kick Xavier's shin if the man didn't make an effort. "I mean, look at these sculptures. Have you seen anything like them before?"

"They are all incredibly detailed." Xavier nodded, finally remembering how his mouth worked. "You, sir, are a true craftsman. For example, that hawk, Luca wouldn't you agree she looks so much like my own, it's incredible. I would truly love to purchase her if she's available for sale."

Mr. Godfrey had sold to royalty before. It wasn't only Remy who was an ardent fan of his work. Pierre commissioned a likeness of Emily when she'd given birth to their eldest son, and Sophia had asked to buy from the store when she seen the small carvings Remy had in his room. But he seemed slightly shocked that Xavier would be interested... *which is a good thing,* Remy thought.

"Please accept it with my compliments, a celebration of your wedding, your highness." Calling to the side of the store, he called out, "Micah, please bring a box, one of the good ones. The Crown Prince of

Balenborn has expressed an interest in my work."

"He won't be long, your highness," Mr. Godfrey turned back to them. "Prince Remy if you care to look under the cloth..."

/~/~/~/~/

It was a considerable time later before Remy, Xavier and Luca finally left the market, two of the stoic guards weighed down by more parcels than Remy had anticipated. Once Xavier had tweaked to what he was doing, they visited at least a dozen stalls, and while Remy could tell he found it difficult to bend and truly relax into conversation, Remy was so proud of his efforts.

Luca was a huge help, exclaiming over every little thing they came across, and grinning at children who laughed in delight and ran to hide behind their mother's skirts. Only Dante and Max stayed on their horses at the edge of the courtyard. Remy caught Dante glowering at them more than a few times and purposefully ignored him. But Remy was feeling a lot better about their trip, and proud of his father's people as he, Xavier and Luca made their way to their horses.

He was almost at the horses when two women, clearly wives of the local storekeepers by their dress, stopped him, and curtseyed. "I don't mean to be rude, your highness, but is it true what they say about Crown Prince Xavier?"

Cautioning himself about making assumptions, Remy smiled, and said, "What something would that be?"

One of the women leaned closer. "My friend Mabel read in a World Council newsletter that it is said the Crown Prince can make a person's knees go weak just by the way he gets on his horse."

Chuckling, Remy nodded. "I have heard that rumor, too, and I feel if you were to watch and see for yourself, you'd know that is definitely true, ladies. I certainly enjoy watching him." And Xavier, to his credit, did make a beautiful show of mounting his horse. The ladies were still fanning themselves with their hands, as the party rode out of Coolarly to the waves and cheers of the crowd.

Chapter Twenty-Three

It's said I'm the prince of charisma, but I swear my husband beats me hands down. Xavier's heart was filled with an unfamiliar warmth. In just a few short hours, Remy had proven Xavier had been right all along to wait for him. Not only had he refused to let Dante reduce him to a cowering fool, *in his own country,* but he'd also shown an adept skill at handling people, treating them with compliments and concern.

And it wasn't faked. If there was one thing that Xavier had learned in his years dealing with society families in particular, fake gave off a specific vibe, and yet Remy was as genuine as he was friendly. People clearly loved him, and because of Remy's ready smile and clear appreciation for what others did, they accepted Xavier and Luca without a second thought.

It wasn't just Coolarly that Remy insisted they stop at, but also the towns of Tomlinson, and Quarter View

– so named because it was where King Francis's Quarter horses were raised. Xavier had been through the town more than a dozen times, and never knew the details that made the places special in Remy's eyes.

Everywhere they went, people were reserved at first, but within minutes they were smiling, nodding, and agreeing as hurricane Remy swept through with a purchase, a smile, and a kind word. Max's stern and worried expression had relaxed, which was totally unlike him, and even the guards were chattering happily among themselves as they continued their way to Balenborn.

The only concern, and one Xavier felt he might have to address sooner than later, was Dante who was getting steadily angrier with every stop that Remy made. He hadn't said anything directly, but at their last stop, Xavier overheard him saying to Max that "if the super shopper doesn't stop spending soon, it'll take us a month to get home, and we'll be that weighed down with useless junk, while Balenborn will be bankrupt." Xavier didn't hear what Max said in reply, but he was furious at the slight to Remy's character.

The chance came when they stopped for an evening meal. From Quarter View there was a long stretch of road, that took at least a full day to ride, through the low hills and beside slow moving rivers. It was the part of the trip Xavier usually galloped through, but with the laden down carts it wasn't possible. Remy didn't seem to mind when they stopped to camp for the night. He'd seen an Orobos on the trail and was keen to see if there was a nest of them nearby.

Luca and Max had agreed to accompany him, and with the guards busy getting the campsite set up, and the cooking started, Xavier finally had a chance to pull Dante aside. He would rather it was Remy, but hopefully he would have a smidgen of privacy with his husband once they retired to their tents.

"Explain yourself," Xavier snarled as soon as he and Dante were out of hearing of the others.

Instead of being shamefaced or cowed, Dante glared at him. "I should be asking the same thing of you. Your highness. Letting your husband parade you around like a pet cow ready for market. What were you thinking? Sire," he added belatedly.

"If you're referring to the way the Prince Consort wanted to introduce me to some of his people, and showing through word and deed how happy he was being my consort, I'm failing to see what the problem is."

"The problem, your high and mightiness, is that you're a man marked by disgrace. True or not, Lady Cecilia's words carry a lot of weight with some people. How the hell do you expect me to protect your personage if you're running amuck around the locals?"

Tilting his head to one side, Xavier eyed his friend closely. Dante had a faint sheen of sweat on his face, and he wouldn't meet Xavier's eyes. And that was without the rude way he was speaking. The friend Xavier knew would never speak so disrespectfully, no matter how many beers they'd shared.

"What is going on with you? You look ill. Have you taken something or eaten something?"

"I'm worried about you, isn't that enough? You haven't even told your husband about the new plot against him. How am I meant to keep either of you safe with you hobnobbing with stall holders all day." Dante turned, tugging at his hair. "It wasn't meant to go like this. None of this was meant to happen."

"What are you talking about?" Xavier was getting more confused by the minute. "I haven't told Remy about the newer threats against him yet, because firstly, you reckon they stem from Balenborn, and we're still in Bentley. And secondly, I haven't had five minutes alone with him since you burst into our private time."

Dante made a noise suspiciously like a snort. Xavier had had enough. "You need to pull yourself together. You're not doing me or yourself any good running on fumes and imagining kidnappers behind every tree. I'm ordering you to go and get yourself a plate of food, and retire to your tent, and I don't want to see you until morning. With luck, you'll be in a far better mood, because I'm warning you now, as a friend not your prince, that if this type of behavior continues around my husband, you can make the trip home by yourself, as a regular guard. Understood."

Maybe it was the way he said it, or maybe the delusions plaguing Dante finally gave him some peace, but after a tense moment where Dante seemed determined to pull out his hair, he nodded tersely and strode back towards the fire.

Xavier immediately looked around for Remy – who was standing directly behind him with Max hovering by his shoulder. "Max, go and get yourself some food," Xavier said noting Remy's pale features and his tight lips. *Damn it, he heard.* "My husband and I will want food in our tent in one hour, if you could see to it, please."

"Yes, Your Highnesses." Nodding as a form of a short bow, Max hurried after Dante. Luca was already by the fire, joking with two of the guards. Xavier held out his hand. "Want to spend some alone time with me for an hour?"

Slipping his hand into Xavier's, Remy nodded. "But not in our tent. Let me show you the Orobos nest Max, Luca, and I found. It's within shouting distance of the camp if anything happens." Xavier was pleased that no one seemed to notice them slipping away – *Let them think we're in our tent. We might get some privacy for five minutes.*

Chapter Twenty-Four

Remy was glad Xavier had spoken to Dante. He'd already decided that he would mention the man's behavior to his husband as soon as they had a chance to speak privately, but he didn't want to come across as a complainer when they were newly married. The fact that Xavier noticed the behavior and didn't just ignore it, like Boris had been inclined to do in the past, was a positive indicator that Xavier was continuing to be supportive of him, in public and in private.

Picking his way through a long-discarded trail, Remy pulled Xavier over to a huge tree he'd found that offered a perfect view of where a mother Orobos had dug into the side of a small hillock and clearly made her nest. "Duck down here," he said quietly, "We don't want to startle any of the lizards if they're home. They'll be highly protective of their territory, and they could attack if they feel threatened."

Noticing Xavier's grimace, Remy ignored it and settled his butt down among the exposed tree roots. "If we keep our voices down, we should be fine."

That got him a grunt, but Xavier sat down beside him, draping his arm over Remy's shoulder. Remy was happy to snuggle in. "I assume you got more bad news from Max and Dante about people apparently trying to spirit me away from you?" Remy tried to keep his voice light, and quiet of course, but inside he just wished people would leave him and Xavier alone.

"Max reported there are some rumblings among a few society families in Balenborn – mostly from people who supported Cecilia's idea that the royal family should marry into a society family." Xavier huffed. "The stupid thing is, with everyone so worried about status and their proximity to the royal family, if I had married anyone from a society family – Cecilia or any of the disastrous dates I went on – then every other family would've felt slighted."

"Which in turn would've caused more problems. Pierre had similar problems when he was courting Emily. The only reason their marriage didn't cause as many problems as it could've done was that everyone knew the pair were basically childhood sweethearts. By the time their engagement was announced no one was surprised."

"Pierre was lucky then. I had to wait until I was over twenty to find my childhood sweetheart."

That was enough to distract Remy from watching for Orobos. "I think that's the sweetest thing you've said to me," he said, sure his grin was bordering manic. "Truly, that means the world to me."

Xavier's cheeks were highlighted with slashes of red. "Yeah, well if I had been more vocal about my attraction to you once you hit eighteen, then maybe I wouldn't have had to suffer the dates from hell, and Cecilia wouldn't have even thought about working for me because I'd already have been married."

"How bad is it?" Remy leaned against Xavier's strong shoulder. There was a tiny part of his brain that wanted to squeal with excitement that he was sitting that close to Xavier, and *it was allowed*, but he reminded himself he was an adult, not a teenage girl like his sister. Or Lady Rosa. She'd definitely squeal, and probably steal squeezes of Xavier's biceps. They were worth squeezing.

Xavier leaned into him, increasing their connection. "If you listen to Max, he believes any problems we might have will be at my mother's celebration party. Snobby looks, you know the sort of thing I mean. It's possible some people might prefer not to talk to you, or me for that matter, but they'll be at the castle, so Max doesn't feel you'd be in any danger. He's just concerned it might upset you if you didn't feel welcome."

Remy chuckled softly. "He's describing what normally happens when I attend a celebration hosted by my parents. I was raised as the spare, remember, so I never had much importance. And as we've already discussed, my value to others outside of the family dropped even further once Pierre and Emily had their children. So, no. It wasn't as though I married you thinking people might actually find me interesting all of a sudden."

"I've always found you exceptionally interesting." Waggling his eyebrows, Xavier gave his half grin. Remy put that down to them spending a lot of time being near people through the day. Lifetime habits were difficult to break. But before he could say anything that quirky smile disappeared.

"Dante is a different issue," and Remy felt there was a note of sadness in Xavier's tone. "Honestly, he's the closest person I can consider a friend outside of family. He knew how much I wanted this marriage. He was supportive of me marrying you. But it's like, since the article came out, he's gone to pieces. He's never been as disrespectful as he has been these past few days. He's my friend, damn it, but in the past, he's never forgotten or ignored the fact I'm the royal heir."

Remy chose his words carefully. "I'm not privy to what you've shared with Dante, obviously, but is it possible he's misunderstood your reason for marrying me?"

"I don't know what you mean."

"Well... you remember how your lovely hawk overheard a certain conversation I might have had with my mother, where I believed at the time you were marrying me perhaps due to political pressure to have a spouse and that you'd never actually want to spend time with me?" Remy was embarrassed to think it now – he and Xavier had come so far. But in his head, it was highly likely other people just hadn't caught up with their attraction to each other yet. "Is it possible Dante is thinking along the same lines?"

Xavier was at least thinking about his answer and not just dismissing his idea out of hand. Remy spent his time looking at the nest, and keeping an eye out for adult Orobos. Little ones were cute with their bright orange color and the speed at which they moved. They were so fast, it was difficult for the naked eye to see their feet touch the ground.

When Remy saw one running one time, he could've sworn the lizard was running on air like so many mages had tried, and failed to do. But the nest area was quiet and the large Orobos Remy had seen disappearing in the undergrowth as the carts had trundled down the road was nowhere to be seen.

"The only person who knew the truth about my attraction to you was Luca," Xavier said quietly. "I consider Dante a friend, but I would never have compromised your reputation or mine, telling anyone how I felt about you when you were so young. And later, I still would've had to explain when I first became attracted to you, so no, Dante wouldn't have known."

Remy didn't want to ask the next question, but given Dante's behavior, he felt he had to. "Is there any chance he believes the slander in the article of lies? Perhaps he has a connection to Cecilia's family or something like that?"

"Dante's from the Sherwood family." Xavier tapped his chin with his free hand. Remy wondered if he knew he was stroking Remy's shoulder with the other one. It was nice. "My mother or Max would be the better ones to ask about family connections

– they weren't something I paid much attention to. But Mother isn't here, and Max..." he let out a long sigh. "I think Max and Dante are involved with each other. If I try and talk to Max about Dante..."

"You could be opening another bottle of pickles." Remy nodded. "I'm not a fan of pickles," he added when he saw Xavier looking at him in his peripheral vision. "To me, if I talk about opening a bottle of pickles, then you know I'm talking about a potential conflict I really wouldn't want to be involved in."

"Pickles. I like it." Xavier nodded. "Like, when someone might get themselves in a pickle – isn't that the expression?"

"Aww, you understand my logic." Remy chuckled, but Xavier was serious.

"We've barely been talking a week, and we've only been married a day." The sigh was long and heartfelt.

"There's a lifetime of things I want to learn about you, but with this mess..."

"We've got... wait a moment." Remy listened carefully. He was sure he'd heard a shout. And then another one and from the way Xavier froze, he knew his husband could hear it, too. "Something's going on at the camp." The sound of shouting got louder, and then there was a clang of blade on blade. "We have to go back," he said as he jumped to his feet.

"We have to be stealthy about it," Xavier said, holding his arm, as he stood up as well. "Have you got any weapons on you at all?"

"A knife." Remy reached into his boot and pulled it out. "You."

"We truly do think alike." Xavier had his knife in hand as well. "Not a lot of good against a sword, but still..." He hesitated. "If they're looking for you maybe you should..."

"I'm not running. I don't look like much but that's not who I am.

Besides, it could be you they're after, in which case I'm not going anywhere especially with your head guard in such a mess."

Xavier must've realized arguing was futile. Walking softly, and keeping to the cover offered by the trees, they moved towards the camp.

Chapter Twenty-Five

Why is this happening now? Did someone follow us from Bentley City? Xavier was running on pure adrenalin as he kept an eye on Remy, making sure he wasn't going to run into the middle of any action before they knew what that action was. He'd been set on by bandits only twice in the past. They weren't common – bandits were usually driven by greed or desperation, and they weren't inclined to attack well-armed and healthy men, especially men wearing uniforms and badges of office. The punishment for that type of behavior was swift and final.

"What the heck?" Xavier was equally confused when he could see the camp area clearly. Remy had stilled beside him although he wasn't looking confused, he was angry, and Xavier could understand the reason for that, too.

The camp was hosting visitors, although hosting and visitors could hardly be considered the correct wordage for the situation Xavier could see. Five men, in dark clothing that included hoods obscuring their faces, with two of them carrying large sticks were clearly in charge. Max was sprawled on the grass, his eyes closed and blood seeping from a head wound. Two of Xavier's guards were standing behind Dante, as if unsure what to do. Xavier looked around the clearing trying to find his brother. Luca was tied up by a tree, a scarf or something similar stuffed in his mouth.

The royal tent, which was a lofty name for the piece of canvas Xavier used for privacy on the road when he travelled, was cut to ribbons. There were slashes all down the canvas. And as Dante was the only one holding the sword, it wasn't looking good for him from where Xavier was crouching. *If he's organized this himself...*

Dante was yelling and Xavier focused on what his so-called friend was saying.

"They were in the damn tent. How hard is it to look? Max, Max tell them. The cocky prince ordered food for an hour in his tent. Why would he do that if he wasn't in there? Max? Max!" Dante ran to Max's side. "You're bleeding, why are you bleeding?" He looked up at the front man of the band of idiots. "You hit him too hard, damn it. You weren't supposed to hurt anyone. I told you absolutely no one was to get hurt."

"Accidents happen." The man shrugged. From his accent Xavier guessed he was from the hill area that ran between Bentley and Balenborn. "We've been following you all freaking day. You told us we could take the prince – where is he? King Francis will pay a fortune to get him back."

"Nothing's going to plan." Dante stalked in front of the fire pit and back again, tugging at his hair. "Absolutely nothing. My strategy was flawless and then that little shit had to stuff it up – dragging Xavier around like he owns him. Shopping!" He turned and flung his arms wide at the man who was watching. "King Francis won't be able to pay any freaking ransom because that boy does nothing but shop."

An inhaled breath reminded Xavier he wasn't the only one hearing Dante lose his mind. Reaching over, he touched Remy's arm, stroking down it, letting him know without words (he hoped) that he didn't agree with anything Dante was spewing.

"And did Xavier take his counsel from me after listening to me for freaking years? Oh no. I don't know what magic that little shit has used, but he's leading Xavier around by his cock, like a prize bull. Damn Remy should've been out of our lives within an hour of leaving the castle and instead, he's still here."

"No, he's not here. That's the problem." The man had a temper of his own. "If he was here, my men wouldn't be standing around like statues waiting for you to get your crap together. Hide out by the bush trails by Coolarly you said. But you all rode through town. Three towns we've followed you through, and did you say anything? Send a message to us somehow? No. Not a damned thing. Meanwhile, my men are tired, hungry, and no closer to seeing the bag of gold and magic crystals you promised us than we were this morning."

"They've got stew," one of the visitors yelled. "We can have that."

"That's ours," one of the guards yelled... Xavier was struggling to remember his name. Peterson. That was it. Private Peterson. "And what's all this about stealing Prince Remy away, Commander? Prince Xavier will be really upset. They've only just got married. We're supposed to be protecting them."

Finally someone with half an ounce of sense. Although Xavier winced as Dante walked over and knocked the man to the ground without a word.

"Nobody understands anything anymore. Xavier didn't want to marry that idiot. Don't you realize – he's a man with *needs*. Needs a weedy second string prince can't hope to meet. The marriage was just a sham to shut everyone up. Sure, bloody Cecilia should've kept her mouth shut about it, but she always wanted to be in the thick of things. Xavier would never have married her if she was the last woman on earth. But damn it all, none of you know the man like I do."

Remy tugged on his jacket and Xavier looked at his husband. Remy's face was paler than usual, but his eyes and lips were hard. He pointed at Luca, and then made tiptoe movements with his fingers before pointing at the trail. Frowning, Xavier was about to shake his head, but then Remy mimed untying his brother.

Holding up his finger, Xavier checked the situation at the camp, showing he was counting men who were against him – six in total, although two guards couldn't be seen, and one guard, the one still standing, was an unknown. Max was out cold, and Xavier was worried about him. If Luca was untied... and they could get to the carts, where Xavier and Luca both had swords...

Holding his finger up at his lips, Xavier indicated for Remy to start moving through the trees around the camp. Dante's ranting was helping, although the man would likely be horrified to know it. But while everyone's focus was on him – and Dante refused to be ignored – he and Remy, and Luca had a chance. Fighting off so many...

Xavier didn't like the odds, but he was angry enough to hit someone, and Dante would make a good start. He also reasoned that the intruders were hoping for a good payday, but only two of them were armed with sticks, so it was possible, once they realized they might have a fight on their hands, that they'd just disappear to find an easier target for ransom.

Remy was behind the tree where Luca was tethered. Still worried about the two missing guards, Xavier stood guard, knife in hand as Remy used his to cut through the ropes holding Luca's wrists behind his back. Quick to understand what was going on, Luca sidled back, and butt walked until he could move behind the tree and stand up. Grabbing his arm, Xavier towed him until they were out of hearing from the camp sight.

"Hades' playground, that was not pleasant." Luca kept his voice low as he tore the scarf from his mouth, sucking in deep breaths. He looked up and grinned. "We seem to be in a predicament, brother, and new brother-in-law. Dante appears to have lost his mind. Any ideas on what we do now?"

"Swords in the cart, if we can get them without being seen." Xavier kept a vigilant eye on what was going on around them. "What happened to the other two guards?"

"Hurt, I think, if not dead." Luca shook his head. "The intruders came out of nowhere. The two missing guards rushed them, being protective, which is what they're supposed to do. Before Dante had a chance to call them off, and what a mind bender that is, the two guards were knocked out. Two of the attackers dragged them into one of the tents. Dante's yelling and carrying on, and then Max tried to intervene. That big guy, the one standing at the back with the stick... he hit Max really hard. We've got to see if he's all right."

"Max wasn't part of Dante's plot?" Xavier didn't think he would be, but he had to make sure.

Luca shook his head. "The amount of horror father's advisor showed when the men turned up – Max had no idea, and that head wound is real enough."

"We have to get back now," Remy said urgently. "Head wounds are no joking matter, and from the sounds of it, there are two other guards hurt, and possibly bleeding out as well. I have some basic medical supplies and a few healing crystals in my bag, but we have to get to them."

The guards are dead most likely, Xavier thought grimly. The fact that Dante didn't care about the men under his command was as bad as him slandering Remy the way he had. He didn't even want to think that Dante, the man he'd called friend, truly believed he was as deviant as Cecilia had painted him to be. "We'll get to the carts, grab swords, and rush them. With luck the bad guys will scatter and..."

Xavier really didn't want to think much beyond that.

Chapter Twenty-Six

Remy was spitting mad. He'd heard the expression and he'd never held with anyone who left globules of their saliva on the ground – it disgusted him. But in that moment, seeing Max hurt, knowing others were too, and hearing the tripe coming out of Dante's mouth, hurting his husband with every foul syllable – Remy didn't want to spit, but he was ready to inflict some permanent damage on the men who thought he was an easy target.

He knew better than to even think of punching anyone. His interlude with Palin still caused an ache in his hand, but when Xavier crept up the side of the cart holding weapons, he held out his hand silently insisting on a sword for himself. He'd prefer his own blade, but Remy wasn't going to be precious and insist Xavier search for it. Not when Dante was getting more unhinged, and the head intruder seemed to be building up a head of steam as well.

"I should just take you freaking hostage, did you think of that? Kill everyone here and take you alive?"

Ooh that doesn't sound good.

"Everyone would blame you – they'd take you before the World Council when it's found out three princes under your care go missing or are found dead, and their truth sayers will know it was your plan all along. How do you like that idea? Because from where I'm standing, there's more of us than there is of you."

"You'll hang." Dante's face was so red, Remy worried he'd burst a blood vessel. "No one will believe you, and scum like you don't end up in front of the World Council. When they catch you, they'll just find a tree and a strong rope."

"We want our payout." The head intruder and Dante were standing so close one sharp inhale and their chests would be rubbing each other. "You promised us that sack of gold and magic crystals and we want it."

Xavier held up his hand – his fingers counting down. Remy had a flash of momentary panic – *do we go on three, five... is it on three or on five, or after?* But Boris's voice, of all people, Boris's voice came into his head. *When you're in danger, don't wait for them to attack, make sure you move first.*

Letting out a huge yell, Remy ran into the clearing. His sword waving above his head, he headed straight for Dante. Remy didn't know the stranger – they weren't likely to ever be friends seeing as the men thought it a good life choice to kidnap people for ransom. But Dante had been stretching his last nerve all freaking day.

"This is my first day as a married man, you stink hole!" Remy swung and Dante managed to duck out of the way of his sword just in time. But the tip of Remy's blade caught his pants, and the ripping sound was truly satisfying.

Dante had already had his sword in hand, but he clearly hadn't been expecting anyone to attack him directly. He swung at Remy, but it was almost as though he was scared of hurting him, *so he's not stupid.* The reason why there was so little crime in any of the lands was because the penalties were usually life threatening. Taking advantage of Dante's hesitancy, Remy pressed forward again.

All around him Remy could hear Xavier and Luca, and the single remaining guard attacking the intruders. He focused on watching his step, driving Dante back to the edge of the clearing, taking care not to tread on Max, or the guard who Dante had knocked out and who was still sprawled across the grass. The clang of metal on metal let Remy know Dante had realized he'd gone beyond any redemption point and was now out to inflict as much injury as he could.

Thank you, Boris. His father's guard didn't have any time for him, and when forced to train him, he'd pushed Remy more than he had Pierre or anyone else under his command. Yes, Boris had expected Remy to fail, but much as he had been when he'd built Daisy's pen, Remy refused to give up. And the fact the man currently trying to separate his neck and his shoulders had believed the article of lies about his husband, Remy wasn't in the mood to be merciful.

Thrust, parry, stab and thrust again. Remy had spent hours training under Boris's judgmental eyes. It was getting late – the light was fading – Remy was hungry, and it'd been a long day, but Dante threatened his existence. He was a threat to Remy's new marriage. And Remy hadn't spent ten years and more, drooling over his husband from afar to lose him now.

"He'll never want you," Dante cried as he fell backwards over a tree root, his sword flying from his hand to land in a clump of grass out of reach. No prizes for guessing who the 'he' was. "He'll stick around long enough to make his father happy, and then he'll be back to his old ways, and you'll be confined in a lonely tower with your damn lizard in Bentley."

"You really don't know my husband at all." Flipping his sword around so he was holding the blade, *thank you Boris for teaching me that little trick,* Remy raised his sword high. Just as he was about to crack the butt of his sword on Dante's head, he saw a movement out of the corner of his eye. He slowly lowered his sword arm and took a step back.

"Ha! You haven't got the stomach for it have you," Dante yelled, struggling to get to his feet. "I'll do you in myself..."

"Dante, lower your voice," Remy warned.

"What's the matter, boy? Is my yelling hurting your precious ears?"

"Seriously, Dante, lower your voice." Remy took another step backwards. "Don't make any sudden moves."

Out of the corner of his eye, Remy saw Xavier and Luca freeze as they were helping Max get up off the grass. He was partially moving under his own steam at least. The unconscious guard had also been revived and was sitting by the fire pit, drinking something from a tin cup.

There was no sign of the intruders, but Remy's focus wasn't even on Dante anymore. He was no longer the biggest danger in the clearing. That honor went to the giant orange lizard who was standing like a statue by the tree line, his only movement his long tongue flicking as he scented the air. Remy immediately noticed the lizard's tail was ramrod straight and about an inch off the ground. He slowly took another step back.

"What in Hades' name is that?" Dante finally realized he wasn't the centre of attention anymore, but he didn't listen when it came to lowering his voice. "Is that a lizard? Your lizard? How the hell...? Did it follow you or something? You'd better call it off. Call it off, I swear, or I'll gut the thing where it stands."

"I told you to lower your voice. That's not my Daisy." Definitely not. The Orobos Remy was looking at was almost twice the size of Daisy, or even Mr. Daisy. "There's a nest near here," he said, keeping his tone low and even. "This one's just come to see what the noise is all about. If you..."

But of course Dante wouldn't listen. "If you think I'm going to be scared of a damn lizard," Dante yelled, scrambling to his feet, reaching for his discarded sword. But the moment he moved, so did the Orobos and in his fluster, Dante missed his sword completely while the lizard moved in. Scrambling on his hands and knees over the tree roots, Dante's boots slipped in the grass.

"Not that way..." Remy tried to say as Dante headed for where the Orobos nest was situated, but it was too late. Dante disappeared from view and so did the lizard. Seconds later there was a loud scream that cut off as quickly as it started.

Shaking his head, Remy winced as he said, "At least the mama lizard will have a good feed tonight." He turned to face his husband. "Is everything okay here? That was a jar of pickles best left unopened for sure."

Chapter Twenty-Seven

"You didn't wait for my countdown." Xavier's heart still hadn't settled into its regular rhythm since he'd seen Remy take off into the clearing, waving his sword like a warrior, yelling like a banshee and that had been at least two hours before. Dante was a first-class swordsman – he had to be to be Xavier's head of guard. To see Remy act so recklessly, so bravely, damn it. Xavier never wanted to see that again.

"It did the trick." Remy was sitting calmly on the mattress, sipping some mulled wine from a goblet. They were in Dante's tent, seeing as Xavier's had been shredded, and it wasn't like Dante would be using his again. Earlier, Xavier had sent the two remaining guards off to see if they could find Dante's remains. The two men came back, their faces looking as if they'd seen a ghost, reporting rather shakily there was nothing left of Dante to salvage.

The other two guards had indeed been killed, showing evidence of blunt force trauma to their heads, and stab wounds in their chest areas. Xavier was angry at Dante all over again for letting something like that happen to men who's lives he'd been entrusted with. But he had been quietly proud when Remy picked up a shovel and helped dig graves for the dead soldiers.

Max, once he'd gained consciousness, seemed to have nothing more than a severe headache. Luca had offered to keep an eye on him through the night in case any further symptoms developed. Max was determined to try and send messages through the magic crystal he always carried. Xavier's hawk had also been sent in the direction of Balenborn with a message in his collar. The hawk would know to go directly to the king and would let no one else touch her. But if help was coming it would be at least a day or more away.

The two remaining guards, Roberts and Jorge, were shaken, but they offered to stand guard, which Xavier commended, and told them so. But his gut was telling him it wasn't necessary. The intruders had run at the first sign of a fight - *Remy's recklessness being a positive again* – and Xavier doubted they'd be back. After everyone had eaten, he ordered both men to their tent and simply told them to remain vigilant. Everyone needed to rest.

Which left him and Remy finally alone, and as was often the case when Xavier was in front of the man, he truly didn't know what to say. So he just said the first thing that came into his head. "I was frightened for you today."

Putting his goblet down on the floor, Remy got up, coming towards Xavier like he'd dreamed of the man doing so many, many times in the past. "I'm sorry I did that to you, especially when you're hurting. You're upset because of Dante and the men that have been needlessly killed. I can't imagine how that must feel." Remy's arms snuggled nicely around Xavier's waist, and his new husband rested his head on Xavier's chest.

"You know," Remy said in the quiet, as Xavier rested his arms around Remy's shoulders and just breathed long and slow, "I'm not sure if you want to talk about it, but I couldn't work out why Dante was in such a hurry for us to leave Bentley. Clearly, he hired those men recently, but they would not have been easy to find. There are a couple of taverns where people like that gang leader frequent, but usually you have to know where to look."

"We've been coming here to Bentley for years," Xavier said glumly, because Remy was right. Dante's betrayal had stung him deeply. Xavier made a point of not getting very close to anyone, but Dante had been the exception. "He could've been making nefarious contacts all over the world, and I wouldn't have known about it. I feel like such a fool."

"His behavior does not reflect on you. But what was the hurry, do you think? I mean, Dante could've just as easily have hired thugs to abduct me next week."

Oh, Hades' playground, he might've done that too. Xavier tightened his hold on his husband as if that would protect him. "I don't know. Originally, we'd planned to leave within a week of the wedding, because I felt leaving any sooner wasn't fair on you. You'd need time to make your plans, spend time with your family..."

"And yet, as soon as Dante burst in on us literally the morning after the wedding, and started going on about the threats against me, that somehow he felt you hadn't discussed with me..."

Remy trailed off and Xavier knew it was up to him to fill in the gaps.

"Let's sit down," he said in a low voice. Waiting until Remy was snug under his arm as they sat side by side on the mattress, Xavier continued. "I need you to know, before I say anything else, that I will never, and I repeat never keep secrets from you. If there are things I haven't told you up until now – information that's come from Max or anyone else – it's only been because I haven't had an opportunity to talk to you privately."

"A common issue with royal couples." Remy nodded. "I know with my parents it got so bad at times, my father issued a decree that he and my mother were to have one hour alone before dinner every day and it didn't matter who was around or what was happening, that was their time. Although, once me and my siblings got older, my mother used to spend a lot of time in my father's office and was privy to any information anyway. But I remember being stunned when I learned my father actually had to order people to leave him alone. His advisors were horrified by the idea, but they accepted it, eventually."

"Remind me to instigate a similar rule." Xavier sighed. "We have so much we need to catch up on. So much to learn about each other. But right now you need to know about Dante." Shaking his head, he added, "Maybe you can shed some insight on why the man turned against me so thoroughly."

"That's not necessarily true." Remy sat up a bit straighter and turned so Xavier could see his face. "I've been thinking about the ranting Dante had been doing before his introduction to Orobos..."

Xavier internally smirked at Remy's description.

"He genuinely thought he was doing you a favor by getting rid of me."

That wiped any idea of a smirk off Xavier's face. "What do you mean? Did he have some twisted idea that you'd insisted on being with me in

Balenborn? That you were behaving like a limpet instead of wanting to stay in Bentley?"

"I know it doesn't make much sense, but then neither did Dante. It was as if, from the way he was speaking, he genuinely believed everything that Cecilia had written was true. Remember, she had not only slandered you, but me as well. I got the impression – did you notice how he kept saying things weren't working out the way he'd planned?"

Xavier nodded. "I was confused about that, too."

"What if he wasn't talking about you and I marrying, as such. What if he was referring to Cecilia being held by the World Council? If I recall correctly, when you mentioned Cecilia to me that first time, she was your personal assistant, who had overstepped in some way or another..."

"She didn't agree with our wedding and basically came out and said she only took the job with me so she could convince me to marry her."

"So you sent her home, to her family estate, I assume."

"Yes. I asked Dante to organize her transport for her with your father's head of household."

"Giving them a chance to talk privately."

Remy made a good point, but something still didn't feel right. "Dante wasn't interested in Cecilia. He'd been chasing Max for the longest time."

"But you don't know if Cecilia hadn't persuaded him in some way, Dante I mean, that your insatiable lusts were a major problem only she could cure."

As much as it felt so good to hold Remy in his arms, Xavier had to pace. He thought better that way. He made sure to stroke down Remy's arm before he stood up though. "Why would he think that about me?" he said as he paced across the tent. "Cecilia had only been with me two years. I've known Dante most of my life. Surely, he would know me better than that."

"Yes, but when it comes to intimate or relationship matters, how much did he know about you really? How much did anyone? Remember, I believed the things written about you in the council newsletter. Those articles all gave the impression you were a serial dater, and you only dated women." Remy leaned forward, his elbows on his knees. "What if... if you think back, have there been times when you've gone off on your own, or asked for private time, or he's gone off and done things on his own? You weren't with each other all the time, am I right?"

"Not usually, no." Xavier frowned as he thought. "When we're at home, I could go days without seeing Dante. He usually only stayed with me when I traveled, like coming here to Bentley or if I had to visit the World Council for my father. The only time he refused to come with me was when I was on my ship. He had a real problem with motion sickness. But the ships all have their own guards, so he wasn't needed for protection then."

"And Max had said that one of the ideas your father's advisors had about you after Cecilia's article, was to spend time on your ship. You told me about that, the first day after Cecilia's article came out."

"I'm still not seeing how this all fits." There really wasn't a lot of pacing room in the tent. Xavier spied a likeness, a small sketch drawing of Dante, sitting on the man's travel trunk. Going over to it, he picked it up, studying it carefully. The only two things in the tent were the chest, and the bed and no matter how badly

Xavier was thinking about Dante, he wasn't about to go through his private things. The trunk would be returned to the Sherwood family when they arrived back in Balenborn.

But the picture had been left out, as if it was important. Xavier shook his head and peered at it again. Although it was night, the tent had been lit with crystal lamps, casting a soft glow. Seen in focus, the details were meticulous but very small. The picture was clearly a likeness of him and Dante. What was unusual was it was a casual pose, definitely not one Xavier had agreed to, showing two men who were a lot friendlier than Xavier had even been with Remy in public, let alone Dante. Royal depictions were never casual.

In the picture, Dante had his arm around Xavier's shoulder – again artistic license as Xavier had always been taller than Dante – and the likeness gave the impression Dante was imparting something secretive in

Xavier's ear. The grin the artist had created for the Xavier figure was definitely another example of artistic creativity.

"Have you found something interesting?"

There was a part of Xavier that wanted to put the picture behind his back, but that would give the impression Xavier had something to feel guilty about. Instead, he crossed the small grass area between the trunk and the mattress and handed the picture to Remy.

"What do you think of this?" Xavier wasn't going to give Remy any hints about what he was thinking – he wanted his husband's unbiased opinion. *Please don't let him get the wrong idea.*

Chapter Twenty-Eight

Remy made sure none of what he was actually feeling showed on his face. "I think," he said slowly, fingering the elegant filigree frame the picture had been fitted to, "if I had seen this, before I'd had a chance to talk to you, or before we'd gotten married, I would have imagined that Dante would be a serious contender for your affections."

He looked up, meeting Xavier's stark expression. "You're going to forgive my asking, but as you pointed out, we don't know a lot about each other, and we only got married yesterday. But I take it you had no idea this likeness had been crafted, and you did not pose for this in any way."

Xavier shook his head. "I have never been in that... that... that position with Dante in my life." He pointed a finger at the likeness as if it was bewitched. "To do something like that would be a gross abuse of my position as his superior. Yes, Dante came from a society family, and one could argue I could marry him as easily as I could have married Cecilia, if I'd been inclined. But to take such liberties with someone I wasn't betrothed to and have it recorded in this way... Remy, my husband, please say you believe me. I wouldn't do something like that. I meant what I said about waiting for you."

"And I believe you, I do." Remy was quick to make a point of meeting Xavier's eyes. "You should also note I am one of the last people who would jump to Dante's defense, however I do think your insistence on keeping yourself for me might have backfired slightly."

"I swear you talk in riddles sometimes, my understanding husband." But it seemed Xavier wasn't as riddled with anxiety once Remy had dismissed any concerns Xavier might have had. "Please explain."

"In the absence of any real information, it would appear some people with avid imaginations, made up scenarios that aligned with their own dreams or deviant tendencies."

"Wait a minute. So, you believe Cecilia wrote about my deviancy, because she was hoping that was how I behaved, and Dante had this likeness done and tried to get rid of you because..."

"There wasn't any room in his imagination for him to share you with me. In fact," Remy was warming to his theme, "if we assume that Dante and Cecilia both believed the same things, whether that be all the time, or just after you announced your marriage, it was equally possible they colluded to get rid of me, so that you could marry Cecilia, and Dante would be your 'hobby' on the side. If Dante knew you weren't that keen on Cecilia, it wouldn't be much of a leap for him to think you might welcome male company once you were married to someone else. Clearly neither of them believed you would marry another male."

"I think I feel sick." Xavier came and sat down beside him again and Remy leaned into his bulk.

"I'm not sure, of course. I don't know these people, but it does explain why Dante kept saying it wasn't meant to go the way it did – whatever 'it' was. Maybe he didn't expect Cecilia to write that article. Perhaps they had some other plan to wreck our marriage in some way. I am almost certain he didn't realize Cecilia would end up in front of the World Council because of what she did, and she probably didn't think she would either. Maybe he didn't think you'd go through with your wedding with me, or if you did, as some form of royal obligation, he believed you wouldn't live with me as my spouse. I don't know..." Remy broke off as someone made a very loud coughing sound outside of the tent.

"Xavier, Remy?" It was Luca. "I do apologize but I've got Max here and he just won't go to sleep until he's had a chance to talk to you. It's about Dante. Can we come in?"

"Another darned pickle we could do without," Remy muttered and while Xavier nodded, he called out "enter," encouraging the two men to come into their tent.

The man who came into the tent was nothing like the impeccable and unflappable Lord Max had appeared to be since arriving in Bentley. His hair was wild, although he'd clearly tried to straighten it, and his clothes were clean but crumpled. But it was Max's face that had Remy getting up and offering Max his spot on the mattress. The advisor was pale, the gash on his head had been cleaned up, but it was still an angry red against his pale complexion. He came in, using Luca's arm as support.

"Lord Max absolutely could not sleep until he'd spoken to you both," Luca explained, leading Max to the spot Remy had vacated and helping the man sit. "I figured you two still had a lot to talk about, so weren't likely to be sleeping..."

"It's fine." Now standing, Xavier's face was giving nothing away as usual. Remy made a mental note to talk to his husband about that when they weren't dealing with death threats and possible abduction attempts.

To make up for Xavier's intimidating air, Remy smiled at the pale man. "Is your head feeling any better, Lord Max?"

"If you're referring to the physical pain, then yes, thank you, your highness." Max nodded and then winced. "But I have to confess, I believe part of Dante's descent into madness," he stumbled on his words, and sniffed before continuing, "I feel it might have been partially my fault."

"You were aware of the plot to abduct my husband and hold him for ransom?" Xavier's glower shouldn't have looked sexy, but it did. Or at least, it did from Remy's perspective. From Max's, probably not.

"No. No. Definitely not, your highness. If Dante had mentioned what he was organizing at all, you have to believe that I would have attempted to dissuade him and reported it to you immediately." Max seemed to slump in on himself. "I'm not sure if you were aware, but Dante had expressed his interest in courting me quite some time ago."

Luca chuckled. He was leaning on the tent support. "Max, everyone knew how you two were interested in each other."

"But that's just it." Max turned to Luca who didn't look as intimidating as Xavier was, so that was probably why he did it. "Dante had expressed an interest in courting me, but I had turned him down more than once. I

365

realize it might've looked like more than that to others – Dante has..." Max stopped again for a moment and then continued, "Dante *had* a charming personality when he wanted to apply it and I considered him a good friend." He looked down at his hands. "That's why the events of the day have been so difficult for me."

Remy looked up at Xavier, but he was still doing his impersonation of an intimidating gargoyle, and when he glanced across at Luca, the man just shook his head.

"It's not easy to lose a good friend," Remy said slowly. "Forgive me, if I'm being insensitive, but the events of today suggested there was a lot about your friend that you didn't know. From what Xavier and I witnessed before taking on the attackers, I wasn't seeing anything that you could blame yourself for. What do you think we are missing?"

"I believe..." Max stopped again. Clearly, whatever he had to say was difficult for him. "I swear, I have never done anything like this before, but Dante begged me... told me he would lose his position, and he was devoted to you, Prince Xavier. Truly devoted."

"It seems you knew more about his feelings than I did. Perhaps you can explain this?" Xavier nodded at Remy. It took a moment for him to work out what Xavier wanted, but then Remy realized he was still holding the likeness Xavier had found.

"This was sitting on Dante's trunk." Remy walked over, handed the frame to Max, and then went to stand by Xavier. "I believe my husband when he tells me he did not pose for this, never acted in any way that was improper with his head guard and had no idea why Dante would commission and hold onto an item of this kind. Something like this, if made public, could be highly detrimental to Xavier's reputation."

"Which has already taken a savaging from the fair Lady Cecilia," Luca noted. He had wandered over and looked over Max's shoulder. "I could tell that was a fake in an instant. You do not smile like that," Luca smirked at his brother.

"Xavier barely smiles at all," Remy said with a smirk of his own. "I plan to change that."

"Oh, Dante." In comparison to the lightness Remy had tried to inject into the situation, Max sounded heartbroken. He stroked over Dante's face in the picture. "I'm so very sorry, your highness. I didn't know about this either." He looked up and Remy could see tears in his eyes. "But he lied to you before we left the Bentley castle, and I knew about that, and didn't correct your assumptions."

Remy didn't think it was possible for Xavier's glower to deepen, but his eyebrows were almost meeting in the middle. "Getting us to leave Bentley castle earlier than planned was a ruse? Why?"

"No, your highness. Not as such. I give you my word, I have no idea why Dante wanted us to head back to Balenborn so quickly."

"What then, Max?" Xavier's tone deepened. "You have been in my father's service long enough to know how much both he and I abhor any form of deception. Why would you lie to me and what was Dante lying about?"

"His fight with Boris, before you two were married." Sniffing again, Max sat up straighter. "If you recall, your highness, I wasn't there because I was in contact with your father after you'd decided to give up your position as the Balenborn heir."

"Boris and Dante were fighting on the trail, yes. I remember you got so upset about it, Xavier, because you felt that my father's head of guard was rude about me and our marriage."

"I also reiterated how worried Dante was about you, when clearly he was lying about everything." Folding his arms across his chest, Xavier said to Max, "What did he lie about specifically? Did the fight between Dante and Boris have anything to do with me and my husband at all?"

"Definitely it did. It started, at least according to what Dante told me, with Boris making a disparaging comment about having to babysit Prince Remy when he had more important things to do."

Remy chuckled. "Boris and I have always had a civil and yet contentious relationship. The man is intensely loyal to my father which is the point of his service. I would also note that my ability to best Dante earlier today was because of Boris's thorough training methods. I was aware he didn't think highly of me due to my position as a spare's-spare so to speak."

"And among men of a similar class and station, making a few ribald comments about the men they serve is probably typical behavior," Max agreed. "However, no one with any honor allows those comments to become public knowledge. In this case though, it would seem Dante misunderstood Boris's comments and..." Max fell silent once more.

Remy could understand the man being upset, but it was late, and he and Xavier had been around people almost all day. Which meant Max truly needed to finish his story so they could get past it.

It seemed Xavier thought so, too. "You've told us Dante lied to me, and you supported that. All we're missing is the details. If you don't mind..."

"I do beg your indulgence, your highness. I feel the weight of what I've been a part of, combined with what Dante actually did is heavier than I believed it would be." Rubbing his hand over his head, which was likely aching, Max said, "Dante was defending himself during the fight with Boris. Boris had been angered when Dante suggested that Prince Remy should be kept in his lizard pen, and Xavier would be better off marrying a lady of negotiable virtue if he had to, rather than the second-string Bentley prince."

Xavier made a noise which sounded suspiciously like the growl of an angry beast, but Remy was totally amazed at what Max had said, and he couldn't help smiling. "Boris defended me? Aww, he must've liked me after all. Not that he'd ever admit to it, but that is so good to know."

"Your highness." Max tried to stand up, and Luca hurried to his side so that he could. "I fear you don't understand the seriousness of what has happened here. Dante lied about what the head of the Bentley guard said and did. He lied to his Crown Prince about the nature of the fight, not to mention he was derelict in his duty of protecting the Crown Prince from any possible dangers while he was in a foreign land. He created a situation where the Crown prince was worried about your safety..."

"With good reason," Xavier said, his fists clenched and his jaw tight. "What did I do, oh, wonderful advisor? You tell me, in all of your wisdom that you impart to my father, in what universe does it become acceptable for not only a man on my staff to treat me so badly, but for my own father's representative to perpetuate the lie? Especially..."

Xavier was breathing heavily, and Remy went to his side, resting his hand on his husband's lower back. The touch seemed to calm Xavier in a small way. At least Xavier's tone was lower when he continued, "Especially, when the only actual danger we've seen so far is that damned Palin who

Remy took care of, and then Dante himself? Tell me. What did I do that was so god-dammed awful that the people closest to me, the people I trusted with my life, have chosen to treat me in such an abhorrent manner? Tell me!"

"Prince Xavier, I'm so sorry..."

"I don't want your apologies, I want answers. My husband, the man I've longed to be with, the man I've waited ten long years to be with, the man who stood up in the face of everything and agreed to be my husband had to fight for his life this afternoon against a man who I trusted – fight for his life! And for what? What basis did Dante have for believing I was the deviant Lady Cecilia seemed to wish I was?"

Max shook his head, and Xavier roared. "You do know something. Tell me."

"Your dating history was spasmodic and unsuccessful..."

"I only dated at all because you and the people around me believed I was considered abnormal by not."

"Dante felt that you were just very good at hiding your appetites. He privately commended you for your ability to keep your needs discreet."

Pointing at Max, Xavier fumed, "So when you said in the privacy of my rooms, that you had informed my father I was behaving myself, you… you thought that was an *exception* on my part. You believed the lies, too?"

Max looked between Remy and Xavier, but Remy wasn't going to help – not this time. He was just as furious as Xavier was. Just quieter about it. *Although that might change as well.*

"I didn't believe them as they were described, no," Max said at last. "I did wonder about your lack of dating history, and I spoke to your father about any possible reasons for your insistence on marrying Prince Remy, but I didn't perceive anything devious or underhanded about the arrangement."

"You should've let me go." For a moment, Remy wasn't sure what Xavier was talking about, but then he noticed his husband was looking at Luca. "Remy was prepared to marry me as a man, not a prince, or a suspected deviant, but a man – the man I am. We would've gone far away. I would never have caused an issue with you as the Crown prince, or anyone in the country.

"I am who I am – quiet, withdrawn and yes, I come across as intimidating, but never in my wildest dreams did I think that the people who were supposed to care for me, would misconstrue what was simply social awkwardness and my cowardice at not approaching Remy sooner... I need you to take Max out of here, Luca, if you wouldn't mind. I fear... I can't deal with this anymore, and if that makes me a lousy future king, then honestly, I don't give a damn."

Luca nodded, and something passed between the brothers – an understanding or something similar that Remy wasn't privy to, but it didn't matter. Luca did as he was asked, and escorted Max from the tent, although in Remy's eyes it was clear the older man wanted to plead his case further. But it wasn't going to help, and in that instant, Remy was glad to see the back of the man. The moment the tent flap was closed, Xavier pulled him into strong arms, and Remy turned his face up for a kiss.

Chapter Twenty-Nine

Xavier felt sick to his stomach. It wasn't that he believed the sheer gutter tripe written about him, but he'd always carried himself as a person of honor, and someone who could be trusted. *Was I so idiotic because I believed people around me did the same?* Xavier didn't know, and instead of making his head hurt by trying to work out the mindset of people around him, he focused on the one person who was important – his husband.

Remy had fought for him, with him, by his side. It was a situation that should never have happened, and Xavier felt he'd aged ten years just seeing Remy launch himself into a position where he could've gotten hurt. Or died. And just thinking about that possibility – of never having the chance to see the light in Remy's eyes when he looked in Xavier's direction – that was the stuff of nightmares, and the day had been bad enough.

So when Remy tilted up his face, so sweet, trusting, and feeling so right in Xavier's arms, Xavier took the kiss offered, and as soon as he had one, he wanted more. He hadn't had a chance to bathe, he was sure he smelled of horse and sweat, but Remy was pushing to get closer to him in every way, and Xavier wanted that, too.

Spinning Remy around, Xavier walked backwards, bringing his husband with him as he used the back of his calves to find the mattress. There was a bit of a clash of lips and teeth when he fell backwards, taking Remy with him, but Remy just chuckled and dived in for his lips again.

Lying on his back, with Remy above him, meant Xavier got pressure in all the right places. His blood heated, and he fisted one hand into Remy's hair while the other one traveled down Remy's back and cupped his butt. He groaned, the added pressure to his crotch sending tingles everywhere.

"You make me feel crazy inside," Remy whispered as he pulled his lips off Xavier's and peppered kisses all along Xavier's jaw. "Do you think I'll ever see you naked?"

"Oh, just the thought of being with you like that..." Xavier groaned again, and the hand he had on Remy's butt might have applied more pressure. "It's just, you know..."

Remy chuckled again, his hands smooth against the rough of Xavier's facial hair. "Being in a tent, in the middle of nowhere is not the safest place to be caught in a compromising position. Hmm... did you ever think about us bathing together, in the same tub, in a room with a door lock on it?"

Rolling them, so they were side by side, Xavier growled, "I'm thinking about it now." The hand that was on

Remy's butt wandered around to the front of Remy's pants, and he rubbed over the bulge he found there. "I fear we're going to make a mess if we keep doing this."

"Messes can be cleaned." Remy's lips had found Xavier's ear and he shivered. "Would you feel more comfortable undoing my pants, if I undid yours?"

"I can do both." Xavier wanted to last longer than ten seconds, which, while Remy was sucking on his earlobe, might not happen. "I'll just..."

Permission granted, Xavier made short work of the fastenings on Remy's pants and then his own. Shoving aside material layers, there was going to be a few wrinkles in their pants when he was done, but in that moment all Xavier wanted was to feel the smooth skin of Remy's cock and rest it against his own.

Taking them both in hand, Xavier did his best to keep quiet, but by the gods he wanted to yell to the heavens, in language definitely not fit for mixed company. His whole life he'd never realized how wonderful it would feel to handle his husband in such an intimate way.

Remy didn't make keeping quiet easy, either. The man was so responsive, so much more so than Xavier ever imagined. His moans were low, as if he was doing his best to not make any noise at all. But the way his hips thrust into Xavier's hold, the buttons of their jackets catching on each other, it was almost as though Remy wanted to crawl under his skin, and by all that meant anything in life, Xavier wanted that, too.

He was craving the feel of Remy's body plastered against his, the both of them naked, rolling around on silken sheets that would tangle around Remy's body... *my gods why do I tempt myself like this?* His imagination was tapping into the dreams Xavier had kept himself going with for the ten years he'd waited... Xavier tightened his grip on their lengths, pre-come slicking his fingers.

"So close," Remy muttered against his shoulder. Xavier would have bruises on his biceps in the morning and he really didn't care. Lost in his passion, Remy was everything he didn't realize he could wish for. His thrusting against Xavier's hold, chest plastered against his, Remy was kissing across his collar bone when he suddenly bit down with a muffled groan, and warm spunk coated Xavier's fingers.

That was all it took for Xavier's orgasm to punch his balls and send him flying. Bending his head, Xavier moaned into Remy's hair, his husband's body still trembling from his own release. It was quite a few moments before he felt inclined to move away, but the stickiness on his hand, and resulting mess had to be taken care of.

"Damn it, I'm not even sure if I've got a washcloth in here," he muttered, looking around the tent. Remy's tired chuckle let Xavier know it could be a good time to improvise. Sitting up, he unbuttoned his jacket with his cleaner hand and removed it and his undershirt. He could find a clean undershirt in the morning.

Tending to Remy, cleaning up their mess for the second night in a row and buttoning him up, Xavier could see him doing something similar, with hopefully fewer clothes, for many more nights to come. It was a satisfying feeling and one Xavier clung to after the events of the day. Moving to throw the undershirt on the floor, Xavier's foot hit the framed likeness Max had been holding and must've left it on the mattress. With a determined kick, Xavier sent that flying to the floor, too, before climbing into bed and pulling Remy into his arms.

Chapter Thirty

Four days later, Remy got his first sight of the Balenborn castle, set on a huge hill overlooking the lowlands and the sea. They'd made good time. Two days into their journey with a depleted crew, men appeared on the road in front of them in the Balenborn uniform, clearly having ridden hard and fast to get to them.

It appeared King Dare was horrified to learn his son and son-in-law had been set upon and had ordered the closest troops he had to meet Xavier's party. Messages from the king ordered that one set of guards were to travel with the wagons, but the king had implored Xavier, Remy, Luca, and Max, to ride independent of the carts so they could get home sooner, with the other half of the guards. Queen Serena needed to ensure her sons were unharmed – and from what Xavier had told him privately that evening, Remy was included in her concern.

Remy's body ached from being constantly on a horse, traveling at speed. The first night after the incident as Remy referred to it in his mind, they'd stopped at a local inn on the Balenborn/Bentley border, and Xavier had apparently made sure that his husband would get a bed under a solid roof for the remainder of their trip. Unfortunately, having a solid roof didn't mean he and Xavier got any more privacy than they'd had in the tent. Luca often spent the evening with them, tankard in hand, while Max stayed in his own room. Remy's concern for the advisor grew the closer they got to Balenborn.

"There it is," Xavier pulled his horse to a stop on the side of the road and pointed at the castle. "We should be there by nightfall. I imagine you'll be keen on a soak in a bath once we arrive."

Looking down at his disheveled jacket and pants that smelled strongly of horse, Remy sighed. "I had hoped I could greet your parents in tidy clothing. But I heard a guard mention this morning that the carts with my belongings in will still be at least another day away." *Leaving me with barely a change of undergarments.*

Xavier maneuvered his horse closer to Remy's and Remy held his steady so his husband could do that. "Please don't fret about your clothing needs. I can assure you that my mother would've already been in contact with yours doing the magic that mother's do, and she will have ensured that there will be plenty of clothes that will fit you ready for when you arrive." He looked across at the castle in the distance, and then back at Remy. "I'm just not sure what sort of reception you'll get from everyone else. I'm not sure what sort of reception I'll get from everyone else."

For someone who looked like a dashing barbarian, someone people would assume would have manners to match, Remy was constantly surprised and pleased with the thoughtfulness and caring Xavier showed. "Does it matter?" He said being sure to keep his voice low. The Balenborn guards completely surrounded them, doing their best to give the impression they weren't trying to listen in, and Luca and Max weren't too far away either.

"I wanted you to feel welcomed in my home. I used to dream of it."

"I will be welcomed by the people who count. Your parents, your sister I imagine, and for anyone else I'll be sure to adopt the Orobos sniff."

"Lizards sniff?" But Xavier looked amused by the idea.

"Miss Daisy could put any royal family member to shame, in any country," Remy said with a grin. "I remember one time a particularly annoying prince – I think it was one of the younger princes from Hinkley demanded that he be taken into

Daisy's presence because he insisted that no Orobos could be tamed."

Xavier chuckled. "I'd have said the same thing."

"Ah, I would to – Miss Daisy stayed with me because she wanted to not because she had to. But Hinkley claimed he'd been blessed with special skills, ones that people had exclaimed over far and wide since he could first walk, about how he could tame the wildest of beasts."

"Oh no," Xavier groaned. "I think I know the prince you mean but go on. I take it Daisy wasn't keen on being tamed by a prince?"

"Miss Daisy refused to acknowledge his existence. She was eating. He was not amused." Remy started to laugh. "When he got within about two feet of her food, she just froze, like a statue, and I thought this is not going to be good. And then, he's spouting all this stuff about how calm she was in his presence, blah, blah, she just ran for him. I swear I've never seen royal legs move so fast. It was hilarious.

"He ran out, screaming at the top of his lungs, and you know how Orobos hate loud noises. Well, the prince wouldn't stop screaming and she chased him across the courtyard, and through the stables until he disappeared up into the hayloft. Then, and this is what I mean by the Orobos sniff, she quite literally turned her back, flicked her tail, stuck her nose in the air and sauntered away as if she had all the time in the world. The prince was finally coaxed down about an hour later."

Xavier chuckled again, causing a couple of the guards to quickly glance in his direction and then look away as if worried about being caught. "So, are you suggesting if we're being snubbed, we should just stick our noses in the air and turn our backs."

"Oh, no. The Orobos sniff is for people who are rude to us either directly or in our hearing. For people who try and snub us, we laugh loud enough that they can hear, while we're wandering away." Looking around, Remy leaned over his horse's neck so only Xavier could hear.

"Think about it. What's the best reaction to people who snub you and think you're going to scuttle off like a cowed rabbit? You laugh and show you're having a good time, especially when the two of us are together, and they will either be riddled with curiosity and worried about what they're missing out on, or they'll spend the rest of the night worried you were laughing at them, and not knowing why. You are the Crown Prince remember, and out rank everyone except your parents."

"You've made it so much easier to go home after this dreadful business, my dear Consort, Xavier said softly. "Thank you."

Remy was sure he was still blushing as they cantered towards the castle.

/~/~/~/~/

Xavier wasn't sure what to expect as their horses finally clattered into the courtyard in front of the castle he called home. And he didn't like not knowing, which was why he'd stopped to talk to Remy before they'd arrived. In his head, Remy's arrival would've been celebrated, as Xavier had been for most of his life, but thanks to one article of lies, that wasn't likely to happen.

He should never have underestimated his mother. She would've received word they were on their way – the messengers at the city gate would've sent word the moment their party was seen on the trail. Xavier imagined the head of the household would be waiting for him on arrival, to take him to where his mother would be holding court, which was what usually happened when he'd been traveling.

But not this time. Queen Serena had a chair outside, surrounded by lords and ladies who liked to stay close to the royal circle. She stood, as Xavier gently tugged his horse to a stop, manservants running down to take the reins as he dismounted and then immediately going around to Remy's side as his husband got off his horse. Remy winced as his feet hit the ground, and Xavier was determined his husband would have a date with a hot bath...

"Xavier, I'm so thrilled you've brought your husband home."

After we've greeted Mother. Taking Remy's hand, which was slightly slick with sweat, indicating his nervousness, Xavier made sure he shortened his stride enough, so Remy didn't have to run. They hadn't even finished climbing the stairs before his mother was there, holding him tight. "I've been so worried," she whispered as Xavier wrapped his arm around her slender shoulders. "Thank the goddess you're all right."

Her hug tightened, letting Xavier know in that instant while he was a man of over thirty years of age, he was still his mother's child, before she stepped back and said in her more normal tone, "Please present your handsome husband. I declare the last time I saw you Prince Remy you barely came up to my knee."

"Your majesty," Remy bowed low and then straightened. "Thank you for welcoming me to your home."

"We'll have none of this your majesty nonsense," Queen Serena laughed, likely more for the crowd's benefit than anything else. "After all of the years your mother and I have discussed you joining our family, I'm thrilled I can finally call you son." She pulled Remy into a close hug that was definitely only reserved for family members, causing a few of the society lords and ladies to chatter among themselves.

Xavier paid them no mind. He was stunned, although not by the hug. He knew his mother would make Remy feel welcome even if no one else did. It was her artful way of rewriting history that had him reeling. "Should've known Mother would be working overtime to put those wretched lies to rest," Luca murmured as he went past to greet his mother.

"Mother, did you forget you had another son? One who was also set upon and tied up until Remy managed to get me loose?"

Queen Serena chuckled again, her smile wide and genuine as she released Remy and hugged her younger son. "I am beyond thrilled, and so very happy that you are all safe and unharmed. After that wretched business concerning that woman who will never be mentioned in my presence again, and then the actual attack on your person... nope."

The Queen shook her head. "We are not dwelling on the unpleasantness today. My son and heir is home with his handsome consort, and we're going to celebrate. It will be a private dinner just for the family this evening, but tomorrow night, we will be celebrating the marriage of my heir and his consort. Come along, you two," she added as she turned to go inside, the crowd parting to make way for them. "Let's get you fed and cleaned up and then we can catch up on what's been happening since you've been away."

It was very difficult for a Queen to be ignored, and Xavier was happy to follow her lead, keeping hold of Remy's hand all the while. But the hairs on the back of his neck were raised as he noticed a few of the crowd were clearly not happy with the way their Queen had greeted them. *I'm sure I'll hear all about it later.* For now, he wanted to find the nearest bathtub for his husband to enjoy.

Chapter Thirty-One

"I can't thank you enough for the new clothes." Remy patted down his new long-line jacket he'd combined with tights and boots, as he smiled at Xavier's parents, feeling more than a little self-conscious. After a hasty bath, they were escorted to Xavier's parents' private family room, where Remy was introduced to King Dare and three of the king's advisors. The only other person in the room was a very subdued Lord Max who had also taken the time to bathe and change his clothes. The mark on his head from his attack was still looked red and sore.

"It was the least I could do," Serena said firmly. "Your mother, bless her, had been so accommodating of Xavier and Luca during this whole torrid business, the least I could do was ensure you felt more comfortable."

Remy nodded, but before he had a chance to say anything, a gray-haired gentleman who looked like he should run an undertakers said, "This torrid business should never have been allowed to happen, your majesties. I insist we move into damage control as quickly as possible."

Xavier, who'd been semi-relaxing in the seat next to Remy, and Remy considered his relaxing only semi because Xavier had been on edge since they'd arrived at the castle – but anyway, that relaxation was now at level zero. But it was King Dare who answered.

"And what form do you believe that damage control should take, Charles?"

"Your majesty, I've stressed this over and over since that terrible article was written."

Remy noticed the man never mentioned the content was all lies. And it seemed the advisor liked the sound of his own voice as he continued along the same vein.

"I realize as a family, you're all very close, but the damage to the Crown Prince's reputation cannot be, and should not be ignored."

Sighing, the King said as an aside to Xavier, "I've been dealing with this crap since that article came out." Dare was sitting on another two-seater with his wife and now he looked up at his advisor, who Remy noticed hadn't been asked to take a seat. None of the advisors had been. "I'm not ignoring the matter, Charles. I'm extremely annoyed at the slander to my son and his new consort. However, Cecilia has been detained by the World Council. What more needs to happen, in your opinion?"

"Please understand that I'm not disrespecting the Crown Prince in any way..."

You can't even look at him, Remy thought.

"...But I do feel, well, the matter has to be addressed." Charles drew himself up to his full height, and looked as if he was addressing a hangman. "I believe the Crown Prince and his consort should give up their titles."

"Give the man a medal," Xavier snapped, pointing his finger at Charles. "I was more than happy to give up my title, and Remy supported me in doing it. We'd decided to become pirates who ran bookshops on the side. So, if that's the best way of dealing with this situation, let's do that, and move on."

"NO!" The king and queen both yelled at the same time, and then they looked at each other and laughed like two people did when they were in sync with each other. Remy loved how Xavier's parents appeared to be as in love as his own.

"You are not giving up your title, Xavier, and I refuse to even consider that idea a moment more," Serena said firmly. "Prince Remy is your consort and will do a magnificent job of it. We've already had reports come in from three towns in Bentley where local folk were delighted to meet the elusive Prince Xavier and his husband. You are going to keep on doing that. And if anyone," she leveled a long look at Charles, "anyone at all mentions that ridiculous idea again, they will be seeking other employment. Am I clear?"

"Yes, your majesty." Charles bowed and stepped back, as if hoping to disappear into the ruby red wall coverings.

"Your majesties, the fact still remains that the Crown Prince's reputation is in tatters." Like a tag team, as Charles stepped back, another shorter and portlier gentleman stepped forward. Like Charles he was gray-haired, but Remy noticed powder streaks in it, as though he was attempting to smooth out an uneven aging issue. "If the prince and his consort were prepared to stay out of sight, perhaps remain confined to the castle or a similar abode nearby..."

Xavier growled, and Remy hated his husband was being talked about instead of being talked to. "No, we are not living as prisoners when we've done nothing wrong," he said softly, making sure to look the second advisor in the eye. "You are all treating Xavier as if there is substance to the article of lies published and that's just not good enough. I want to know what moves have been made to shut that publishing house down for printing the travesty in the first place.

"I want to know what has been done in ensuring they print a full-page retraction before they are closed down. I want to know what moves, if any have been made towards the Lady in question's family, and while we're on the subject, the Sherwood family after Dante's despicable acts during our trip here. In other words, gentlemen, I want to know what attempts, if any, have been made to show how supportive Balenborn is of its royal heir."

There was a moment's silence, and Remy was seriously rethinking the pirate owning bookshop idea, when Serena started clapping her hands while Dare burst out laughing. "There you go, Harrison," the king said, "Perhaps you can answer the Crown Consort. What has been done along those lines?"

Harrison, who was the overweight advisor, went a shade of red that couldn't be healthy. "Sire, as you know, this is unprecedented..."

"Which is why the responses to those events need to be equally unprecedented," Dare cut in quickly. "Prince Remy has good ideas, so I don't want to hear excuses. I want to know which of the demands your Crown Consort has made have actually been executed. In other words, answer his questions and face him when you do it."

The third advisor, the one who'd stayed silent so far, was scribbling madly on a piece of parchment he'd pulled from his robe. Harrison, his face now a very bright red, turned to the seat Remy and Xavier were sharing, bowing slightly.

"Crown Prince Consort Remy," Harrison managed to get the title out without stuttering, "It was considered taking action against the Lady's family, however, as she was in the Crown Prince's employ at the time, the family have disavowed any knowledge of her actions. As to the Sherwood family, likewise when they were approached, they claimed no knowledge of their son's actions and vowed to have Dante's records struck from their family register. As for the publication..."

"Wait a moment." Remy put up his finger. "The disavowing on the parts of both families involved have been verified by the World Council, I assume, to ensure there is no further danger to Xavier and myself or any other member of the royal family?"

Harrison glanced over his shoulder at his colleagues. There was no help there. "The World Council shouldn't be involved in this instance as it is a local matter..."

Remy didn't get angry very often at all, but he was fast moving in that direction. He hated how rigid Xavier's shoulders were against his. "I am going to assume that is a roundabout way of saying no, you didn't get confirmation from the World Council magic users that the two families concerned in bringing disgrace and dishonor to the fair country of Balenborn, have had their accounts verified. In fact, I'll go so far to suggest that what you did do, in response to your King's orders most likely, is write a politely worded request to the family heads concerned, asking if they knew about the atrocities, and received an equally polite response as the families distanced themselves from what their family members had done. Possibly even by return messenger."

"The next day actually, your highness." The advisor who was still scribbling, looked up long enough to answer. "But that is what transpired, yes."

"And yet in the meantime, when my husband has done nothing wrong, you want to imprison him, shun him and hope the world forgets he exists, all based on the word of a validated liar." Remy turned to Queen Serena. "Did my mother tell you we were able to secure a World Council representative to attend our wedding? My mother was determined that her children only marry people they are genuinely connected to, and the representative did verify most definitely that Xavier and I were married because we cared about each other – further vindication I would imagine that the lady in question who wrote her fiction was lying in every word."

"You had the World Council verify the reasons behind your marriage?" Harrison looked as though he was two breaths away from a stroke. "Why would you do that?"

"My husband believes in me, Harrison, something you and your cohorts never did. Even Max, tainted by Dante's arguments thought there was something deviant about me, when all I was doing was waiting for my husband to grow up." Xavier spoke up at last, the hand he rested on Remy's shoulder was warm and solid. "Remy and his family have stood by me completely, just as my own family has done. As my father's advisors it is your job to ensure those people who do support me have valid reasons for doing so. I insist, no – as your Crown Prince, I am *ordering* you to call in a representative from the World Council, a magical truth sayer, and I want both the Sherwood and that lady whose name will not be mentioned's family interviewed at length. Only if there is absolutely not one single taint of scandal associated with them, should they be allowed to continue to enjoy the benefits and rights accorded to them by virtue of their position."

"But they'll be so upset." Harrison turned to the king. "Surely you can see, to cause dissent among the society families..."

"My son gave you an order, Harrison. Carry it out. Now." Dare made shooing motions with his fingers. "All three of you, out. Carry out those orders immediately. I want an extensive report from the World Council representative on my desk concerning the honor and validity of the claims made by both families, no later than in two day's time."

It was clear Harrison wanted to argue, and even Charles looked a little gray against the black of his high collar. The scribe was still busy writing, but he managed to bow as he left with his colleagues.

Once the door was closed, Dare looked at Max and shook his head. "In all the years I've known you, I'd never believe you could be taken in by a set of biceps and a ready smile."

"I offer no excuse and take full responsibility for my actions," Max said stiffly. "I admit, I took the weight of Dante's words, over the actions of your eldest son, and it pains me to say that, but it's true. I believed I knew Dante and the way he justified his thoughts and actions... smiles and a pair of biceps, yes."

He lapsed into silence for a moment and then added, "Prince Remy's idea of having Prince Xavier interact with the locals of Bentley went very well. Prince Remy has a natural charm, and once he warmed to the idea, Prince Xavier proved to be friendly and genuinely complimentary of various stall holders and the people they came into contact with. In each case, rather than appear intimidating, the locals seemed to consider Prince Xavier a protector, and someone they could look up to. Indeed, even on the trip home, once we met up with the guards you sent to us, I heard more than one mention of how much happier Prince Xavier has been since he'd married."

"Spending considerable years, waiting for the object of your affection to grow up can cause an individual to be more standoffish from others." Serena grinned, even though she could have no idea how close to the truth she'd gotten. "Remy, Xavier, I feel the King and I need to speak to Max privately about his own fate. He's given us many years of faithful service, and the recent events have been his only transgression, but they can't be ignored, either.

"I imagine you two would like to dine alone and enjoy some time in comfort before the celebration tomorrow. And please, I would like you both to visit your sister and her new daughter in the morning. Both mother and the little one are doing well, and I know Imogene can't wait to meet you, Remy, so she can welcome you into the family, too."

"We'll be in our rooms for the evening." Xavier was up and pulling Remy up so quickly, Remy almost stumbled. "If you could ask for food to be delivered promptly and then give orders for us not to be disturbed for the rest of the night, hopefully you'll be listened to if they won't listen to me."

"Isn't young love wonderful," Queen Serena giggled as Remy was towed from the room. "Do you remember when we were like that?"

"We still are," the King said, or at least that was what Remy thought Dare said. But he wasn't sure as Xavier was rushing him through the castle.

Chapter Thirty-Two

"I don't know how you do it." Jackets and boots off, Xavier and Remy were sat cuddled up on his large two-seater by a roaring fire, waiting for their dinner order to be delivered. "How do you get your words out, in a logical order, and not stumble or…" There it was again - Xavier's words had deserted him. "You took on my father's advisors so eloquently. I've never been so proud of you in my life."

"I was angry on your behalf, which made it easier." Remy smiled up at him, and then went back to staring at the flames. "They were so keen to see damage done to the royal family, while hiding behind their moral outrage, and secret glee. It's infuriating – they never once considered you were innocent."

"The royal family is expected to hold itself to a higher standard than anyone else," Xavier said glumly. "And then society families try to emulate the royal family behavior, giving the reasons my father's advisors have for the way they view things. I mean, a deviant crown prince could set off a wave of copycat behavior among young society members – or something like that. I find all the posturing very tedious."

"You have to remember, in many cases I was ignored by society peoples, because of my status as the second son," Remy was agreeing in part. "Like you asked of me, no one ever wanted to get to know me as a person at those events, which is their loss in my humble opinion. Personally, I've never understood why our upperclass family members all hold themselves as being superior to everyone else. Very few of them contribute to the common good, and many of them use their extensive, mostly inherited funds to hush up their own wrongdoings."

Remy sounded despondent for a moment, but then he brightened. "At least your mother suggested we meet more regular people, rather than socialize with the elite. That sounds like a lot more fun. Lunches in the local taverns, wandering among the craft stalls. You do have them here, don't you?"

Xavier had to smile at his husband's exuberance, Remy was so unlike anyone he'd ever met before, except perhaps Luca. *Maybe it's something to do with being the second son.* Xavier never remembered Remy's brother Pierre being excited about anything. "We have excellent craftspeople in Balenborn and in outlying townships. I'm also keen to take you down to the docks, to see the ships, meet the fisherman that congregate there, and become part of that world, too."

"That will be different. Bentley was landlocked so it will be a new experience for me." Peeking up at him, Xavier knew Remy was teasing him when he said, "Are you still keeping your options of us running off and becoming pirates open?"

"If Charles had his way, he'd probably pack our bags for us." But Xavier chuckled. "I would love it, if our lives were simpler, especially after what Cecilia and Dante did, but if I hadn't been born a Crown Prince, then I wouldn't have been allowed within ten feet of you."

"I would've noticed you, even if you'd worked in the stables." Remy sighed. "Speaking of which, I wonder how Daisy is doing. Actually, scrap that. I know how Miss Daisy is doing – she'll be sitting on her eggs, holding court among all those who visit her. Hopefully one of the stable lads will actually make friends with her, rather than act all scaredy around her all the time. She seems to like human company. Well, some human company."

Xavier was struck again with just how much Remy had given up to be with him. *I'm so incredibly lucky.* "We will go back and visit her soon," he promised. "There're a few things I need to do first – tomorrow's celebration is the hardest bit, but I'll also need a new head of guard, and mother will likely want us to do day trips around home for a while. What happened with Dante scared her, at least that's what father said."

"Ah, yes, you went and talked to your father while I was changing." Remy nodded. "Is everything all right, or is there stuff said you can't share with me?"

"I will always share everything with you, my husband," Xavier said fiercely. "Never let anything that anyone ever says indicate any differently. You will always know what I know, where I am and what I am doing. I know what the gossips around this castle are like, and I refuse to give you any cause to be concerned about my feelings for you."

Xavier didn't realize how angry he was at the very idea, until Remy stroked his arm. "Hey, I grew up in a castle, too. I am well aware there will be people who will seek to separate us, either because they want you for themselves, or because they just can't bear to see us happy. But so what. I don't care. I am not going to hide how I feel about you, and if that's not princely, well then, they can kiss my royal butt."

Chuckling, Xavier pulled his husband close, nuzzling in Remy's wild hair. "You protect me so effortlessly."

"I support you," Remy corrected gently. "I know you can and will do good things both as a prince and a king. I saw you with the people back in Bentley, once we were away from the trappings and rituals that are so imprinted in the royal lifestyle. You care about people. You just needed me to come along and give you examples on how to show it."

"You know tomorrow night's going to be a disaster, don't you." If it wasn't for his mother's determination to show how supportive she was being, Xavier wouldn't go.

"The celebration is important to your family, so we will go, and have a wonderful time, even if those around us would prefer we didn't. You're not hiding away, Crown Prince Xavier. You've done nothing wrong, and tomorrow night we're going to show just how close we are to everyone... whether they like it or not," Remy added with a laugh.

Xavier chuckled, too – his husband's good humor was contagious, but there was a nest of vipers living in his belly that would not quieten until the celebratory part of their lives was over, and he and Remy could start enjoying their married life together.

"You'd think our dinner would be here by now," he grumbled, suddenly needing to show Remy just how much he was cared for. Something he needed privacy for.

"It'll get here in due course." Clearly Remy had more patience than Xavier did. "In the meantime, why don't you tell me more about the docks and the places we can visit once the party is over with?"

/~/~/~/~/

For all of his bravado, Remy was not looking forward to the celebration Queen Serena had organized. It wasn't that he didn't appreciate what she was doing – considerably more than any of the advisors had bothered with. And he wasn't even concerned about being shunned, ignored, or snubbed by people he didn't know and probably wouldn't want to get to know. He meant what he'd said to Xavier about that sort of behavior being common around him.

But Remy cared about Xavier, and it seemed his handsome, intimidating husband had a sensitive side he'd never anticipated. Which meant there was a good chance that if people were going to be awful, they wouldn't know just how much their Crown Prince as hurting. Xavier wouldn't say anything. Remy could see it in his mind's eye. His husband would look down his noses at the ingrate and walk away. But he'd be aching inside, and it hurt Remy to think about it.

"Is something wrong with dinner?" Xavier asked. "I can order you anything you like from the kitchen." They had migrated from the love seat to a small table and chairs Xavier had set in the bay window of his private living area. Night had fallen, and Remy loved how Xavier had only lit two light crystals with the bulk of the light coming from the flickering fireplace. The dim lights created intimate shadows, letting Remy imagine he and Xavier were the only two people in the world in that moment. Heady stuff with a man like Xavier for company.

Looking down at his half-eaten plate, Remy shook his head. "It's lovely, beautifully prepared. I guess I'm just not that hungry. Tired though," he pressed a hand into his back, "And I will be really happy if I can have a few days horse-free. I believe my spine might have scrunched in on itself by at least two inches, and I wasn't that tall to begin with," he added in case Xavier thought he was complaining.

Pushing his own plate aside, Xavier laughed. "I seem to recall a certain conversation where someone thought I was that old I couldn't recognize the name on the marriage contract I'd arranged. Yet, somehow, my back is fine." That was definitely tongue-in-cheek, making Remy smile. Holding out his hand, which Remy took, Xavier said, "How about you stretch out on the bed, and I'll see if I can rub out the scrunches in your spine."

"Is that a form of rub down, like one might do to a horse?" Remy knew he was being cheeky as he stood up. He didn't care how Xavier rubbed him, so long as he did. His husband had very capable hands.

"That wasn't the sort of rub down I was thinking of, no," Xavier said, keeping a perfectly straight face, as he led Remy into a huge room dominated by an equally large bed. "If you want to take off as many clothes as you feel comfortable doing, and hop onto the bed, I'll go through to the bathing area and get a towel and some oil."

He disappeared through another door. Remy looked around. Bed. A large trunk-style chest stood against one wall. There was a chair, with Xavier's scabbard and harness draped across the corner, and by the heavily draped windows, there was what looked like a standing coat rack. Yet, when Remy got nearer he could see it was a metallic depiction of a tree with tiny birds nestled among metal and fabric leaves. Whoever had made the piece had an amazing eye for detail – the eyes of the birds seemed to be alive, the wings positioned as if the creatures would take flight any minute.

I'm dithering when I'm supposed to be undressing. Remy was only dressed in his pants, undergarments, and undershirt, which didn't leave a lot to remove before he was naked. *Do I want to be naked with Xavier? Yes*, he decided, he should be. Xavier was his husband. If anyone had a right to see him naked it was the Crown Prince of Balenborn. But Remy had never been naked in front of anyone that he could remember. Partially naked, and only with Xavier, but never everything bare and exposed.

Our relationship is never going to progress any further if I can't even be naked with my husband. Inexperienced he might be, but Remy had guessed there was a lot more he and Xavier could be doing in the bedroom than the hand and mouth action Xavier had done so far. *And he is getting oil...*

Remy understood oil could also be used for massaging sore muscles – it wasn't necessarily going to be used for more intimate actions – *but a man can hope.* He stripped off his shirt and placed it on the trunk. His fingers lingered by the button holding up his pants, and then with a burst of courage, he flicked the button open, and pushed his tight pants down his thighs.

I said I wanted to feel Xavier's skin against my own. I've dreamed about the idea long enough. With that line of thought ringing through his head, and because he might as well be efficient about it, Remy pushed his undergarments down in the same direction as his pants and stepped out of the two layers of material.

Scooping up his clothes one handed, Remy looked for where he could put them, before deciding the top of the trunk was as good a place as any.

Glancing at the door that Xavier had gone through, Remy saw it was still closed, so he climbed up on the bed, and refusing to second guess himself, laid on his belly in the middle of the mattress. He was acutely conscious of his bare butt sticking up behind him – the first time he'd ever been in such a position.

Burying his head in his folded arms, *at least I won't be looking at Xavier when he sees me splayed out like an offering. Gods of magic and mechanics I do hope he likes what he sees. If he jokes about this in any way, I'll never show my face or get fully naked again.*

Chapter Thirty-Three

NAKED! Xavier shoved his knuckle against his lips so he wouldn't moan out loud. He'd heard the occasional comments about Remy as the man grew up, and not one of them have ever spoken of the prince's courage. But seeing Remy laid out, his soft skin highlighted by the dim lighting – so much skin – Xavier didn't know how Remy managed to look so sexy in his innocent pose, but damn, he really did.

Xavier wasn't the type to get naked often either – he'd learned since he was twelve that anyone could and did just knock on his door and wander in on him if they felt their business was important. He'd already taken off his shirt in anticipation of being on the bed with Remy, but seeing his husband's courageous nakedness, he was determined his pants were going, too. But he had one thing to do first.

Crossing over to the bed, Xavier leaned down, kissing Remy's naked shoulder. "You look so incredible I don't have words. I do know I am the luckiest man in the whole world tonight. Excuse me, just one more moment and I'll be with you."

"Huh?" Remy raised his head, looking over his shoulder. Xavier was busy heaving on the heavy trunk that, apart from the bed, was the only solid piece of furniture in the room. Remy's clothes were still balanced on it. "What are you doing?"

"Making sure we can't be disturbed," Xavier grunted as he pushed against the trunk again. "I will not have the gift of your naked body spied upon by any eyes except my own." The trunk slid slowly across the polished wooden floors, likely leaving scratches, but Xavier was hardly going to stop and inspect the floorboards. "I. Will. Not. Have. Your. Body. Disrespected." One final grunt and the trunk slammed against the door. Xavier brushed his hands together. "I'd like to see anyone get through that."

Flicking his hair back from his eyes, Remy grinned, showing off his straight teeth. "I certainly appreciated the muscle flex. You have a very...er... powerful build."

Xavier glanced down at his torso. Slightly sweaty but not bad enough to warrant another wash. Sliding his hand into the waistband of his pants, he quickly shoved them down his legs, moving towards the bed as soon as they cleared his feet. "I believe I promised you a rub down." He climbed up onto the mattress. "Lie back down again beloved and let's see what's happening with your sexy back."

"I never knew backs could be sexy until I saw yours." Remy settled himself back into the position he'd been in when Xavier had come into the room. "To be deliberately touched..." Remy moaned as Xavier lightly slid his hands down "I feel positively decadent."

"You look positively edible." Taking a chance that Remy wouldn't object, Xavier swung his leg over Remy's butt and straddled him, giving him a better position to run his hands up and down his husband's back. Remy reminded him of a sleek cat, moaning and stretching out as Xavier ran his fingers across muscle groups and skimmed across bones. Reaching over for one of the two bottles he'd put on the small shelf by the bed, he was aware of how his very solid and unapologetic cock was sliding over the swell of Remy's ass. The urge to rut against all that silkiness increased.

Grabbing the oil, Xavier slicked up his fingers, and then applying a bit more pressure, gently coaxed Remy's muscles into a more relaxed state. Massaging someone wasn't anything he'd ever done before, but the oil made his rough fingers slide effortlessly over his husband's skin.

"You have amazing hands." Remy's voice was low, and Xavier could hear the pleasure in his tone. "After being on my horse for so long... not something I'm used to. But I'll happily ride all day every day if I can come home to something like this. Incredible." Remy's butt did a little wiggle.

He's going to unman me. "I did have some messages waiting for me in father's office earlier." Xavier had both purpose and distraction on his mind. "Have you ever met King Mintyn of Marinkaw? He got married recently to Prince Syrius of Rosenhip."

"Big man, very abrupt, doesn't like fancy celebrations?" Remy hummed. "I've met him in passing. Is he coming tomorrow?"

"No, although, he did send his apologies and a small celebratory gift for us both, along with a personal invitation to visit anytime we're in the region. King Mintyn's never been the type to worry about society gossip, so I know his offer was genuine." There was a personal note as well, but Xavier didn't think Remy needed to know how ribald Mintyn could be. He'd had a bit to do with Mintyn over the years and considered him a friend of sorts. The man never talked much about himself, but he was fun to share a drink and a cigar with.

"That was nice of him." Remy wiggled again, and it was only thanks to a decade of self-control that Xavier didn't just do what the animalistic side of his brain was demanding.

"Yes, the gift – he thought it would be useful for us... being newly married... and perhaps not experienced or familiar with various aspects of intimacies... in our private times together."

Leaning up his front half, Remy looked over his shoulder at him.

"King Mintyn sent us an erotic toy as a wedding present?"

"No," Xavier chuckled at the thought of opening something like that in his father's office. "He... uhm... his note suggests..."

"But you've had experience in intimate matters – before, you know, before... oh, my goodness." Remy scrunched around a bit further. "It wasn't a manual was it, or a book of possible positions? I've heard such things exist, but I've never seen one."

"No, it wasn't a book." Xavier redistributed his weight a bit more easily on his knees and used his hands up Remy's back to encourage the man to lie down again. "He sent some oil."

"Like the one you're using?" Remy sounded pleased. "It feels amazing on my skin."

Oh, save me. Xavier focused on the feel of his fingers on Remy's back rather than the heat of his husband's butt enticing his length. "The oil Mintyn sent was something his magic users had created to aid in his wedding night with Prince Syrius. Like you, Prince Syrius was... er... innocent of the pleasures between men."

"From what I recall about King Mintyn, I doubt Prince Syrius would've stayed that way for long." Remy sniggered. "Just as you do, King Mintyn struck me as a very capable man in all areas of life."

Hmm. Xavier made a point of leaning further over Remy's back, aware Remy would feel almost every inch of his length along the crack of the delightful ass, as he slid his hands up the nape of Remy's neck. "The oil has special properties." He couldn't resist a small thrust of his hips, dropping his voice a full octave.

"According to the instructions received it would allow someone of my size, in all areas, to penetrate the most intimate of places on my husband's innocent body without causing pain or discomfort. In fact, it's been reported, and this is purely anecdotal evidence only, intense pleasure is felt by both parties, if such liberties were permitted."

It wasn't so much the groan, as the full body shiver Remy gave that set Xavier's senses on fire. But he cared enough about his husband to add, "It doesn't have to be tonight."

"I think it does." Remy's behind came up from the mattress, brushing against Xavier's balls. "I'm in real danger of making a mess here, and that's just with the regular oil and your fingers on my back."

"That's why I brought a towel as well."

/~/~/~/~/

This is it. Remy had spent a lot of his intervening years from the age of fifteen to his present situation hearing all manner of ribald comments and innuendo that seemed

437

intimate in nature, from the men and women who worked in the stables, the gardens, and even in the kitchen on the odd occasion. But he'd never truly understood the actions behind the comments.

Feeling the weight of Xavier's length like a brand on his back had given Remy a clue as to what might happen. Testing a theory, he wiggled his butt again, lifting it just slightly off the mattress. *Yes.* That was a definite moan coming from behind him.

Keeping his eyes closed, and his head resting on arms, Remy sank into the sensations as Xavier worked further and further down his back. By the time his husband had reached the swell of his butt cheeks, Remy was a melted puddle of goo although his insides felt as if there was a volcano threatening to erupt.

The touches were firmer now, more deliberate, caressing around Remy's behind – the curves, with dips into the crack that divided them. Running purely in instinct, Remy arched his butt up, meeting the heavenly strokes of Xavier's rough hands, opening himself up – he hoped – so Xavier could touch him *everywhere*.

And he did. Remy gasped when he felt the brush of Xavier's finger across his hole. Xavier's legs were like a cage on either side of the top of his thighs, but all Remy wanted to focus on was the feel of his husband's cock bouncing and prodding at Remy's skin, as if looking for direction.

There was a lean, Xavier was reaching for something, the present from King Mintyn most likely. Remy didn't want to think about the warrior king. He wanted to keep his eyes closed and just enjoy the sensations. His breathing was coming faster – his heart was pounding so hard, Remy was sure Xavier could hear it. Lying still was difficult especially when Xavier's finger was back and this time the oil he was using was totally different.

Heat. That was Remy's first impression. A glowing warmth that seemed to send tingles from his hole to his balls. There was a bit of pressure – Xavier's finger – and he was pushing inside of Remy's body.

There was no pain – Remy had no idea what to expect. It's not like he'd ever fingered himself there. But he'd anticipated there would be a certain element of uncomfortableness. There wasn't. The magic was working – the crackle across his skin, the warmth that seemed to be expanding from Remy's hips outward. Xavier's breath was coming faster, and while Remy wanted to look, he imagined instead a serious Xavier totally focused on his task.

A second finger was added to the first. *How many does he need to use?* Remy hadn't spent a lot of time near Xavier's cock. They hadn't had a chance for more than frantic fumbling on the trip to Balenborn, and that magical way Xavier used his mouth on him their first night together. Remy got the impression Xavier's cock was bigger and rounder than his, but then the man was like that all over, he reasoned.

The new oil had a pleasant musky scent – definitely not sweet, but just inhaling it was arousing and relaxing all at the same time. Not sensations Remy had enjoyed together, so he made a conscious decision to just roll with it. The feelings inside were increasing in intensity, causing Remy to fidget. He wanted to say something, to hurry Xavier along, but his mouth didn't want to let out anything but a moan as a third finger joined the first two.

"Tell me you're ready for me, please." Xavier's voice sounded as if it was dragged across gravel, sending another shiver down Remy's spine. He couldn't talk, he just moaned, nodding his head rapidly even as his eyes were still closed. Seconds later he felt a blunt press of something that wasn't Xavier's fingers, but Remy could feel his body just open right up, and Xavier slid in. *Magical.* Remy's gasp turned into a long moan as his body lit up in pleasure.

/~/~/~/~/

Magical. Xavier's moan mirrored Remy's as the magically infused oil slicked down his length – there was pressure, of course there was, but only the slightest of resistance. And from the way Remy was twitching and moaning, there was no way his husband was feeling any pain.

I should have had him on his back so I could see his gorgeous face, Xavier thought when he was in as far as he could go. His toes curled and he froze, sure if he moved another just a fraction he would blow. He'd had sex before, although he couldn't remember with who – it was a decade before and not a thought needed in his bed with his new husband. But the sensations of being in Remy's body, being accepted, supported, dare he think even loved, was adding elements to their passion rendering it far more than simple sex.

Leaning over Remy's back, Xavier was glad of his height as he nuzzled into Remy's neck. Remy's eyes were closed, but he twisted his neck around to the point it was probably uncomfortable, his lips curled up for a kiss Xavier was quick to give him.

It was a messy mash of lips. Remy was panting hard as Xavier thrust in gentle strokes, and Xavier was finding it difficult to take a full breath himself. Resting his elbows on either side of Remy's face, he nuzzled and kissed, and did his best to keep breathing, as his hips rocked back and forth in a motion that had never felt so good.

"Xavier. Again." Remy's butt was flexing in tune with his. Xavier took Remy's lips with his own, his tongue seeking access in the warm mouth, thrusting into it in sync with his hip action. Remy's arms unfolded, fingers clutching Xavier's forearms with surprising strength. "Xavy, Xavy, Xavy. Oh, my gods, yes."

Remy's body stiffened, the channel Xavier was happily thrusting into tightening and holding his length in a vice. It didn't last, Remy's body relaxed just as quickly, but that final pulse of pressure blew Xavier's control to the moon and back. He came with a groan against Remy's neck, his balls happily unloading, marking Remy's insides.

Being sure not to crush his husband, Xavier's lower arms curled around, holding Remy close as he tried to calm his rapid heart. "I've loved you for so long," he whispered against Remy's ear.

"I'm so glad," Remy murmured, "I'd hate to be in love all by myself."

Behind him, Xavier grinned, enjoying the closeness and the warmth that melted his heart. The real world could stay on the other side of the door for now. In his room, in their bed, he was loved and supported, and that was more than anything Xavier had ever hoped for.

Chapter Thirty-Four

It was the following day. If Xavier was to be believed, it was going to be a disaster from the moment they left their room. That meant, as soon as the trunk was removed from blocking the door – so much easier with two people – Xavier morphed from the loving sensitive husband he was in their room together, into the intimidating force of nature Remy remembered from his visits to Bentley. Xavier wasn't being unkind to him in any way. But it was as though he'd got an idea in his head Remy was going to be hurt by someone rude or thoughtless, and Xavier was stalking through the castle as if his sheer presence could prevent it.

Personally, Remy thought his husband was being a bit fatalistic. For example, he truly enjoyed their visit with Princess Imogene. She was a lovely woman, with a blunt tongue and a loving nature – someone who was clearly adored by her husband Prince Consort Cyril. After she'd scolded Xavier for thinking he could give up the core of who he was over the lies of someone who had the writing skills of a cockroach, she presented the baby, clearly expecting her brother to hold the tiny human.

Not even Xavier could see a threat in his new niece. In fact, the baby appeared to be the only person who could make Xavier smile. Remy kept his private "aww moment" to himself as he watched the big man tickle the baby's fingers and toes. Remy wasn't sure how much the baby could see or do, but her chubby little hands seemed to want to connect to Xavier's facial hair.

Lunch was also fun – they were back in their room because the King and Queen were busy with the final preparations for the party and apparently Luca had been sent off to run some last-minute errands. Xavier shed his intimidating nature along with his jacket, as soon as their bedroom door was closed, pulling Remy into his arms. Remy could feel the tension seep from Xavier's shoulders as he wrapped his arms around Xavier's torso.

But time waited for no one, or so Remy had heard, and as the evening got closer, Xavier's tension increased. He didn't say anything, but when Remy helped him with the chest harness that his mother had indeed replaced, he could feel the worry pouring off him in waves.

"It'll be over soon enough." Remy smiled, even though his own nerves were reacting to Xavier's. "We'll make an appearance, appreciate all your parents have done, and dance. I will want to dance with you, frequently."

"I won't be dancing with anyone else." Xavier looked stricken for a moment. "I wish, honestly, I wish with everything I am, that this evening's celebration could be a true one. You deserve that and so much more."

"Did you socialize with the society families who are going to be here tonight, before this business happened?"

Xavier shook his head. "I would have rather socialized with your Miss Daisy. There are a few of the men, who've served in the navy with me who are decent sorts but even then I was in charge of them, and so there was always a barrier between us. My title." Xavier sighed.

"And tonight, that title will be the barrier we need to guard against any rude or offensive behavior." Remy chuckled. "The good news is, everyone will be watching everyone else, and no one will want to be gossiped about tomorrow. They can give it out, but they can't take it."

Nodding, Xavier said, "So we can hope this will just be a stiff and uncomfortable evening then, that we'll be highly glad of when it's over."

"I'll look forward to us being alone, definitely," Remy couldn't resist stroking Xavier's jacket one last time. "But I fully intend that the two of us will enjoy ourselves while we are there. It's our wedding celebration party – we only get one."

"Two." Xavier grumped. "Your mother already gave us a reception. Please don't punch anyone though," he added. "We're in Balenborn now. That's my job."

"How romantic." Remy's grin got wider just thinking about it. "Let's go and have a good time. It's a state of mind as much as anything else," he added when Xavier didn't smile. "If you plan on us having a good time, then we will. Together."

"That's the only plus of the evening."

/~/~/~/~/

When there was an event at the castle, guests were heralded in. One of the footmen called out their names from the elaborate invitations that had to be presented when the visitors arrived. Usually the King and Queen would sit on their thrones on a small stage. The visitors would pay their respects to their royal family, before grabbing goblets of wine or beer, and making small talk with their acquaintances until dinner was announced.

Regardless of who they were, visitors were expected to turn up within thirty minutes of the time on the invitation, otherwise they weren't admitted – and they were also struck off future guest lists. Queen Serena did not see the need to hold off dinner for disrespectful guests who couldn't be bothered to turn up on time.

In the past, there were a few times when Xavier, and his brother and sister were expected to share the stage with their parents. When

Imogene's and Cyril's engagement was announced, was one example. Xavier's recognition as heir to the realm on his twenty-first birthday was another. Festive celebrations, in May and November usually involved having the whole family on the reception dais.

The celebration of his marriage was yet another reason Xavier and Remy would share the stage with his parents. "Don't look so worried," his mother said, reaching up and patting his cheek. "We're so excited to have Remy join our family. This is a great opportunity for him to meet everyone who think they matter and get it out of the way all in one event."

"Mother," Xavier said as Remy smiled. "Have you forgotten the huge blemish on my reputation that everyone coming tonight will know about? The nasty things that have been published about my husband?"

"We're not discussing that," Queen Serena said brightly. "To discuss it, or worry about it, is to give weight to someone whose opinion truly doesn't count. And besides," she added to Remy, "If I catch anyone snubbing either of you, you can bet your pants, those people will not be allowed back here again."

Looking back at Xavier again, she said softly, "I know you don't want to be here, my darling son, but I promise you, the longer we keep acting normally, the sooner this dreadful business will just die away. Your father and I are determined to show everyone who is anyone in Balenborn, that you are supported, loved, and perhaps most importantly, we believe in you... and our lovely Remy. Now, don't smile, I'd worry your face might crack under the strain, but don't go inviting trouble, my darling, all right?"

Don't go inviting trouble? I never do. Helping Remy to his seat – Xavier made sure his husband was sitting between himself and his mother,

Xavier tugged his chair closer to Remy's before sitting down himself. There was no sign of Luca, which was unusual in itself – Xavier could've done with the moral support and Luca's ready laugh. But he wasn't around. Max, in a dark suit, and still not looking fully recovered, stood on one side of the stage. The doors of the massive ballroom were opened, and the footman took the first invitation, calling out the first names.

"Lord and Lady Belgrave, and their niece, Lady Jasmine Morgan." Another card, another group of people by the door. "Lord Winter and Lady Eugenie..."

"My gods, it's like a cattle drive out there," Xavier mumbled. "It looks like Mother invited every single society family in the country."

"We know two family groups who won't be here," Remy said as the first party started moving towards the stage. "I don't have to actually say anything, do I?"

"Normally, the meet and greet is purely a formality, but this is supposed to be a special occasion. If they linger, Max will introduce you." Xavier huffed. "It'll just be our luck every single person coming will want to be introduced."

"Then I'll keep my responses neutral and brief so they can just move along." Remy caught his eye and smiled. "Who knows, we might make some new friends."

Or maybe people will be just plain nosy. Pirates don't have this problem. The next half an hour couldn't go fast enough.

Chapter Thirty-Five

The meet and greet was as bad as Xavier feared. Everyone did indeed want to be introduced to the Crown Prince Consort, but barely anyone said more than the customary "how lovely to meet you," to him. What was obvious to Xavier was that the only reason people were lingering was so they could show off their unattached women folk, as if expecting Xavier to leap from the stage and plunder the woman concerned right there in front of the King and Queen with his wicked and deviant ways.

Corsets were so tightly strung, some women could barely breathe. Bosoms were thrust in a manner that had to be unnatural, laced, and buckled to emphasize their prominence. Tall heels on slender boots drew attention to figures that Xavier had no interest in noticing, and that's without the coy glances, hair flicking, and eye lash fluttering that was all pointed in

Xavier's direction. Xavier was getting increasingly uncomfortable and made a point of holding Remy's hand from five minutes into the situation that could only be described as awkward.

His mother, bless her wonderful kind soul, intervened where she could, asking questions of the simpering persons, ensuring she became the focus of their curiosity, rather than Xavier and Remy. Remy had noticed, of course. Nothing escaped his sharp gaze, but his smile stayed steady, if a little tight, and he nodded and greeted people if spoken to.

"Just five minutes more." Queen Serena leaned over Remy, putting her hand on his knee as she spoke to Xavier. "You're doing brilliantly well, both of you my wonderful sons. But there is just one more party I'm expecting… Ah, thank goodness, here they are now."

"Their Majesties, King Caspian and King Consort Nikolas of Gunkermal, and Prince Luca of Balenborn," the footman cried. Everyone hushed, as they turned to see the new arrivals. No one had known there would be visiting royalty at the event – Xavier hadn't known although, seeing Luca's grinning face, he understood why his brother hadn't been there for the meet and greet torture. For the first time since the dreadful evening had begun, Xavier felt a spot of hope.

Dressed casually, in comparison to the overdone outfits of most of the guests, Nikolas and Caspian wore heavy long coats favored by ship captains, tights and boots, their swords strapped to their sides. Nikolas's smile was huge as he reached the dais. "Your majesties," he said, bowing to Dare before reaching for and kissing Serena's hand. "I'm so glad we could get here so quickly. While it's lovely to see you both, may I...? He indicated in Xavier's direction and Serena nodded with a smile.

Xavier stood, encouraging Remy with him, bowing low as was only proper to a visiting king and consort. Laughing loudly, Nikolas waited until he was upright, to pull him into a hearty hug, air kissing him loudly on either side of his face. "Xavier, my wonderful friend, there is no way you need to bow to me. We've been drunk together. And look at you now. I can't believe you've finally got your prince by your side. All those years of pining have finally paid off. Introduce me please. I'm not sure if I've met the lovely Crown Prince Consort before."

"Once, very briefly when I was very young." Remy came forward bowing low and then offering his hand, but Nikolas hugged him, too, air kissing on either side of Remy's cheeks greeting him as an equal. Xavier could see Remy was stunned, but hopefully no one else would notice – the being stunned that is. Everyone saw the friendly way he and his husband were being treated.

"King Caspian," he bowed to Nikolas's husband. "I'm not sure if we've..."

"Like your husband with mine, very briefly a long time ago." Caspian's smile was as wide as his husband's. Leaning close, he whispered, "We heard about that dreadful business and knew we had to come. I've had some experience in dealing with negative rumors ruining my reputation. It was sheer fluke poor Nikolas went through with our marriage at all."

"You are too kind, but it's truly wonderful to see you." And Xavier meant it. The society families could gossip all they liked, but if Xavier and Remy had the support of visiting royalty, it made their pettiness look lame.

"Now the guests have arrived, your majesties, shall we go through for dinner?" Max broke in politely.

"Yes, let's." Queen Serena rose, King Dare smiling broadly, doing the same.

She rested her hand on her husband's arm. "Luca, you're with us. I'm sure these four friends have got a lot to catch up on."

"It looks like we're escorting each other into dinner." Xavier held out his arm to King Caspian. "Your Majesty, may I?"

"Seeing as my husband is monopolizing yours, let's go through and call me Caspian, please." The man grinned as he slid his hand around Xavier's elbow. "Nikolas has been telling me so much about you on our trip here, so I feel I know you personally and life is far too short to be worrying about titles among friends."

Sure enough, Remy and Nikolas were chatting easily, although Xavier noticed Remy was watching out for him from the corner of his eye. Something changed in that moment – something profound. Xavier realized that Remy and his mother were right. Despite the judgmental glares from people around him, and their erroneous assumptions about him, he could have a good time at his wedding celebration because he had the loving support of family and friends.

"Let's go and find our seats," he suggested to Caspian. "Does Nikolas know anything about Orobos, do you know? My Remy is an expert on their care and habits, and truly I have found them fascinating to hear about."

"I'm not sure," Caspian said with a fond look at his husband. "But Remy is from Bentley isn't he?"

Xavier nodded as they followed the royal party through one set of doors into the dining area.

"Then Nikolas will have taken it upon himself to help Remy learn about ship life. It's made huge changes in my life. No titles, no worries, no responsibilities – just us and the crew under the open sky sailing the wide oceans. Nikolas and I were married at sea, did you know?"

Xavier didn't, although he wasn't surprised. Nikolas would spend his whole life on his ship if he could. But he happily listened as Caspian explained how he and Nikolas came to be married and then became the joint rulers of Gunkermal. His respect for the young king grew as the story unfolded, and by the time he and Remy had said goodnight to their friends at the end of a long evening, Xavier also found a measure of peace from their visit.

Sure, there had been a few incidents that could've become ugly. One woman, who insisted Xavier dance with her 'to be sociable', hadn't taken his refusal lightly, pulling her husband in, who'd then made a few ugly comments about Remy's lack of ability to bear children. Remy simply smiled, while Caspian stood up with that whole "do you know who I am" look that froze the man in his tracks.

With Nikolas standing at his side, and both of them with hands on their swords, the abrasive couple quickly disappeared into the crowd.

Xavier only wanted to punch one person – Lady Cathaway, the woman he'd told Remy he'd been on a date with before. He'd been stunned speechless when she parked herself in the seat next to Remy at one point in the evening and loudly asked about their plans to have children. She offered herself up as a surrogate provided the children were conceived naturally with Xavier. "It's not that I want to raise children, you understand," she proclaimed to everyone who'd listen, "But I'll carry royal offspring if it means I get to see how much of my dear friend Lady Cecilia's stories are true."

The punch didn't need to happen. His mother, Queen Serena who looked so beautiful in the elegance of her dress and manners, turned and favored the woman with just one piercing glance.

"There are strict orders in this castle that woman's name will not be mentioned in my presence. Leave my home immediately, and if you ever want the chance to be invited into our court again, I'll expect your written apology to both me, and my sons Xavier and Remy, on my desk in the morning."

It was a beautifully delivered rebuke, and it put a stop to any further approaches. As the evening went on, Xavier could finally relax. The society families had expected his friends and family to shun him, and for him to remain hidden away, probably for decades.

Instead, his mother and father had shown their support of him, just like Remy had done from the day he agreed to be Xavier's husband. Nikolas and Caspian's arrival was a generous gesture of true friendship, and a lesson for Xavier, too. The King and King Consort of Gunkermal were a living example of molding their lives according to their needs, rather than anyone else's. Xavier vowed he and Remy would live the same way. Maybe not the pirate life, and running bookshops they'd dreamed of briefly, but a happy compromise all the same.

Holding out his hand to his husband, Xavier smiled – a full face smile and to hell with what his brother thought of that as well. Remy's eyes lit up. "Are you ready for that dance, my beloved?"

"With you, always."

Chapter Thirty-Six

"Oh, my goodness, this is incredible." Remy turned, looking at his husband in delight. "How do we get this thing of beauty moving?"

They were on Xavier's ship. It had been a busy week since the party, but after a few private discussions with his parents, Xavier and Remy were going on a trip of their own.

Nikolas and Caspian's visit had inspired Remy's imagination, letting him know how wonderful life at sea could be – in particular the freeing aspect of being out under the open sky, with only the waves around them.

Caspian's eyes had lit up when the four of them had shared breakfast the morning after the party, describing how he'd seen amazing birds flying overhead, and the wonderful creatures that swum alongside the ship at times. Having never even been on a boat, Remy was excited to share that experience with his husband.

Thanks to the visit from the king and his consort, Xavier was so much more relaxed. Nikolas and Caspian only stayed the one night – Nikolas sighing, as he mentioned them having to go back and prove they weren't dead. He was joking, but Remy could see the same reluctance in him and Caspian in going back to their positions and the responsibilities that waited for them, as Xavier had expressed in private a few times. He and Xavier promised that visiting Gunkermal would be their first port of call.

In the meantime, Remy had Balenborn to investigate. If they saw society family members while out and about exploring the city and the small townships beyond, Xavier would nod politely as they moved on. But Remy never felt as though he was being ignored or snubbed in the way Xavier had worried about. It was as if people were genuinely curious that he and Xavier seemed so happy together, and wanted to be closer to them because of it. In the meantime, local tradespeople and craftsmen were learning the Crown Prince Consort had a friendly smile and a true appreciation of the skills they had.

But the ship... it was evidence of true crafting skills. Built sturdy, it still had a grace to it, something Remy likened to his husband, although he never mentioned the comparison. Built of magically enhanced wood, it seemed like everywhere Remy looked there were little corners, places where carved details, and intricate iron pieces changed the vessel from functional to one with a personality – Xavier's personality.

In particular, in their state room, there was a copy of the beautiful iron coat rack Remy had admired in Xavier's bedroom. Just the day before, Xavier had taken him to visit the crafter who'd made them – a big burly man who wielded a huge hammer as he twisted his metals in intriguing and fascinating ways. After melting under Remy's smile and eager questions about the process, the man offered to craft an Orobos that would twist around the lower branches of Xavier's piece, to give Remy a reminder of home.

But now, they were on Xavier's ship, standing on the wheel deck, watching the crew bustling around below them. Xavier stood behind him, a solid presence and one that even after only a few days, Remy knew he didn't want to live without. Turning to face his husband, Remy asked softly, "Are you happy, my husband?" *Was I worth the wait? Do you see a long and happy life for us both until our time comes to an end.*

"Yes, to that question and all the ones I see in your eyes," Xavier kept his voice low as he looked down to meet Remy's gaze. "I want to head out there," he indicated the horizon with a flick of his hand, "To see the world through your eyes. I want to meet the people who matter – people living their lives with passion and purpose. I want to watch your face when you see the sea creatures playing in the wake of our ship for the first time, and every time thereafter. And I want to hold you in my arms as we stand on the deck under the night sky."

"All under the watchful eye of Brutus, your new head of guard." He gave a cheeky wave at the huge man standing to the side of the watch deck. Remy had never known Boris, his father's head of guard had a brother, but after learning Xavier had to replace Dante, and wanting someone who was focused on his job, not charming everyone in a mile radius, King Francis sent Brutus. It was like having Boris around, only more so.

To his credit, Brutus didn't act like Remy was a waste of space, like Boris had been known to do, but then Remy was now married to the Balenborn heir, so that might have had something to do with it. Remy wasn't worried either way – he was just glad Xavier had someone to watch his back who wasn't affiliated with any of the society families in Balenborn. He wasn't going to forget the blatant flirting the night of the party for a while.

"Excuse me, Sire, we're ready to cast off." A mature man called up to the wheel deck. "Just waiting on your orders, Sire."

"Let's get moving then, Richie." Xavier nodded. "Head out to the open sea if you will, and then set sail for Gunkermal. No rush. My husband has never been on a ship before and wants to enjoy the scenery."

"The scenic route, yes, Sire." With a wave and a smile, the man hurried towards one of the masts. Seconds later huge rolls of canvases unfurled and crackled against the slight breeze. There was a clanging of gears, and chains on the left side of the ship, and Remy turned so he could grab onto the wooden railing as the ship started to move. He felt Xavier coming up behind him, probably closer than was considered acceptable in public, *but we're on a ship, so it really doesn't matter.* Grinning, Remy glanced over his shoulder, before looking back to the horizon again. Then he had a thought. "Who's steering this thing? I thought you were going to do it."

"It seems Brutus is a man of many talents," Xavier leaned in, whispering in Remy's ear, "Which is handy for me because it means I can hold you, and make sure you won't fall overboard."

Looking at one side of the ship, and then the other, Remy looked back over his shoulder again. There was at least a chain length on either side of him before he got anywhere near the sides of the ship. "That's not likely to happen from here, is it?"

"I'm not taking any chances with you, beloved." Xavier smiled, and Remy melted all over again. Xavier had a beautiful smile. "Besides, it's no hardship, holding the man I love as we sail off into the sunset."

It was the middle of the day, but Remy understood the emotions behind Xavier's words. As he looked out to the horizon once more, his own smile widened. There was a whole world beyond their ship, and Remy couldn't wait to see it. And what made the adventure so much more exciting, was the man standing behind him, making sure Remy didn't fall.

"You'd better stay close, then," he said as he leaned back against Xavier's chest. "There's things out there I want to try that I don't even know about yet."

And Remy knew, as the wind filled the giant sails, that Xavier would be right by his side while he tried new things, just as Remy would stand by his husband no matter what came their way. It's the sort of thing people in love did for each other and unbeknown to either of them, they had both been in love for a long time. *It's just lucky we were in love with each other,* he thought with a grin. *Because now we can be in love together. Forever.* Just like it seemed both of them had dreamed.

Epilogue

On a cliff above the Gunkermal Port

The tall man clad in a dark cloak used his telescopic eyeglass to sweep across the hills and cliffs, down to the hustle and bustle of the dock below. There were ships in, but there only one the observer was interested in. "Hmm, you're finally home, and look at you striding around, acting so important. I wonder if you'd be so cocky, if you were naked on my bed." He chuckled. The man he had his sights on had always come across dominating in every way. It was only because of...

"Captain. Captain." Letting the arm holding his eyeglass drop, the man scowled at the huffing body climbing up the hill towards him. "There's been another one of those messages. The ones with the fancy crest. It was waiting at the Byron Bar."

"Give it to me." The tall man held out his hand for the message waving in the air. He never worried about anyone reading his messages. His crew weren't literate, one of his many disappointments. "Tell the crew we'll stay moored out of sight for a few days. They can go into town, but they are not to cause any trouble. Understood?"

"Go to town. No trouble." The huffing man was already heading back down the hill. Sighing, the remaining man flung back his cloak from his face, breaking the wax seal on the message. Scanning the few short sentences, he looked back down at the docks.

The royal party, King Caspian and his Consort King Nikolas were laughing with each other as they made their way from the ship to a waiting carriage. But the man on the hill looked beyond them and smiled as he saw the object of his dreams organizing the removal of bags from a pile on the gangplank.

"I think it might be time to visit my brother, seeing as he asks so nicely. I wonder if I'll get invited to stay for dinner." The man laughed softly. "For a chance to get closer to you, my bristly friend, it would be worth the risk of getting arrested."

Snapping his eyeglasses closed, it and his message were placed carefully in one of the deep pockets on his pants. The man wrapped his cloak around his body again and checked that his hood was obscuring his face. With one last look at the object of his attention still supervising the luggage transport down by King Nikolas's ship, the tall man slipped away into the shadows of the trees, away from the Gunkermal castle.

To Be Continued...

About the Author

Lisa Oliver lives in the wilds of New Zealand, although her beautiful dogs Hades and Zeus are now living somewhere else far more remote than she is. Reports indicate they truly enjoy chasing possums although they still can't catch them. In the meantime, Lisa is living a lot closer to all her adult kids and grandchildren which means she gets a lot more visitors. However, it doesn't look like she's ever going to stop writing - with over eighty paranormal MM (and MMM) titles to her name so far, she shows no signs of slowing down.

When Lisa is not writing, she is usually reading with a cup of tea always at hand. Her grown children and grandchildren sometimes try and pry her away from the computer and have found that the best way to do it is to promise her chocolate. Lisa will do anything for chocolate... and occasionally cheezals. She has also started working out, because of the chocolate and the cheezals.

Lisa loves to hear from her readers and other writers (I really do, lol). You can catch up with her on any of the social media links below.

Facebook –
http://www.facebook.com/lisaoliverauthor

Official Author page –
https://www.facebook.com/LisaOliverManloveAuthor/

My new private teaser group -
https://www.facebook.com/groups/540361549650663/

My MeWe Group -
http://mewe.com/join/lisa_olivers_paranormal_pack

And Instagram - https://www.instagram.com/lisa_oliver_author/

My blog - http://www.paranormalgayromance.com

Twitter – http://www.twitter.com/wisecrone333

YouTube (I am so awful at this lol, but it makes me laugh) - https://www.youtube.com/channel/UCuPx1orrUiUHt_ECNaX8SWw and

TikTok - https://www.tiktok.com/@lisaoliver135 (These could be easier to watch because the videos are shorter lol)

Email me directly at yoursintuitively@gmail.com.

Other Books By Lisa/Lee Oliver

Please note, I have now marked the books that contain mpreg and MMM for those of you who don't like to read those type of stories. Hope that helps ☺

Cloverleah Pack

Book 1 – The Reluctant Wolf – Kane and Shawn

Book 2 – The Runaway Cat – Griff and Diablo

Book 3 – When No Doesn't Cut It – Damien and Scott

Book 3.5 – Never Go Back – Scott and Damien's Trip and a free story about Malacai and Elijah

Book 4 – Calming the Enforcer – Troy and Anton

Book 5 – Getting Close to the Omega – Dean and Matthew

Book 6 – Fae for All – Jax, Aelfric and Fafnir (M/M/M)

Book 7 – Watching Out for Fangs –Josh and Vadim

Book 8 – Tangling with Bears – Tobias, Luke, and Kurt (M/M/M)

Book 9 – Angel in Black Leather – Adair and Vassago

Book 9.5 – Scenes from Cloverleah – four short stories featuring the men we've come to love

Book 10 – On the Brink – Teilo, Raff and Nereus (M/M/M)

Book 11 – Don't Tempt Fate – Marius and Cathair

Book 12 – My Treasure to Keep – Thomas and Ivan

Book 13 – Home is Where the Heart is – Wesley and Castor

The Gods Made Me Do It (Cloverleah spin off series)

Book One - Get Over It – Madison and Sebastian's story

Book Two - You've Got to be Kidding – Poseidon and Claude (mpreg)

Book Three – Don't Fight It – Lasse and Jason

Book Four – Riding the Storm – Thor and Orin (mpreg elements [Jason from previous book gives birth in this one])

Book Five – I Can See You – Artemas and Silvanus (mpreg elements – Thor gives birth in this one)

Book Six – Someone to Hold Me – Hades and Ali (mpreg elements but no birth)

Book Seven – You'll Know in Your Heart – Baby and Owen (mpreg)

Book Eight – Worth It – Zeus and Paulie (mpreg)

Book Nine – When Three Points Collide – Ra, Kirill and Arvyn (M/M/M) (mpreg elements, no birth)

Book Ten – Special Enough – Odin and Evan

Book Eleven – Reconciliation: Seth's Story – Seth and Luka (mpreg is a small part of this story)

Book Twelve – Being Loki - Loki and Anubis

Book Thirteen – Give Me A Reason – Helios and Bruno

The Necromancer's Smile (This is a trilogy series under the name The Necromancer's Smile where the main couple, Dakar and Sy are the focus of all three books – these cannot be read as standalone).

Book One – Dakar and Sy – The Meeting

Book Two – Dakar and Sy – Family affairs

Book Three – Dakar and Sy – Taking Care of Business

Bound and Bonded Series

Book One – Don't Touch – Levi and Steel

Book Two – Topping the Dom – Pearson and Dante

Book Three – Total Submission – Kyle and Teric

Book Four – Fighting Fangs – Ace and Devin

Book Five – No Mate of Mine – Roger and Cam

Book Six – Undesirable Mate – Phillip and Kellen

Stockton Wolves Series

Book One – Get off My Case – Shane and Dimitri

Book Two – Copping a Lot of Sin – Ben, Sin and Gabriel (M/M/M)

Book Three – Mace's Awakening – Mace and Roan

Book Four – Don't Bite – Trent and Alexi

Book Five – Tell Me the Truth – Captain Reynolds and Nico (mpreg)

Alpha and Omega Series

Book One – The Biker's Omega – Marly and Trent

Book Two – Dance Around the Cop – Zander and Terry

Book Three – Change of Plans - Q and Sully

Book Four – The Artist and His Alpha – Caden and Sean

Book Five – Harder in Heels – Ronan and Asaph

Book Six – A Touch of Spring – Bronson and Harley

Book Seven – If You Can't Stand the Heat – Wyatt and Stone (Previously published in an anthology)

Book Eight – Fagin's Folly – Fagin and Cooper

Book Nine – The Cub and His Alphas – Daniel, Zeke and Ty (MMM)

Book Ten – The One Thing Money Can't Buy – Cari and Quaid

Book Eleven – Precious Perfection – Devyn and Rex

Book Twelve – More Than a Handful - Karl and Tanner

Spin off from The Biker's Omega – BBQ, Bikes, and Bears – Clive and Roy

Balance – Angels and Demons

The Viper's Heart – Raziel and Botis

Passion Punched King – Anael and Zagan

Soul Deep – Uriel and Haures

Found – Raphael and Seir

Demon Masks and Angel Wings – Michael and Orobas

Love Before Time – Lucifer and Gabriel

Arrowtown

A Tiger's Tale – Ra and Seth (mpreg)

Snake Snack – Simon and Darwin (mpreg)

Liam's Lament – Liam Beau and Trent (MMM) (Mpreg)

Doc's Deputy – Deputy Joe and Doc (Mpreg)

Cam's Chance – Cam and Fergus (Mpreg)

Stone Cold Obsidian – Dian and Kee (Mpreg)

Brutus's Surprise – Brutus and Heath

City Dragons

Dragon's Heat – Dirk and Jon

Dragon's Fire – Samuel and Raoul

Dragon's Tears – Byron and Ivak

The Magic Users of Greenford – a new trilogy.

Book One - Illuminate

Book Two – Eradicate

Book Three – Validate (coming early 2023)

My Arranged Marriage Fantasy Romance Books
(not Fated Mates)

The Infidelity Clause – Nikolas and Caspian

Don't Judge A Prince by his Undergarments – Mintyn and Syrius

An Article of Lies – Xavier and Remy – you just read it ▯

Quirk of Fate

Summons – Edward and Mammon

Reggie's Reasons – Reggie and Dirkin

The Mating of Blind Billy Hipp – Billy and Dathan

Quirk of Fates Shorts

Saving Moses – Tucker and Moses

Hellhound Collar Series

Collar and Scruff (Prequel) – Raoul and Jason (Now on Amazon)

Better Than Sweets (Book 1) – Java and Cyril

Precious Blue (Book 2) – Beau and Blue (mpreg elements in last chapter.)

Tangled Tentacles – in Collaboration with JP Sayle

Book one – Alexi – Alexi and Danik

Book 2 – Victor – Azim and Victor (mpreg)

Book 3 – Todd – (MMM, mpreg) Todd, Lucas, and Ki)

Book 4 – Markov – Markov and Cassius

Book 5 – Kelvin – Kelvin and Magnus (mpreg - Markov)

Assassins To Order With JP Sayle

Marvin – Marvin and Ajani

Ben – Ben and others – (due out April 2023)

Standalone:

I Should've Stayed Home: Irwin's Story – Part of the Nocturne Bay collab series – Irwin and Kolton

The Fall of the Fairy Tale Prince – Charlie and Lex (A spin off from Dancing Around the Cop and Change of Plans in the A&O series)

Stay True to Me – Con and Ven

Rowan and the Wolf – Rowan and Shadow

Bound by Blood – Max and Lyle – (a spin off from Cloverleah Pack #7)

The Power of the Bite – Dax and Zane

One Wrong Step – Robert and Syron

Uncaged – Carlin and Lucas (Shifter's Uprising in conjunction with Thomas Oliver)

Also under the penname Lee Oliver/Lisa Oliver

Northern States Pack Series

Book One – Ranger's End Game – Ranger and Aiden

Book Two – Cam's Promise – Cam and Levi

Book Three – Under Sean's Protection – Sean and Kyle

Book Four – Newton's Law – Newton and Tron

Printed in Great Britain
by Amazon

20876389R10278